STELLA AND THE TIMEKEEPERS

M. SHAWN PETERSEN

BEYOND WORDS
Hillsboro, Oregon

BEYOND WORDS

8427 N.E. Cornell Road, Suite 500
Hillsboro, Oregon 97124-9808
503-531-8700 / 503-531-8773 fax
www.beyondword.com

Text copyright © 2019 by M. Shawn Petersen
Cover and interior illustrations copyright © 2019 by Beyond Words Publishing

Managing Editor: Lindsay S. Easterbrooks-Brown
Editors: Emily Einolander, Gretchen Stelter, Emmalisa Sparrow Wood
Copyeditor: Kristin Thiel
Proofreader: Michelle Blair
Cover and Interior Illustrations: Robyn Waters
Design: Devon Smith
Composition: William H. Brunson Typography Services

First Beyond Words edition May 2019

For information about special discounts for bulk purchases, please contact Beyond Words Special Sales at 503-531-8700 or specialsales@beyondword.com.

Manufactured in the United States of America

10 9 8 7 6 5 4 3 2 1

Library of Congress Cataloging-in-Publication Data

Names: Petersen, M. Shawn.
Title: Stella and the timekeepers / M. Shawn Petersen.
Description: Hillsboro, Oregon : Beyond Words, [2019] | Summary: After her
  parents' disappearance, eleven-year-old misfit Stella Merriss learns she
  is half-angel, half-mermaid and must join an elite angel apprenticeship
  program, where she finally finds a sense of belonging.
Identifiers: LCCN 2018050753 (print) | LCCN 2018055224 (ebook) | ISBN
  9781582707082 (eBook) | ISBN 9781582706788 (pbk.) | ISBN 9781582707136
  (hardcover)
Subjects: | CYAC: Belonging (Social psychology)—Fiction. | Angels—Fiction.
  | Mermaids—Fiction. | Apprentices—Fiction. | Fantasy.
Classification: LCC PZ7.1.P449 (ebook) | LCC PZ7.1.P449 Ste 2019 (print) |
  DDC [Fic]—dc23
LC record available at https://lccn.loc.gov/2018050753

The corporate mission of Beyond Words Publishing, Inc.: *Inspire to Integrity*

CONTENTS

Contents

PART THREE **SAVING A SAFE HAVEN**

PART ONE
ON THE RUN

1

AND THEN THERE WAS ONE

When Stella's eyelids flickered open, she was looking up at blue sky, floating on her back in a sea so tranquil that, for a moment, she thought she might be dreaming. As she lifted her head, it took her aching body but a moment to help her remember—she was in a small boat with a few inches of standing water in the bottom. Clutching the side, she hauled herself up and peered out across a vast ocean that disappeared into empty sky at the horizon. Devoid of wind, sound, or signs of life, Stella found herself completely alone.

Stella had set out in the dinghy with her parents, but now they were gone. She whirled around in a panic, causing the boat to rock. Sloshing water broke the silence as she searched for any sign of her parents. She called their names, but there was no response. Not even an echo out on the open water. Her voice seemed to die in the open flatness. Ripples undulated from the small craft across the glassy surface of the water until they dissolved into a loneliness unlike anything Stella had ever experienced in her eleven years of life.

Everything was murky in Stella's mind. She tugged at her long golden locks—a habit she had when thinking—trying to somehow knock loose the memories of her last moments before she had lost consciousness; she was sure they were floating around in her head somewhere. Then, in a flash, she remembered: her father, Arago, was rowing furiously through frothing mountain-sized waves, working to keep the dinghy from capsizing. Her mother, Andri, suddenly crying out, "The lighthouse!"

Shaking her head, Stella came back to the present, certain her mind was playing tricks on her. But the evidence sat right in front of her: the oars in their brackets, her father's knapsack, the food basket packed by her mother, and, of course, her parent's absence.

The impact of her situation soaked in slowly like light drizzle on a dry sponge. Then another snippet played out on the screen of her mind—Andri yanking her arm out of Stella's desperate grasp and standing up at the exact moment the dinghy crested a wave, plunging down the other side of a steep wall of water. Andri plunging into the sea and disappearing, as if a mouth had opened and swallowed her up. Stella springing to her feet in an attempt to save her mother just as the dinghy crested another wave. Stella flying backwards, stars exploding across her vision, her head striking the bench with a crack. The last thing she saw was Arago releasing the oars, rising to his feet, and calling out Andri's name. Then everything faded to black.

Tears glistened her cheeks, "Are they really gone?" she wondered aloud. What had happened to her father? She'd seen the horrified look on her mother's face before she was catapulted overboard, and now her father's absence . . . had he dived in to try to save her? Or was he swept over by a wave as well?

This is what I get for wanting to run away from them, she thought. This was the thirty-first time in her short life her family had moved, and Stella had wanted to stay behind, even if that meant her parents leaving without her. They had lived everywhere, from the deserts of Arid, where food was scarce but gold jewelry plentiful, to the outskirts of the bustling metropolis of Ilya, where nobody would talk to them or give her father work, even when he begged. When Arago had found employment mining for diamonds on Viola Island, Stella hoped they were finally home.

Stella loved the quaint Violan house perched on the grassy hill where she and her parents lived. She fondly remembered its gently sloping slate roof, wide, well-supported elmlock timber eaves, and the open-air pavilion under which she would daydream as thunderstorms blew through causing the blue starcrester flowers to dance with the lightning; she imagined that she was finally home. But the inevitable occurred, like it had every other time—Andri shook Stella awake one night, helped her climb out the window, and said, "Run, run, run—meet us at the old tree." And like every other time, it was her parents and her against the world—a terrible pattern to live by—running from every place she'd ever settled without ever knowing why.

The initial shock of climbing out of her own window wore off when Arago and Andri joined their daughter at the old tree. Stella could hear explosions and see the orange glow of houses on fire in the distance as she and her parents covered their mouths and noses with wet handkerchiefs to keep from breathing in the thick smoke. They snuck through thorny underbrush that tore at their clothes and scratched at their skin as they made their way to the port. Stella protested when Arago booked immediate passage from Viola Island on the cargo ship *Emprezza*, and protested even more when, several days into their journey, her parents pilfered one of the lifeboats to steal away—once again—in the middle of the night. When Meriwether, the captain of the ship, came upon them lowering the dinghy, Arago knocked him out with a single, expertly placed strike. Stella had never seen her father attack anyone before, and it frightened her.

I don't want to do this anymore, she thought as the dinghy pulled further and further away from the cargo ship they had left behind. *Maybe I'll just stay.*

Without uttering a word, Andri responded, *But we've already left, sea star. Where are you going to go—into the water to swim back? You don't know how to swim.*

As far as Stella knew, she and her mother were the only ones who could communicate telepathically. As she'd gotten older, it wasn't always a welcome gift, and she'd learned how to shield her thoughts from her mother when she needed to.

Stella's emotions were a tangle as she thought about the events of the past few nights, but her physical needs were starting to overtake her racing thoughts. Her head hurt, her tongue felt as dry as petrified wood, and her stomach rumbled fiercely.

When they first boarded the dinghy, Stella had been so seasick she couldn't even bear the idea of food. But her father slid a bracelet from his wrist and onto hers. "This'll make you feel better, angel," he said, "and protect you." The bracelet had sent an electric current prickling along her skin, and soon her head stopped spinning, but her appetite hadn't returned until now.

Stella spotted the food basket still lashed to her father's bench. Inside, was her father's jacket, which she set aside to get to the foodstuffs beneath. After gulping down some water from the waterskin, she used her teeth to rip a hole in one of the water-proof sheaths and pulled out a loaf of pearlgrain bread and a slab of smoked silver fin.

She devoured them as the sun climbed higher in the sky and began to burn her face. She reached for her father's jacket and held it up to give herself some shade. In the buttoned breast pocket of the jacket, she could feel a lump that she knew was Arago's special timepiece, something he always carried.

Thinking of her father, Stella looked at the bracelet still hanging from her wrist. She pulled it off and examined it. Why had it made her feel better? Was it a special bracelet to prevent seasickness? It looked too fancy to be anything other than an adornment, with its wing-and-sword design. The sun hit it and the bracelet gleamed iridescent. The longer she stared at it, the angrier she got. Maybe at one point it had made her feel less nauseous, but it certainly hadn't protected any of them from the sea. And the bracelet wasn't going to help her find more drinkable water or food or reach land. What was she going to do? At that moment, all she wanted to do was throw the bracelet as far away from her as possible, or break something, or let out a primal scream . . . anything to relieve a little of the frustration and grief she felt. But to what end? Taking a moment, she paused, took a deep breath and held it.

With a sigh, she realized that her anger wasn't going to get her anywhere, so instead of chucking it into the water, she slid the bracelet back into her father's jacket pocket, stuffed her fists into the oversized sleeves and rolled them up to her elbows. The ear-piercing squawks of sea dunkers rang in her ears. She looked up and tracked the flock circling over her head, and she then realized—birds were a sign of land nearby. Scanning the horizon, Stella spotted a shadowed speck of land. *I'm not in the middle of nowhere anymore. I'm near land!* The birds chased each other through the sky, and she felt a small, determined smile tugging at her mouth. It occurred to her that she could survive this disaster no matter how insurmountable the circumstances might appear. All survival would require of her was action on her part. She took up a position on the bench with the intention of rowing to land.

With her peripheral vision she registered movement in the water. Her left arm instinctively went up to block the unexpected attack. White-hot pain blinded her as a small shark clamped its razor-sharp teeth into the flesh of her forearm. She let out a cry as the shark's jaws set, pulling her off balance. Tasting blood, the shark went wild, nearly causing the little craft to capsize and sending the food basket and her father's knapsack overboard. Stella braced her feet against the side of the dinghy and fought the creature's tugs. Blood ran down her arm into the standing water at the bottom of the boat, turning it pink.

Without stopping to think, Stella threw a punch much like the one she'd seen her father throw at Captain Meriwether back on the *Emprezza*. Instead of landing on the side of the shark's head, though, it hit the shark squarely on the snout. The surprised predator released her arm, and Stella tumbled backward, again finding herself on the bottom of the dinghy. Dazed, she reached for the bench with her good arm and pulled herself upright, staring in fascination at the bite marks that were leaking blood.

I'm okay, she assured herself. *Just stay clear of the sides and get to land as fast as you can without getting attacked again.*

A frenzy of sharks circled the dinghy. *They're being drawn by the scent of blood* Stella thought. Hadn't there been sharks circling the dinghy before she'd lost consciousness? Squeezing her eyes shut, she rejected that disturbing memory and wouldn't allow herself to think of what that might mean for her parent's survival. Instead, she focused on finding a weapon to fight them off with. She scrambled to release an oar from its bracket and set to battering the frenzied creatures, who were becoming more aggressive and numerous by the second.

As she swung the oar, she felt the weight of her father's bracelet thumping against her leg. She reached into the jacket pocket, grabbed it, and slipped it on to be sure she didn't lose it. No sooner had it touched her skin than an electric current surged up her arm, and she found herself enfolded in a globe of light. As the globe glowed brighter, it seemed to generate an energetic barrier that the sharks ricocheted off of.

What the . . . ? She panted, collapsing to her knees and peering at her wounded arm. It was clotting, the blood slowing to a seep, but she was acutely aware of how much the limb was throbbing. The boat was sprinkled with debris from the aggressive sharks leaping and nearly overturning the dinghy. She grabbed a long length of seaweed and managed to bandage the wounds—a folk remedy her mother had shown her when she was young. Light-headed from the loss of blood, but possibly also from whatever the bracelet did, she collapsed onto the bench. She took a few moments to rest and then grabbed the oars.

Right. Time to get out of here. Despite the pain and fatigue, she snapped the oar she'd used as a weapon back into its bracket and plunged them both into the sea.

As the oars broke the water's surface, the sharks resumed their frenzy, but the globe of light pulsed, shielding her from further attack, and sending any would-be attackers twisting and spinning back into the sea.

Looking skyward, Stella shook her head in disbelief. "I don't know where you got this bracelet, and I don't know where you are," she said aloud, "but thank you, Dad." And with that, she started rowing.

2

WINGS AND TAILS

With each stroke, the little craft edged closer to land, and soon, what appeared to be a lighthouse rose up in the distance. To push past the pain, Stella pictured herself rowing up to the structure—a trick her father had taught her when she'd fallen off her cycle as a kid but wanted to keep playing: imagine doing something, and you just may end up doing it. Stella wasn't sure how long she'd been rowing when she caught sight of the tall white structure jutting out of what seemed to be a pile of rocks. Though her left arm still throbbed, she kept the dinghy moving toward it in a straight line. It was slow going, and several times she nearly gave up, but now, looking up at the looming white tower with its ample square windows and whirligig weathervane, she saw someone scanning the horizon from an observation deck, and hope surged through her. She released the oars to wave, crying out, "Help! Help! Help me, please!"

The person disappeared from the window, and Stella's heart sank. But spotting him was enough to rekindle her determination, and grabbing hold of the oars, she continued for the little rock island. As she passed into the shadow of the lighthouse, the wind shifted, and somehow, it was as if it carried the crisp scent of hope. She heard the voice shouting before she saw where it was coming from.

A burly man with broad shoulders, powerful arms, and a bushy dark brown beard was . . . flying? Yes. He was flying toward her, flapping two enormous white wings. As he neared the dinghy, he called out over the sound of waves splashing against the rocks, "Stella!"

She nearly fell off the bench. *How in the world does he know who I am?* Stella was too dumbfounded to answer him.

"I've been expecting you," the flying man called out. "I'm Magnus, the lighthouse keeper. Your parents and I are old friends. You're safe now." Pulling up alongside the dinghy, he hovered close enough for her to see the furrowed lines on his forehead as he took in the boat and her appearance. "Where are your parents?"

Though she mustered the courage to say it aloud, the word caught in her throat, and she couldn't unstick it. "G-gone," she finally managed, her tongue rough as sandpaper.

His eyes widened, and he gave a curt nod, as though he'd discuss it with her later, but for now, it was time to get down to business. "I won't be able to reach you with your globe turned on," he said. "Take off the bracelet."

Too tired and relieved to worry or argue, she pulled it off and slid it into her pocket, the globe dematerializing into nothing. Magnus swooped in to pick her up, cradling her against his chest. The blue sky and his kind face were the last things she saw before her body shut down and she, again, lost consciousness.

When Stella woke, she was surprised to find herself in a bed with a mattress as soft as a cloud. It was by far the fluffiest bed she had ever slept in, and she realized her body no longer ached from fatigue and her arm no longer hurt from the shark bite—but she was confused.

Had someone with wings carried her from the boat? She had what appeared to be a fresh seaweed bandage on her arm, and she had the impression of a bushy beard and hair, kind eyes, and . . . wings. Right? She quickly reassessed recent events to assure herself she wasn't imagining things: she'd escaped the *Emprezza* with her parents, lost them both (one possibly intentionally), been attacked by and fought off sharks, and then rowed to a lighthouse where she'd been taken ashore by a . . . What was he? *Who* was he?

She sat up, shaking her head. Things couldn't get weirder.

The room had bright-white walls, like the exterior of the lighthouse, and was sparsely furnished. A single chair stood next to the bedside table, her father's jacket draped over its back. Seeing a glass of water on the table, she sat up farther, reached for it, and sipped.

Light streamed in through a small window near the foot of the bed. Stella felt woozy as she slid slowly from under the covers and placed her feet gingerly on the floor. Standing slowly, she wobbled toward the window, where she was able to see most of the island, which jutted up from the sea in harsh, rocky formations. Except for a small strip of beach, it was devoid of trees or plants—vegetation of any kind.

She spotted two figures on the narrow beach. Their heads were bent together, appearing to be deep in conversation. She instantly recognized the large frame of the man who'd saved her—but where were his wings? Had she lost her mind?

His female companion shook her head at something he said to her, she dropped a handful of seaweed into a bucket of water at her feet, then bent over and rinsed the grit from her hands. The man turned from the woman, his back now toward Stella, and two beautiful wings unfurled through his shirt.

Stella's heart started to pound. So she wasn't crazy, but this? This was crazy. And he had called himself Magnus—yes, she was starting to recall the events leading up to her waking up in this bed. This winged man had rescued her!

With a few graceful flaps, he was airborne and, in no time, disappeared from view as he flew off into the distance.

Stella watched in amazement as the woman, leaving the bucket on the beach, waded into the water and dove into the surf. The water was clear enough for Stella to see her body as it arced, serpent-like, in the breakers. A tail breached the waves where feet should have been, before disappearing into the deep.

3

TWO HALVES MAKE A WHOLE

As soon as Stella recovered from what she had seen on the beach, she began searching her room. She needed to know more about this strange place—and she needed to know now. Bare though it was, she found one treasure—in the drawer of the bedside table she found a sealed envelope with her name written on it in large, swirling letters that Stella recognized as her mother's handwriting. She tore open the envelope and pulled out the letter:

My dear Stella,
If you are reading this, it means you're in the protective care of our friend Magnus and we aren't with you for some reason. I am sorry that we haven't been truthful with you about who we are—about who you are. All we ever wanted was to protect you from the ugliness of the world, but we've also kept some of the magic from you, though we never meant to. You, my darling sea star, are unique. Mermaids and angels are not just stories we

told you to entertain you—they are very much real. In fact, your father is an angel, and I am a mermaid. We were not supposed to fall in love, to start a family together, to have a beautiful daughter who was both mermaid and angel, but we did. It's why we have lived our lives without family and without roots—we broke the rules dictated by the angels and have been on the run ever since.

When Magnus showed up at our door with your notice of apprenticeship, we knew the angels were making a rare gesture to offer you safe haven, despite how we had turned our backs on them.

Go to them, Stella. It's the safest choice for you now. My family will want to take you to Abalonia. Sylvain and his forces will want to exploit you. Don't be tempted. Steer clear of them at all costs. The angels are your only way forward. Go with Magnus to Sentinel Island. Your life depends on it.

Please know that no matter what you hear about us, we love you. We always have and always will—into eternity. We never wanted to hurt you and hope you will hold happy memories of us. I love you with all my heart, from the shore to the clouds to the depths of the sea.

Until we find each other again,
Mom

Stella peered down at her body. She looked like an utterly normal girl, yet wondered if she could sprout wings and fly, like Magnus, or if she could grow a tail, like the woman on the beach. The whole thing was disorienting and even a bit exciting. *Why didn't my parents tell me about any of this before?*

She wished they were here now to help straighten this mess out like they always had before. Stella collapsed on the bed feeling the weight of her grief. The day passed with her face buried in a pillow as she worried about her parents and what she was going to do without them.

The room darkened as dusk settled over the lighthouse. Stella's eyes strained rereading her mother's letter when she heard a door open downstairs. She hastily refolded the paper and stuffed it under the pillow. Footsteps clomped up the stairs, and then a lilting female voice said, "I'll check on her." Stella's heart hammered as the door opened. She found her herself peering into the aquamarine eyes of the—she gulped—mermaid she'd seen just a short time ago.

Stella was struck by a faint sense of recognition, but she jerked away when the stranger reached for her arm.

"No need to be so worried. I only want to examine it." The tone and timbre of her calm voice were soothing, familiar, but Stella couldn't quite place why.

"Who are you?"

"I'm Esmeralda," the stranger replied, "but everyone calls me Esmi. I'm your aunt."

"My aunt?" Stella exclaimed. She didn't have an aunt . . . did she? But it made sense. Her aunt's eyes were the same aquamarine as her mother's—as her own. And the voice was similar too.

Didn't your mother tell you about me? Esmi asked, the question echoing telepathically in Stella's head.

Startled, Stella stared at Esmi. How did she know how to speak like Stella and her mother did?

Looking more closely, Stella realized the resemblance was not only in the color of their eyes but in other ways too, like how the stranger sat—with one leg tucked under the knee of her opposite leg. The same way her mother had done a thousand times before.

No, my parents never talked about their families, Stella said, thinking of the family mentioned in the letter that her mother warned would want to take her.

Ah, Esmi replied. *I'm glad to see you speak Mermese.* Brushing Stella's hair off her face and combing it with her fingers like Stella's mother did, she added, *Well, I wish you'd known before now, but it's true: I'm your aunt.*

Sadness washed over Stella. She ached at the thought of her missing mother and wished only that she could be here in the room with them. When Stella would've done anything for a sibling, she wondered how her mother could have abandoned her sister. And how in the world had she been able to keep such an enormous secret from her own daughter?

I was wondering if you could tell me where your parents are, Esmi said.

It felt like Stella's heart stopped, and the sadness was joined by a new kind of grief as well as confusion—she still wasn't sure what had happened.

They're gone. I . . . I think they're dead. When they went overboard, we were surrounded by sharks.

Did you actually see the sharks kill them?

Returning to the dinghy in her mind's eye, Stella tried to remember exactly what had happened. Eventually, she said, *No*, and then a more assuredly, *no. It was dark and raining hard. Waves were crashing everywhere, and Mom was swept overboard . . . and Dad . . . Dad went over too, but I'm not sure if he was caught in a wave or . . .* She stopped and put up the mental wall she used to build between her mind and her mother's. Behind its privacy, she decided to leave her story at that for now. If he went over on purpose, she wasn't sure what to say about it anyway, wasn't sure she wanted anyone to know he'd left her willingly, abandoning her.

Her aunt reached out, tentatively this time, but stopped short of touching her. *I'm so sorry. We'll figure out what happened.* She paused before asking, *May I examine your arm now?*

Stella extended her injured arm to her aunt. She wouldn't have admitted it aloud—or even telepathically, for that matter—but she was ready to let someone take care of her after all that had happened, at least for a few minutes, anyways.

Gently taking hold of Stella's arm, Esmi brushed her hand over it. Prickly pain made the hairs on the back of Stella's neck stand up as Esmi massaged the seaweed cuff—again, just as her mother had whenever she hurt herself ("blood owies," her mother had called scrapes and scratches) when she was little.

Her eyes burned with unshed tears, and Stella drew in a deep breath. The scent of the sea—the scent that always lingered on her mother—filled her nose, and instead of the familiar scent comforting her, she had to fight the tears that did their best to spill over. She wrestled down the lump in her throat and watched as Magnus slipped quietly into the room and leaned against the wall, careful to not disturb the tender moment between aunt and niece.

Esmi squeezed Stella's hand. "I taught Magnus about the healing properties of seaweed." She continued to gently rub Stella's arm from elbow to wrist. "It's highly regarded among our kind. Merfolk, I mean. The rest of our school—or I guess you'd say family—are excited to finally meet you, the princess."

"Me? I'm no princess."

"You are. As am I, and so is your mother. But you're an original—the only princess to ever have mixed angel-merfolk blood."

"Well, this just can't be true or my parents would've told me."

Esmi lifted an eyebrow. "Did they tell you about me?" Stella shook her head, looking to Magnus for help.

Nodding his head, he said, "It's true."

The world seemed to stop for Stella, with only the sounds of her pounding heart and the far-off squawks of sea dunkers in her head.

Esmi broke the silence. "Everyone's excited to have you join them in Abalonia. Your grandparents, the king and queen, are particularly looking forward to it. You may be unique, but you're still their grandchild and royalty."

Stella stiffened. She fought with her parents, sure, but she wasn't used to telling other adults that she wasn't going to do what they wanted her to. Luckily, Magnus jumped in.

"Unfortunately, they'll have to wait," he said, his statement clearly surprising Esmi.

Esmi made a startled sound before looking over her shoulder at the lighthouse keeper. "Why would that be?"

"Stella has received a notice of apprenticeship on Sentinel Island," Magnus said. "She can't go to Abalonia."

"She absolutely can," Esmi said, turning away from the angel. "Her parents are missing. Merfolk custom dictates the next of kin make decisions about her future until they're found. Surely it's for her grandparents to decide what she does, and they certainly won't want her at the Citadel."

Stella took that moment to harness her courage and speak up. "Both my parents want me to go with Magnus to Sentinel Island."

She didn't know what "the Citadel" was, but she knew her parents must've had their reasons for wanting her to go there.

Magnus smiled, but Esmi trained her wide eyes on Stella. "Excuse me? A moment ago you didn't even know I was your aunt. Now they've told you they don't want you with your school?"

Stella wasn't sure how to react to an angry aunt, but she figured proof was her best shot. She leaned over, grabbed the letter from under the pillow, and offered it to her aunt with a shaking hand. "Here. This is from my mother."

Esmi snatched it from Stella, her eyes flashing as they darted back and forth, taking in the words on the page. "We won't stand for this," Esmi hissed.

"You don't have a choice," Magnus said calmly. "It was clearly what Arago and Andri wanted."

The mermaid sprang off the bed to face Magnus. "This is outrageous. My sister must have been forced to write this!" Stella shrank back from her aunt's fury, which seemed to fill the entire room.

"I assure you that wasn't the case," Magnus thundered back, pushing himself away from the wall to stand toe-to-toe with the mermaid. Although he towered over her, Esmi wasn't intimidated; she was as fierce as they came, with fiery, unpredictable merblood in her veins. "Your sister and her husband felt Sentinel Island would be the safest place for their daughter."

"But it's for *angels*," Esmi objected. "Stella can't manifest as an angel. She's not even ready to transform herself into a mermaid."

"She's capable of both, and you know it."

Esmi crumpled up the letter and hurled it at him before she stormed out of the room. Her footsteps echoed throughout the lighthouse as she hurried down the stairs.

Crouching to pick up the note, Magnus turned to Stella and held the paper out to her. "I apologize for the argument, but I'm glad you were made aware of your parents' wishes."

Stella took the note from Magnus and tried to smooth out the wrinkles. She was over the two of them talking about her like she wasn't there—like all adults loved to do, apparently—so she was glad Magnus was at least addressing her now, even if her aunt had stormed off. "I read that letter for the first time today, but sure, I guess I was 'made aware,'" Stella said, not willing to let it go without at least mentioning how late in the game she was getting all this info. "Can you tell me what this all means? I don't even know what Esmi meant that I can't *manifest* as an angel yet."

He smiled. "Of course. It just means *to appear.* Sentinel Island is for those who are able to appear as angels by harnessing their superior consciousness." At her confused look, he added, "*Consciousness* means your awareness of yourself, others, and your environment. Because your father was an angel and your mother a mermaid, you have the potential to manifest yourself at the highest level on the consciousness scale—by having both wings and a tail. To my knowledge, this is something no one has ever done before."

Stella was pretty sure her head was going to explode . . . but it did sound pretty cool. "So I'm going to learn to man-i-fest"—she spoke the word slowly, trying it out in the sentence—"wings at Sentinel Island? That's awesome."

"Well, your father once lived there. In fact, he lived there when I did."

"Did you know my mother too?" Stella asked.

"Not too well," Magnus replied, sitting on the edge of the bed. "She didn't like me much. She thought I was going to take your father away because he broke the law."

Stella thought of the letter. "You mean because he fell in love with my mom?"

"Exactly," Magnus said. "Your father and I went on a mission together under the sea—it was a joint mission, angels and mer-folk working together, and we took a serum so we could manifest as our friends in the water realm. We were all working together to stop Sylvain, but we were supposed to return when we'd fulfilled our part of the mission. But he didn't come back, so I was sent to collect him. That's the first time I met both your mother and Esmi, by the way."

She took a long moment to think about that. Sylvain was the name her mother had mentioned in the letter. She was almost afraid to ask, but she figured knowing was better than worrying about the unknown: "Who is Sylvain? What was he doing that you had to stop?"

"A person has to be trained to think before they act—you know what I mean?"

Magnus looked at her for confirmation, and Stella nodded. Her parents had taught her all about that.

"Well, sometimes, when you act without really thinking it through—when you don't draw on your awareness and instead listen to the untrained thoughts in your head—you risk drifting from your life's purpose. Then you do stupid or even bad things that are harder to correct, harder to turn away from, which is what happened to Sylvain. He wants to control the world. His forces are at work even now, seeking to destabilize the universal order. Missions, like the one your father and I were on, are help-ing to thwart his plans."

She got what he was saying, and she was interested in the information about her family, but some of the other stuff was starting to feel like a lecture. She wanted to know more about her family—or school as Esmi had called them. "Did Esmi know where my dad was after that mission?"

"Yes, but she didn't tell me, in order to protect her sister. Your parents had already married, and the law forbids our kind from marrying those from other realms."

"But why? That's not fair."

"Fair or not, he broke the law, and that mission was the last one merfolk and angels worked on together. We only joined forces to stop Sylvain, and most of our leaders were still . . ." He paused, clearly searching for what he wanted to say. Finally, he said, "It was a delicate alliance that was broken when your mother and father disappeared together."

"Did they know they were breaking the law?" Stella didn't know whether to be horrified by all the damage her parents had done or thrilled they'd loved each other that much—probably a little of both.

"They knew—or at least your father did, but he did it anyway." Magnus fell silent again and stared off, as though remembering it all. Squaring his shoulders, he continued, "I went back to the Panel of Judgment to plead his case, which is how I came to be banished to this lighthouse." He smiled ruefully. "I've been stuck here since before you were born. Then your notice of apprenticeship showed up. That's when I tracked you all down—just a few weeks ago."

"So you found us on Viola Island?"

"Yes. Your letter came to me with a request to find you, but it had been more than a decade since I saw any of you. That's why I sought Esmi's help. Together, we found you."

"But why? We were safe there. No one else had found us. It was clearly you and that 'notice' that made my parents decide to leave. Why is it so important I go to Sentinel Island now?"

Magnus smoothed his beard as he looked at her, his expression serious. "Stella, Sylvain's forces were coming for you on Viola Island." Stella thought about the fires and explosions on the night they left the island, finally realizing what had caused them. Seeing her eyes widen in understanding, Magnus nodded gravely but said no more about it. "Only eight landling apprentices are summoned to the Citadel each year, and this year, you're one of them."

4

FILLING IN THE BLANKS

No pressure at all, Stella thought. The only thing she hadn't been average at her entire academic life was being the new student. In an instant, she was half mermaid, half angel, a princess, and one of only eight landlings—whatever that was—to go to some weird angel school? If this was true, she wanted to jump with joy, because this would make her special—abnormal, strange, and, yes, maybe even grotesque, but also extraordinary. She'd spent her life being picked on, teased and excluded in every school she'd ever attended. Maybe at this new school, she'd be accepted. She sighed at the thought. Was this a dream? Was someone playing a joke on her? She wished she could tell her parents the good news. But wait—they already knew. So why hadn't they told her about all of this?

About a million questions were running through her head, but she went with the easiest: "What's Sentinel Island like?"

"Wonderful." A big smile split Magnus's face so that Stella couldn't help but smile back. "It's full of excitement and knowledge and—" He leapt to his feet and pulled an envelope out of his pocket.

"Here," Magnus said, handing it to her. "This is your notice of apprenticeship." Stella took the letter and noticed that the envelope was embossed with the same wing-and-sword sigil that was on her father's bracelet. She opened the letter and read:

Dear Stella Merriss,

Congratulations! You have been recruited to Sentinel Island's prestigious angel apprenticeship program. Your recruiter will accompany you to report to the iron gate of the Citadel before the end of the Pageant Day Parade—be prompt! The training year begins on the first day of fall and ends on the last day of spring. The first year of your training is a probationary period during which you may be escorted home at any time should our rigorous standards not be met. Because the probationary year of your training will require all of your focus, no outside contact is permitted. Regular progress reports will be sent to your parent/guardian.

The Citadel provides room, board, and training gear, so pack only enough for your journey, bringing no more than five personal items with you. Your required garments are available at Josephine's Fine Garment Shop, located at 13 Halo Lane on the island, and must be picked up before orientation. Please familiarize yourself with the seven Laws of the Universe (see back) and bring the enclosed permission form, signed by your parent/ guardian. A response is required for your space to be held.

Sincerely,
Orica Astras
Apprentice Coordinator

Stella flipped the letter over to scan the laws printed on its back:

The Seven Laws of the Universe
· the law of vibration
· the law of rhythm
· the law of perpetual transmutation
· the law of relativity
· the law of polarity
· the law of attraction
· the law of cause and effect

Homework already, she thought. Aloud, she said, "How am I supposed to send a response?"

"Don't worry. As your appointed recruiter, I've already taken care of it," Magnus said, without offering further details.

"Oh-kay," Stella said slowly. "When is the Pageant Day Parade?"

"Ten days's time on the last day of summer. A ship is coming soon to take us to Sentinal Island. For now, you must be starving. Let's eat." Magnus led Stella to the quaint kitchen where they had a meal of steamed red clampers and talked more about what life was like on Sentinel Island.

Stella was helping Magnus tidy up the lighthouse when a scream outside the window made them both jump. Rushing to peer out, they watched as Esmi, gasping and desperate, dragged herself from the water onto the beach, her face awash in agony. It had been nearly two days since Esmi had stormed off. As she pulled herself farther onto dry land, they could see the trail of blood she was leaving in the sand. Magnus barely squeezed through the nearest window, and then jumped, wings appearing and spreading, and flew down to her side.

As Stella raced down the stairs, she saw through the many small windows dotting the walls of the stairwell that the bay churned with sharks. When she reached the beach, Stella noticed that one side of Esmi's tail bled where it had been torn. Magnus cradled her head in his lap as she whimpered. Glancing up at Stella, he ordered, "Go get the bucket of seaweed."

Frantically, Stella tore up the beach, grabbed the bucket from where her aunt had left it the day she'd first laid eyes on her and headed back, seawater sloshing over the sides, dousing her shins with a cold, brackish brine as she struggled over rocks and across the sand to where her aunt now lay unconscious and Magnus pressed on her tail to stop the bleeding.

Magnus fished out a handful of seaweed and hurriedly wrapped Esmi's wounded tail. "Go upstairs, into the bathroom, and fill the tub with water from the middle faucet; it's salt water."

Stella sprinted away. She only looked back briefly once she'd reached the lighthouse, and watched Magnus pick up Esmi's limp body, manifest his wings, and lift off, kicking up all kinds of sand. Inside the bathroom, Stella rotated the faucet handle and salt water poured into an old cast iron bathtub. Magnus entered the tiny room, careful not to bump Esmi against the doorframe, and gently lowered the unconscious mermaid into the water. "In order for her tail to grow back, she must remain wet," he explained.

"What happens if she . . . dries?"

"She would lose her foot," he said, grimacing. "Tissue regeneration occurs with fish and merfolk, but seawater and seaweed are necessary for a mermaid's recovery."

While Esmi stayed submerged, her tail cocooned in the protective sheath of knotted seaweed Magnus had put in place, Magnus and Stella quietly slipped downstairs to the kitchen. He busied himself at the counter and then said, "See if you can get her to sip some of this." He handed Stella a mug whose hot contents emanated a horrible smell. She looked inside. Bits of twigs, gnarly roots, yeasty scum, dried leaves, and what looked like a worm floated in brackish water.

"What is it?" she asked, wrinkling her nose.

"Herbal tea—just make her drink it."

Stella nearly gagged carrying the funky-smelling liquid to the bathroom. She held her breath, tilted Esmi's head back, and coaxed her aunt to swallow the medicinal concoction. Throughout the evening and part of the next day, she took turns with Magnus tending to the injured mermaid.

By midafternoon of the following day, a fog had rolled in over the small lighthouse island, blanketing everything in fluffy cotton as Stella took up her post next to the bathtub.

You must leave this lighthouse immediately, her aunt said, emerging from her healing coma with bulging eyes and startling Stella. The message gurgled up weak but insistent. *You are in grave danger.*

Leaning over the edge of the tub, Stella asked, *What kind of danger?*

The sharks . . . they're coming for you.

Stella had spent the last couple of days getting used to several new realities, but it seemed the surprises would never stop. *Sharks* were coming for her?

"It's all part of Sylvain's plan," Esmi continued, speaking aloud now, clutching the side of the tub to pull herself up to look at her niece. "Leave now. Go to Sentinel Island, like your parents wanted. The angels will keep you safe."

Then, she slipped back into unconsciousness, leaving her frightening words pounding in Stella's ears.

5

EVIL COMES TO TOWN

The three volcanic peaks called the Dragonspurs jutted skyward above the clouds, belching out ash and soot. The smoke plume camouflaged the arrival of Lord Sylvain's army. Sylvain himself led the squadron of soldiers. This was the last of three possible locations to be scouted as his headquarters from which he would execute his plan to conquer and rule the three realms. He had deemed the other two unsuitable. If Victor's preliminary reports were accurate, this lakeside village would meet Sylvain's needs to perfection.

His black cloak billowed and snapped around his frame, his dark wings cutting through the wind as he flew. The skin that covered his face was practically translucent, and the shadowy eye sockets encased ruthless midnight eyes. When he was a teenager, Regent Macklin, his appointed mentor in the sky realm, had declared him too obsessed by personal ambition for an angel, but it went beyond just personal desires—he would have done anything to get his way, and his mentor had known it even then.

Sylvain wondered what Macklin would think of him now. His drive had spurred him to start a revolution to overthrow the Celestial Council, earning him the respect of the vilest beings in the three realms. He was in the process of unifying this evil and needed to establish a seat of power from which to do so.

In his wake, a posse of ten officers copied Sylvain's every aerial maneuver. Stars of various colors and sizes sewn to their collars proclaimed their ranks. The highest-ranking among them was Victor, a fallen angel and therefore general of the sky realm. Although five stars adorned his collar, a sixth was surely imminent. It rested on whether Lord Sylvain chose the general's selection as his headquarters.

Positioned farther back, an aerial squadron of one-hundred Red Eyes, the soldiers of Sylvain's growing army, flew in sync. Their wings pounded out a rhythmic beat. Their form-fitting uniforms shimmered like wet coal in the smoky-gray air; their faces were hidden by tight masks with eye slits through which peered their menacing, glowing red eyes—a byproduct of the procedure they underwent as recruits in Lord Sylvain's army.

Lord Sylvain spotted his destination through a momentary opening in the cloud cover. Halting, he raised his hand, signaling his fleet to fall into formation behind him. Although Lord Sylvain gathered details about military strategy from his officers, he investigated every angle personally, never trusting anyone's advice implicitly—the final decision was always his.

He focused on the town below, and a sneer lifted the corners of his mouth as he basked in his power; he relished how the fear he caused could be used to control others. *Absolute authority is given to the one who knows how to wield it* was his motto.

"Have you planted the explosive charge inside the volcano's crater?" Lord Sylvain asked his general.

"I have, my lord," Victor said. Though he would never show any outward signs of weakness in front of his red-eyed subordinates, there was a slight tremor in his voice that he knew only Sylvain could detect. Victor passed the detonator to his master. "Just press this button and the explosion will set off a volcanic eruption."

"Excellent." All at once, a brilliant golden light engulfed Sylvain and transformed his dark visage into a kind, beautiful face with shimmering white wings. With a flap of his now-beautiful appendages, Sylvain descended into the village.

Despite the rain, the simple villagers were bustling about their business. Fishermen sold freshly caught silver fins and lake buttertails from canoes, farmers hawked medicinal roots and fragrant leaves, basket weavers barked out the value of their wares to would-be buyers, and market-goers crowded around stalls to haggle over prices.

The stalls consisted of nothing more than skinny poles fastened together with leather straps and walls fashioned from handwoven cloth. Empty wooden crates were strewn about. Flies buzzed over fish guts, bones, and heads in the barrels where the fishmongers had discarded them. Fish scales littered the ground, sending little twinkling prisms through the air, while the scales themselves clung to the boots of every passerby who walked the square's cobblestones. The whole marketplace reeked.

Such primitive landlings, Lord Sylvain thought as he closed in on the scene. *How easily they will be taken in.*

Leaning against a stall pole, with a child in her arms, a beggar tilted her face skyward. "Angel!" she shrieked, leaping to her feet. "Up there. Look!"

Shoppers and merchants turned to stare in disbelief. Fables about angels had been passed down from generation to generation, but none of the townspeople had ever had a personal visitation from one. Whispers grew louder, turning into a murmur of voices, until a chorus of shouts rose above the hubbub: "Look! Angel! It's an angel!"

Lingering in midair above the muddy cobblestones, Lord Sylvain scrutinized the chaos with a smile. *I do believe I have found the perfect place from which to plan my takeover.* He looked out at the rich brown dirt field, the crystal-clear river that bubbled through town, and the sturdy brick buildings with their star-shaped roof tiles. *No one else around for miles, no prying eyes from nearby villages to see what's happening, and hardly any visitors. By the time anyone realizes we're here, it'll be too late.*

Awestruck, the villagers gathered around, dazzled by Sylvain's luminescent robe, the glow of his radiant face. His compassionate smile conveyed love and kindness, and as he extended his arms out to his sides, they reached with their own arms, hoping to touch him. The crowd instantly fell silent.

"I have come from afar to save you from a grave danger," he announced. "I have been instructed to rescue you. Follow, and you will not only be unburdened of your toil and wretchedness but I will lead you to a paradise beyond your imagining."

The crowd, mesmerized, nodded practically in unison, willing to do whatever he asked of them.

"But we must go quickly," Sylvain said, "for the land on which you have made your homes is about to be destroyed by the volcanoes. Leave everything and come now. Your every need will be provided for."

Sylvain lowered his hands and pressed the detonator that he'd slid into his sleeve. Dirt and rock instantly shot skyward from the tallest of the three Dragonspurs. The volcanoes had rumbled for years but hadn't erupted in generations. The villagers screamed, running for cover as the ground shook, collapsing market stalls and toppling over stacked goods. Debris from the eruption started pummeling the village with a thunderous rain.

"Be not afraid, my friends," Lord Sylvain called. "Follow me. I will lead you to safety, but we must hurry."

Lulled into a trance by the angelic apparition, the crowd began following him along the village's main road, slowly at first, heading away from the lake toward the mountains beyond.

Once the villagers were well beyond the confines of the town and in a narrow pass, Red Eyes appeared above them. When the landlings caught sight of them, screams ripped through the air. The crowd pushed and shoved, knocking one another to the ground. Massive flying transporters came into view and landed. Walkways extended from the bodies of the vessels. Panicked villagers attempted to run, but the terrifying Red Eyes quickly corralled the landlings and herded them into the cargo holds of the airships. The village had just been evacuated by a fallen angel and his grotesque army.

In town, a roundup of stragglers had begun. As a contingent of Red Eyes hunted door-to-door for anyone who remained behind, Sylvain returned to the center of town.

Taking up residence in the largest house in the village, Lord Sylvain created an energy portal in the garden, to make journeying back and forth between the three battlefronts quicker, and settled in.

With the disappointing news about the girl getting away from his frenzy of sharks, Lord Sylvain held his water realm general, Requino, personally responsible for the failed mission. Besides catching Stella, Requino had been directed to form alliances with the merfolk and recruit mersoldiers to join Lord Sylvain in seizing control of all three realms. Unfortunately, for Requino, he had let his leader down on all accounts.

It should not be taking this long to gain power in the water realm. Requino should be able to find more recruits. I need to have a conversation with him about his commitment to my leadership. I also need a general on land, or we will remain too weak in this realm, Lord Sylvain thought. He walked through the garden to check his portal, plucking a thorn from a plaguewood tree—the gnarly trees overwhelmed the garden as soon as the corrupted energy of the portal had taken root.

The energy portal buzzed to life, and Requino stepped through and greeted his leader. They walked inside, and Sylvain directed him to sit.

The pungent smell of guano permeated the room—Lord Sylvain called out to his pets, a colony of numbats, which had already made themselves at home among the rafters in the high ceilings.

Nervously, Requino stared up at the shrieking black mass before he was called back to attention by Sylvain's heated gaze.

"So, have you captured the child?" Sylvain inquired.

"Er, not quite sir." Attempting to steady the quivering in his voice, Requino shuddered when a few of the numbats landed on his head.

"In our last meeting, you assured me there would be an all-out offensive to capture her. What became of that?"

"The sharks attempted to get her, but she seems to wield some great power that keeps her beyond reach. Now, both an angel and a mermaid have interfered. They are—"

"Enough!" Sylvain snapped, slamming his hands down on the table so violently that the bats took flight. "Do I need to remind you of what happens to those who fail me?" Slowly rising to his feet, he unbuttoned the top few buttons of his shirt and pulled it open, exposing the skin of his upper chest. A faint shadow moved beneath his skin, and a devilish smile broke across his face.

"N-no, my lord," Requino said, stuttering. "But—"

"There are no 'buts' in my service, General Requino. Return to the water realm this instant. Seize her. I want her brought to me without further delay. Is that understood?"

"I will bring her to you." Requino rose and backed out of the room, bowing as he went, his eyes fixed on the writhing tattoos that looked back at him from underneath Lord Sylvain's skin.

Lord Sylvain watched as the general hurried through the portal and back to the water realm to fulfill his assignment. With such a frightful incentive, the general surely would be motivated to capture the elusive Stella Merriss at last.

6

THE FLYING *CAPEARLUS*

Stella burst into the observatory at the top of the lighthouse and doubled over, panting. So affected by her aunt's warning that she wished she could sprout—manifest, as Magnus would say—wings and fly to wherever her parents had wanted her to go. "I have to go to Sentinel Island. My life depends on it."

Unfazed, Magnus stood in place, looking through his sky scanner at the sea and horizon.

"Did you hear me?" Stella asked, clutching the stitch in her side. "Esmi woke up." She paused, but he seemed focused on whatever he saw through his device. "She says only the angels can keep me safe from Sylvain," she said, trying again to get his attention.

The lighthouse keeper remained silent.

Her hands on her hips, Stella scowled at him. "Why don't you answer me?"

"The *Capearlus.*" Lowering the sky scanner, he handed it to Stella.

With it trained on the horizon, she put an eye to it and looked—a ship came into view. Puffy sails billowed above a long, sleek hull that gathered to a point, where the bust of a mermaid perched. Instead of bobbing on the surface, the ship rocketed through the air just above the water.

"It's flying," Stella exclaimed.

"Not flying, hovering."

Lurching hard to the right, it rounded the island at lightning speed, leaning so far to one side that Stella was sure it would tip over. Instead, it shot back upright, catapulting something into the air from its mast. High above, a parachute opened into a rainbow of color, and a parachutist came into view, his long, blue coat fluttering behind him in the wind. They watched as he landed gracefully on the little beach.

Magnus grabbed Stella's hand, and they ran together down the hundreds of stairs, out the door, and through the hot afternoon air to meet the new arrival.

On the beach, the parachutist with dark skin and kind, brown eyes unclipped the parachute's harness and slipped it off. Black curls covered his head, and the gold buttons on his coat winked in the sun.

"Glad you could drop in, Captain Finnegan," Magnus said, greeting him with a bear hug. "So, this is how you raise your consciousness high enough to fly like an angel?" he joked, gesturing toward the parachute.

Captain Finnegan stuffed his parachute back in his pack and propped his hands on his hips. "Landlings may not be able to fly like your kind or swim like the merfolk, but we have our own special traits."

"Yes, you certainly are talented at 'liberating' angelic technology," Magnus said, raising an eyebrow.

Addressing Stella, the captain said, "Magnus tells me you're both a flyer and a swimmer, or at least your parents were."

Stella shrugged. Her aunt had just warned her she needed to go immediately to Sentinel Island to stay safe, and she did not know this person. Who was he anyway? She wasn't going to reveal anything to him—maybe he was one of Sylvain's spies.

Observing her silence, Magnus said, "She doesn't yet know her own capabilities, but once she's on the island, surrounded by all those other angels, she will. It's just a matter of raising her consciousness."

Stella shot Magnus an anxious look. Wasn't she supposed to be in danger? Should they be telling this stranger—this landling—about her? Which made something occur to her. "Wait—you're a landling. How do you know about all of this angel and merfolk stuff?"

Finnegan smiled. "I know lots of things." He winked and motioned to the angel. "Magnus showed up on my ship, the *Capearlus*, a few days ago and asked me a favor. He told me he'd left you here to sleep off a nasty shark bite you'd taken on the arm."

"Come on, Finn, let's go inside," Magnus said, slapping his friend on the back, "and grab some food and talk about the journey that lies ahead of you."

They strolled to the lighthouse, with Stella following along despite her concern over what appeared to be dawdling on Magnus's part. Inside Magnus ladled chunky buttertail stew into bowls. The captain slipped out of his coat, gave it a quick shake, and draped it over the back of a chair before taking his seat.

When a moan of pain echoed through the lighthouse, Finnegan scrambled to his feet, a look of alarm spreading across his face. "What in the world was that?" A ghost? Is this place haunted?"

"No, the lighthouse isn't haunted. It's only Esmi." Magnus, laughing along with Stella, got up and ambled to the bathroom to check on her. "Tell the Captain all about it, Stella. He won't bite."

Stella eyed the landling suspiciously before starting in. "Sharks nearly bit off her fin. Magnus says she'll recover, but she needs constant care—"

"—so I'm going to have to stay here," Magnus finished, returning to the table. He gave them both a look so serious it seemed to literally weigh them down. He pointed at Captain Finnegan. "I need you to take Stella to Sentinel Island."

Stella felt as shocked as Finnegan looked.

"Now wait just a minute!" Finnegan said, his head jerking toward Stella. "I agreed to take both of you, not just the princess."

"I know, but who could've foreseen Esmi's shark attack? She needs me or else I'd go." Magnus held his breath, his eyes pleaded with the captain.

After Stella watched Finnegan do a bit of mental handwringing, he glowered at Magnus. "Oh, all right. Just this once. But you owe me—big time!"

Magnus's tensed shoulders relaxed, and then he grabbed Finnegan's hand, shaking it so hard his arm was nearly wrenched out of its socket. "Thank you, and I'll repay you. I promise," Magnus said, relieved. Then he turned toward Stella. "You'll be safe with Finn and the trip will only take a week or so. Are you okay with this?"

Stella looked at the large angel. "Yes," she said, her words laced with worry, "are you sure? Sounds like Captain Finnegan here has"—she cleared her throat—"maybe taken things from the angels . . . ?" She wasn't sure what Magnus had meant when he said Finnegan "liberated technology," but it sounded shady.

The captain huffed out a laugh. "He was referring to my boat. Angel technology is what makes it fly . . . er, I mean, hover over the sea. I only hover it on open water, though. Near land, she sails like any other landling vessel."

Stella cast a doubtful glance at Magnus.

Finnegan noticed. "Like all the merfolk, she distrusts my kind," he said, shaking his head.

"Of course she doesn't," Magnus said, his tone calming. "She was raised a landling like you—just not a pirate landling." He smiled at his friend. Then, to Stella's relief, he stopped talking like she wasn't there and turned to address her. "Finnegan here is an old friend, and I trust him with escorting you to Sentinal Island, as much as I trust myself. As a sort of landling ambassador to the angels, he helps the sky realm get things that can only be found on land, and in return, we, um, I mean—the angels—let him use a few things most landlings don't even know exist."

Stella watched Magnus's face flash red at the mention of his own exile from the sky realm, and she suddenly felt sorry for him. It occurred to her that Magnus was taking care of her, making sure she arrived safely to Sentinel Island, not for her, but for Arago, her father, his friend. Compassion for the lighthouse keeper bloomed in her heart, and she suddenly felt a touch better about leaving with the captain. She was still anxious about it all, not least of which was her aunt's recent proclamation that she was in immediate danger, but relief flooded through her when the captain spoke again.

"I'd offer to stay," Finnegan said to Stella, "but I know Magnus wouldn't hear of it. Besides, my body doesn't do well on firm ground—I need a ship beneath my feet."

Stella was grateful they'd be heading for the one place her parents thought she'd be safe, but she couldn't help but worry about the journey ahead. Without Magnus, would they be able to get away if attacked by the sharks or, worse, by Sylvain himself?

7

SETTING SAIL

The salty air whooshed over them as Magnus, holding Stella with one arm and Captain Finnegan in the other, confidently flew them to the *Capearlus*, whipping Stella's hair about until it was a tangled mess.

Seeing his angel form up close, Stella was struck by his magnificence. His impressive wings were made from feathers of white and gray with alternating feathers of silver. The silver feathers shimmered inside the globe of crackling energy that engulfed him. When they drew closer to the *Capearlus*, the sharks reappeared, hurling themselves at the angel flying above it, but the height at which he flew and the bubble of golden energy protected them.

Once they landed on deck, the sailors aboard grabbed hold of the mooring line to get them back out to sea. The wind swept across the bow, smacking Stella full in the face. Sails danced above her. While the crew worked in clusters to haul in the ropes, two sailors climbed the masts. She watched in awe at their skill and courage as they braved the heights.

Magnus placed a huge hand on Stella's shoulder and squeezed reassuringly, bringing her attention back to him. "Better get back to Esmi."

Stella felt a rush of sadness and wrapped her arms around his waist. "Thank you for everything. Be sure to let Esmi know I took her advice and went to Sentinel Island. Tell her to write to me."

He leaned out of the hug and smiled a bit sadly. "You know there's no outside contact during the first year of training, especially from a mermaid," he said. "You'll learn more about it once you get settled at the Citadel."

First, Stella had lost her parents, and now she was losing both her aunt and Magnus.

Lifting her chin with his fingers, Magnus peered into her eyes. "You'll be fine because you're strong—strong as your father, maybe stronger. I know it seems like your world has fallen apart, but your life is just beginning."

With another squeeze to her shoulder, Magnus expanded his wings and lifted off the deck. Stella watched his figure shrink away as he flapped his glorious wings and headed back toward the lighthouse—back to her aunt Esmi.

"Set a course for Sentinel Island," Captain Finnegan hollered, sending deckhands scattering to their posts. "Anchors aweigh!" He conferred quietly with a crew member and then turned to Stella. "Follow me, Miss Stella. I'll show you to your quarters."

He led Stella through a doorway and down some stairs, into the belly of the ship. It took a moment for her eyes to adjust to the darkness belowdecks, but she could make out that the corridor ended at three doors. From a cord around his neck, Finnegan drew out a skeleton key and opened the middle door.

"Welcome to the captain's quarters," he announced, stepping aside to let her through. Inside smelled like an old library. Large paned windows in front of her illuminated dark bookshelves along the walls, and two small wrought iron chandeliers, hanging by chains, swayed with the ship's movements. Making his way past a large desk and two wooden chairs, Finnegan waved Stella into another room. "You'll be sleeping here. At night, I'll bunk with my crew, but during the daytime, I'll be working at my desk—I hope you don't mind."

"Nah, it won't bother me," Stella said. "She looked around the cozy chamber, noting its built-in quilt-covered bed, a dresser, and some diamond-paned windows. Plonking herself down on the bed with a sigh, she bounced a few times to test its springiness.

"Here," Finnegan said, walking over to hand her the key. "It's called a universal key. Its form changes to fit any lock, which means it opens any door. You keep it. This door stays locked, understand? For your own safety, don't let anyone in."

"Really? Wow, thanks," Stella said, awestricken, staring at the antique key. "It's a really great gift." Stella put the cord around her neck and tucked the key into her shirt.

Blushing, Finnegan changed the subject. "Let me give you a tour of the *Capearlus* so you can get your bearings."

Thirty minutes later, they were back from their tour, which had been windy and filled with many introductions to happy sailors singing off-key. She had also enjoyed a tasty fish sandwich from the galley. Stella now peered out a window in the captain's main cabin, marveling at how the ocean floated past from inside this hovercraft and imagining what it would feel like to fly like Magnus.

At his desk, Finnegan had charts, gadgets, and boxes spread out. Holograms of ships at sea, faraway lands, and moving constellations hovered around his head. She'd never seen any-thing like it before. As the captain studied them, he recorded his impressions in a big book. Looking over his shoulder, Stella attempted to decipher what he was writing.

The captain drew in a deep breath, pressed a button, and all the holograms disappeared. Removing his glasses, he rubbed the bridge of his nose. "Whoever is after you are a dangerous bunch," he said quietly.

Stella's shoulders slumped in defeat. "I don't understand why they are after me. Magnus, Esmi, even my mother in her letter, never bothered to explain why anyone would be after me. Maybe it's because I'm a freak that doesn't belong in either world—a freakish half mermaid, half angel."

"I have some news for you. Your mermaid-angel parentage may be unique, but you aren't unusual in your freakdom." He smiled kindly at her. "It doesn't matter where you go—everyone's a freak in their way. The trick is accepting it."

She shook her head. "I want to go home."

"And where exactly *is* home for you?"

"Viola Island, where my parents and I were happy."

"But they're not there anymore, are they?" He said it gently, but it still cut deep.

"No." The reality was that if she were to return to Viola Island, it wouldn't be like before.

"Home isn't a place. It's a feeling inside you. It's being com-fortable in your own skin. We all want to belong, every last one of us. If you only realized it, you'd already belong."

"I only ever felt I belonged when I was with my parents," Stella said, wishing she could be with them now. Her chest tightened from the overwhelming sadness she felt knowing they were truly gone.

Finnegan paused, then pointed at the cord around her neck. "Do you know the universal key unlocks more than doors?" Stella held up the key. "It unlocks mysteries inside our minds too. I received it from a soothsayer in Ilya. He told me, 'Take this token and keep it until you know your purpose; then pass it on to another questing individual.' Even after that, it still took years for me to find my purpose."

"And what's your purpose?"

"To sail the seas in service to others and to explore."

"Explore new lands?"

"New territories both outside and those dimensions on the inside, deep within." He raised his brows mysteriously, and then he gathered up his books, charts, and graphs, and told her, "Don't forget to lock the door after me."

Stella lay down on her bed, wondering why someone who didn't even know what it meant to be half mermaid, half angel— hadn't even known angels and mermaids existed—could be at the middle of anything, let alone a great war. It frightened her, but she was determined to explore within. Maybe she'd not only find her home but also herself.

8

A MERARMY

The next several days sailed by uneventfully as the wind pushed the *Capearlus* on its course. Stella mostly stayed in her room, unable to eat, wavering between sadness for her parents and anxiety about her future with the angels. At times she would fidget with her father's timepiece or reread her mother's letter, which she had tucked into a pocket of her father's jacket along with her notice of apprenticeship. Early on the sixth morning, pounding on the door next to her room startled Stella awake, and one of the crew cried out, "Captain, you're needed on deck right away."

The door next to hers slammed and footsteps—she assumed them to be Captain Finnegan's—thundered away. Sitting up, she peered out the window and was surprised to see that in the golden light of dawn the *Capearlus* was floating motionless on a calm sea. In the open water, as far as she could see, leaping dolphins exploded into the air like cannon fire, racing toward their vessel. Terror-stricken, Stella pulled on her father's jacket and ran up on deck. Standing at the helm at the back of the ship, she saw Captain Finnegan peering through a telescope while all twelve of his sailors awaited orders. Afraid Captain Finnigan would send her back belowdecks, she shrunk behind a wooden barrel to remain unseen and watch what the captain would do.

Moments later, the waters around the ship started to gurgle and froth forcibly as hundreds of muscular mermen and mermaids surfaced from the depths while seated atop giant seahorses covered head to tail in bronze-green turtle shell armor. In utter awe, Stella noticed how the merfolk were seated upon sidesaddles that were similar to a land horse saddle but shaped to accommodate their large fins. Their scaly tails glistened a variety of metallic hues—some pearly alabaster, some lustrous rainbow, still others opalescent jade. Leather chinstraps affixed silver helmets to their heads, and the rising sun reflected off them in a dazzling array. With tridents, spears, and swords raised skyward, it was obvious that the merarmy was battle ready.

The flotilla turned to face their commander, a black-haired mersoldier in an abalone-shell breastplate. When he thrust his golden trident above his head, his troops came to attention. The dolphins stopped jumping and surrounded the merarmy, their heads poking from the water.

"Who is in charge?" the mersoldier commander shouted in a loud, authoritative voice.

"I am Finnegan, the captain of the *Capearlus*. Who are you?"

"I am Lazaretto, commander of the merarmy cavalry. I am here to warn you of an impending attack to your vessel. You must flee. We will defend you while you make your escape. Make haste to Sentinel Island!"

"Without wind, my ship won't sail."

"Worry not, we will help. Throw out lines for the dolphins and prepare to move out."

Without hesitation, Captain Finnegan hollered, "You heard him, crew, ready her for sailing, then assume your battle stations!" The crew tore off in all directions.

The mersoldier commander addressed the dolphins. "First team, take position beneath the surface and push the ship. Second team, take hold of the lines and pull!"

Lazaretto then turned to rally his troops. "Despite our history with the sky realm, today we fight against Sylvain and his followers who wish to stir chaos and division throughout all the realms. Merfolk will stand with landings and angels alike and we will prevail!"

The dolphins screeched a battle cry that joined the boom of the soldiers pounding their weapons against their shields in a cacophony that rent the air. Falling into lines fifty soldiers long and columns twenty soldiers deep, the mersoldiers took position to make their stand.

The rays of the dawning sun illuminated an army of sharks and stingrays fast approaching from the rear. Their numbers were so many, that Stella couldn't begin to count. The *Capearlus* suddenly lurched, knocking Stella off balance from her hiding place, but soon the ship started to slowly glide away from the approaching enemy army. Realizing her vulnerability, Stella grabbed a nearby gaff hook to defend herself. In that moment, the enemy was upon them.

"Harpoons!" Lazaretto commanded. Barbed spears whistled from barrelled weapons Stella had never seen before, carried by a section of the merarmy. Many found their mark, but the enemy attacked in such large numbers it hardly slowed their advance.

"Charge!" Lazaretto ordered. The front lines of the cavalry raised their spears and tridents, urging their mounts to meet the oncoming enemy.

As the armies clashed in full force, screams and savage war cries filled the air. The sea churned in the wake of the swift-swimming, battling creatures. Half the mersoldier lines held the advancing enemy off, as the *Capearlus* kept pulling away. The remaining soldiers tightened their lines around the ship, a last stand of defense if needed.

As the forces clashed, the mersoldiers' shields created an impenetrable wall the sharks and stingrays couldn't pass. Tridents prodded the sharks into a herd and cut a swath through the opponent's front line. The mersoldiers held a temporary advantage over the sharks and stingrays. But a second school of larger sharks moved in with a ferocity and coordination that surprised even the merfolk.

Working in formation, sharks surrounded and attacked the soldiers. Lazaretto's soldiers regrouped and chucked weighted ropes, which wrapped around the sharks' tails, causing them to sink. The enemy stingrays lashed their tails around the wrists of the sea cavalrymen, who, in response, cleaved off the stingray's tails to free themselves. Although the mer-army had stretched giant nets across the water, some sharks and stingrays broke through and made their advance on Captain Finnegan's vessel.

Despite the dolphin's efforts, the *Capearlus* was moving away from the scene too slowly. When Lazaretto realized his forces couldn't hold off their opponents much longer, he reached into a pouch attached to his waist. Pulling out a conch shell, he put it to his lips and blew a triple blast.

All of a sudden, a pod of huge white narwhals breached, emitting deafening high-pitched screeches that caused everyone in the vicinity—including merfolk, deckhands, and Stella—to cover their ears. The screeching momentarily rendered the sharks and stingrays motionless, and the narwhals took that moment to slap the water's surface with their tails, creating a great wave that reached the craft's hull, buoying it forward at breakneck speed.

Stella found herself soaked, the sails' masts nothing but rubble, and everyone on deck scrambling to keep their footing. The tsunami carried the *Capearlus* over a great distance until a shout of "Land Ho!" echoed across the deck. Though veiled in mist, a giant rock appeared before Stella's eyes.

They had arrived at Sentinel Island.

9

THE DAHU

Rand Eyvindur peeked nervously through the slit in the curtain to look at the crowd. Anxious reporters shifted on their feet, crews held their cameras aloft, and a velvet rope sequestered the wealthy businessowners, fashionably dressed socialites, and distinguished politicians to an area at the back of the auditorium.

"What if I trip?" Rand wondered aloud. An eleven-year-old prodigy, he had already obtained a doctorate from Ilya University. Yet despite his brilliance, at moments like this, he was overcome with self-doubt. He nervously rearranged the notes in his pocket, which by now were smudged, and wiped his chestnut hair off his sweaty forehead.

"Relax. You'll do great." Jakin Abernathy, his guardian, bent down and laced Rand's shoe. "Imagining unlikely scenarios will only increase the likelihood of them coming true. Why attract them by wasting effort thinking about them? Would the media or all these people even be here if they didn't support you and your cause?"

Rand's tense shoulders relaxed. "I suppose you're right."

"Besides," Jakin continued, "only one person matters tonight." Pulling back the stage curtain, he pointed. At the center of the front row stood Meenah Battelle, twirling slowly to expose the full-length, luxurious lion skin coat that was draped over her frame. The pelt had a rich, golden sheen.

Oohs rose from her admirers.

Her biggest fan, her assistant Hort Grouse, smacked away the hands that reached out to touch the costly coat. "Hands off!" he said, not-so-subtly making space between his idol and the gawkers.

"The big cat was once thought to be extinct," Meenah said, chuckling as she did. Hort joined in a moment later. "I may have nabbed the last Aridian lion in existence to create my fabulous coat."

"Oh no," Rand groaned under his breath. That the coat completing Meenah's ensemble was from one of his favorite animals set his blood boiling.

Jakin tried to calm him. "If you impress her, it will guarantee financing, not only for this expedition, but all others to come."

"But—"

"Tut—tut—tut—if you want to prove the existence of all your lost and forgotten animals, and save them too, I suggest you do as rehearsed," Jakin said. "If you do, you'll have a lifetime of financial backing."

Rand didn't want to argue with Jakin, who had adopted him five years ago, but he didn't have the chance to decide for himself as the voice of the master of ceremonies echoed through the auditorium. "Please put your hands together for our very own cryptozoologist, Dr. Rand Eyvindur."

The crowd erupted in applause, and butterflies rioted in Rand's stomach.

"Go get 'em," Jakin said. With a gentle shove, he pushed Rand onto the stage. The shy, science-minded kid transformed into Dr. Rand Eyvindur, cryptozoologist extraordinaire looking for the next animal that was thought to be only myth.

Rand waved to the crowd and, when the roar died down, reached for his notes. His responsible side dictated he follow his guardian's advice. However, his compassionate nature urged him to stick up for the Aridian lion whose pelt had become just another piece of Meenah's wardrobe.

He cleared his throat and decided to present what he had prepared. *I'll deal with the pelt issue later*, he told himself.

"Thank you, all, for coming today," he began in his most grown-up voice. "My university counselors were surprised when I announced cryptozoology as my major. Considering that studying mythological creatures is often thought to be philosophical instead of scientific, their shock was understandable."

A titter rose from the audience.

"However, finding the giant seahorse during my last expedition not only captured the realm's imagination, but it also legitimized my work, demonstrating the existence of these so-called mythological creatures.

"Today I am announcing another expedition to locate another creature." With Rand's nod to Jakin, his guardian opened a red velvet curtain, revealing a large screen. A single word in capital letters was splashed across it: *DAHU*.

"Dahu," Rand said. "Not many of us have ever heard of a dahu. They're such elusive creatures that it was theorized they were mythological. These animals are reclusive by nature and survive only in mountain ranges high above where few venture."

Jakin pressed the remote. The image that appeared featured the head of what looked like a cross between a goat and a deer. "What makes a dahu unique is how ideally its body has adapted to its environment. It's perfect for living on steep slopes."

The next image was an illustration of the animal's entire body. "As you can see, the legs on one side are shorter than those on the other. The difference allows the dahu to stand upright on the slopes, while at the same time making it impossible for it to turn around on the mountainside without losing its balance and toppling over."

Many in the crowd giggled at the renderings. Several rolled their eyes. A voice called out from the audience, "Dr. Eyvindur, have you pinpointed where you might find one of these dahu?"

Rand sported a broad grin. "Indeed I have. We will be traveling to the three Dragonspurs volcanoes, as we have received credible reports of sightings from this area. Our plan is to find a specimen and bring it back to study, so we know more about them."

"How do you plan on capturing one?" asked a reporter.

"Assuming he finds one, that is," someone said, a remark that was met with low laughter.

"I believe its capture will be best executed by using its uneven legs as the means to trap it." Rand's blue eyes sparkled. Despite the disbelief on the faces of some, a murmur of excitement buzzed through the auditorium. "My team will leave tomorrow by train to commence the search."

A commotion from the front of the crowd grabbed everyone's attention. Meenah was rushing up to the stage; when Hort attempted to follow, Meenah pointed and commanded him to stay. Like a good pet, he obeyed, slinking back into the crowd.

Meenah strode across the stage and pushed Rand aside as the bewildered crowd looked on in disbelief.

"I wanted to come to the dais this evening and publicly announce my support for Dr. Eyvindur's expedition," she said, petting her lion skin coat. "As an animal lover myself, I commend the good doctor for devoting his life to the rescue of these rare and helpless beasts, no matter how short his life has actually been." She smiled indulgently, as if he'd just said the sky was green and she pitied him for it.

She pulled a check from her penguin skin purse and waved it in the air. "As a show of my support, I will be underwriting this expedition to bring in the dahu." She gestured to her pants and knee-high boots. "I wore these jodhpurs in support of this adorable little beast. I mean, doesn't it look like a miniature horse? What a great photo shoot that will make! I even plan to travel with the team to document the whole thing."

She waved the check toward Rand but did not hand it to him. "Also to show my support for the endangered and mythological creatures of the world, I'd like to announce my new start-up: Fashion Farm. It will be a safe space for all of these rare beasts to live in captivity. We will care for them as well as breed them."

From the wings, Jakin swept onto the stage to stand between Meenah and Rand, placing his arm around the boy's shoulders with the obvious intent of trying to defuse the blowup building in Rand. Smiling for the cameras, he said, "Thank you for your generous support, Meenah. It means the world. To both of us." As he squeezed Rand to his side.

"Of course it does," she said, bowing her head ever so slightly.

Rand could restrain himself no longer. He knew Meenah well enough to read between the lines and understood that her real purpose for the Fashion Farm was to slaughter his animals to create new fashions. "It'll also provide you with rare hides for your fancy clothes." The crowd gasped at Rand's boldness while reporters leaned in hungrily for the juicy, scandalous gossip surrounding the infamous Meenah.

Meenah's voice was low and threatening as she said, "Be careful, or I will be sure you can't afford to traipse after your little animals." The sounds of pencils scratching fast across paper sounded throughout the room as reporters quickly recorded every word the trio uttered.

Jakin clapped his hands on Rand's shoulders as if to physically hold him back. "Pay no attention to him, Ms. Battelle. He's just sensitive."

Rand was nearly bubbling with anger, but he held his tongue about her "fashion," instead explaining, "A dahu isn't a horse. Horses have a single-toed hoof. Dahus are cloven-hoofed ungulates."

She arched a brow at him and offered him the check. "Here. And for goodness' sake, Jakin, buy yourself and the child some decent clothes. You must be presentable for the departure ceremony at the train station tomorrow." Shooing Rand and Jakin off the stage with a dismissive flick of her wrist, Meenah turned back to the avid audience and cluster of reporters, and smiled broadly over the dais. "Now who has further questions?"

Jakin grabbed the check and hustled Rand outside, where they stood in somewhat stunned silence.

It was Jakin who finally broke the silence. "Good job. Now we have funding."

"But at what cost?" Rand asked with a droopy voice.

Jakin shrugged. "We got the money we wanted. Besides, she's launching her new business venture. She'll take care of all the mythological animals you discover."

Rand stiffened. "Her intentions are pretty clear—she wants to slaughter them. My animals will provide her with one-of-a-kind fashion. If she's to be believed, the coat she wore was from the last Aridian lion on the planet! I'm guessing she won't wait for my animals to die of old age either."

"She was exaggerating. Let's use her funding for your expedition and then figure out how to ensure all the animals you find aren't intentionally harmed."

"All right, but if they are, then I'll quit. I won't be a part of the murder of any of these rare and beautiful creatures."

10

REQUINO'S FAILURE

Lord Sylvain was seething. Word had arrived that, aided by the merarmy, the child escaped again. Now he paced in front of the glowing fire roaring in the fireplace, its light creating macabre shadows that flickered on the walls. A pronounced limp—an old injury—made him no less imposing. His wide-neck robe revealed what appeared to be tattooed beasts on his chest. He muttered angry words about the child's escape and in response the beasts roiled beneath the surface of his skin.

"I know you crave vengeance against this failure, but not yet," Sylvain consoled the creatures. "Patience. We must wait until he comes to us." The monsters responded to his musing with roars, hisses, and growls. "Requino should have recruited at least a few merfolk by now. Even if we could not have rivaled their numbers, we should at least have a spy within their ranks."

In the courtyard, the energy portal hummed, indicating the general's arrival. Sylvain turned and saw Requino skulking toward him as if summoned to his execution, his knees quivering with each step. The tattooed monsters skittered across Sylvain's skin, making him smile, a grotesque parody of happiness, at his beasts' knowledge of what was to come.

"Did you get her?" Sylvain asked, knowing full well what the answer was.

"No, my lord," Requino confessed.

"Did you not have the assistance of our allies in the sea?" The tattoos pressed against his flesh, craving the opportunity to leave their cage and pounce on this poor excuse for a general.

Sweat poured off Requino as Sylvain continued, "Did you not assure me you had an infallible plan? Am I mistaken that you promised you would bring her to me by now?"

"No, my lord. She was surrounded by—"

"Have you had any success recruiting high-level merfolk to our cause?"

The general shook his head and stammered, "N-nothing yet."

"I have had enough of you and your incompetence," Sylvain growled. Despite his mangled leg, he lunged forward, seizing Requino by the shoulders, and hurling him against a bookcase on the far side of the room.

He whistled, and numbats came flying from the rafters. In a single, dark mass, the colony of bats descended on Requino, sinking their fangs into his exposed flesh. His screams turned to whimpers as the venom paralyzed him, and only a few moments later, he fell silent. The numbats retreated to the shadowed rafters, their beady eyes following their lord's movement toward his motionless general.

A figure emerged from the gloom, a black rucksack hanging by his side. Tattoos completely covered his bald head and face. The spirals and lines appeared to undulate not on top of but beneath his skin.

Sylvain turned to him and commanded, "Camibu, capture the general's consciousness and commit him to skin prison."

Camibu knelt beside Requino's unmoving body. From inside his rucksack he removed a syringe, inserted the needle into the general's temple, and extracted a black, undulating liquid from his brain, nodding at his master.

Back in his chair, Sylvain looked over at the general's body—now just a shell, his eyes staring vacantly. Everyone was disposable.

"Please remove your robe, my lord," Camibu said. He approached the chair with a needle contraption in one hand and a vial containing Requino's consciousness in the other.

Sylvain let his robe drop, exposing his back, as he leaned forward toward the flames. Camibu's cold hand felt for the raised scars of the prison that spread across the ribs on both sides of Sylvain's spine. The ghoulish faces of two prisoners peeked through the prison cell bars.

"Good day, generals. Another prisoner will be joining you momentarily." From Sylvain's shoulders and chest, beastly monsters slithered close to the needle's point, waiting for the fresh addition to their under-skin world.

11

THE DOCKS OF
SENTINEL ISLAND

As the *Capearlus* bobbed into port, its masts splintered and sails in tatters, Stella took in the activity on land.

"It's Pageant Day," Captain Finnegan said, cutting into her thoughts, "so the port will be crowded. Vendors from all over sell their goods here, but the real excitement will be happening behind the Marble Veil, the wall shielding the angelic parts of the island from the landlings who find their way to this port. The Celestial Council raised it to keep the others out, preserving their sovereign authority over the advanced angelic technology. Only angels and those with special permission can pass through the gates of the Marble Veil. Pageant Day is still a wonderful celebration, even without seeing those angelic secrets. You'll learn more once your apprenticeship gets underway at the Citadel."

"Do you have a pass?" she asked.

Finnegan pulled a small identification booklet from his pocket and waved it at her. "The Celestial Counsel granted me a permit when I became a courier between landlings and angels."

Stella checked her own pockets and confirmed she still had the letter from her mother, her notice, the bracelet, and her father's timepiece—just touching these objects made her feel closer to her parents. She quickly slipped his bracelet back on her wrist for safe keeping.

Clouds slid past the island, shrouding it in an aura of mystery. Winged sea dunkers dove into the surrounding waters and then bobbed to the surface, gobbling down their fishy breakfasts. Sentinelian falcons circled overhead, squawking their discontent at the visitors.

While deckhands cleared a path through the scattered debris on deck, a tugboat pulled the *Capearlus* past a jetty and into the jam-packed harbor. Wooden skiffs from Lialia, flatboats from Vast Bog, Ilyan yachts, Laphian catamarans, Gollankan cargo ships, Vilunian pleasure craft, and even sailboats from Arid with their golden canvases aloft clogged the waterway, each awaiting their turn to dock. Stella watched deckhands from other boats drop gangways in place and scurry to unload each craft. Once a boat's cargo was unloaded, it pushed back from the wharf and was replaced by another.

The harbormaster blew his bugle, then shouted into a brassy, conical loudhailer, "Make way, make way!" Hulls thumped as the myriad craft moved to open up a passageway for the tugboat and the *Capearlus*.

"No worries, Stella," Captain Finnegan said, trying to reassure her and pulling her close to him as they drew alongside a quay. "You have your invitation. You'll receive a warm welcome."

"I'm not so sure about that," she said, looking at his weathered face.

"Your father?" Finnegan asked.

She nodded. Arago had been a high-level officer who fled, turning his back on his kind to be with her mother. Somehow, Stella thought not everyone would think that was romantic.

"You should never be judged by the actions of others, only your own," Finnegan said, smiling.

Evidently her face betrayed some of her inner turmoil, because Captain Finnegan patted her back and reiterated, "You'll be treated well."

From the deck, Stella studied the market's grid layout of passageways with stalls featuring every imaginable landling product: sumptuous Aridian gold jewelry, Laphian construction tools, handcrafted Marvelian paintings, one-of-a-kind Lialian swords and daggers, Hollowildian wind and string instruments, Vilunian fabrics, and luxurious clothing from the fashion capitol of Ilya. The display of color and activity was dizzying enough to dazzle any market-goer, but for Stella, who up until now had led a sheltered life, these amazing sights were so inviting that she wanted to jump ship, sprout wings, and explore this new amazing land that was to be her home.

From one side of the quay to the other, the market was encircled by a gleaming white marble wall with a large iron gate at its center. A small queue formed in front of it, and Stella assumed each person had a permit to go behind the Marble Veil. Beyond the wall and its iron gate, homes, shops, and warehouses adorned with red-tiled roofs climbed the steep hillside.

Following Captain Finnegan and the crew down the walkway, Stella noticed that the sailors from the *Capearlus* headed off in various directions to their own activities. The captain told her that his crew hadn't set foot on solid ground in a long time, so she and Finnegan were left to wriggle through the mob as they made their way toward the iron gate, like fish swimming upstream against a strong current.

Smells of sizzling meat, exotic perfume, and sweat hung over the market and made Stella's stomach vacillate between hunger and nausea. Finnegan wove his way through the crushing crowd pulling Stella along. Due to the slow progress they were making, Stella was able to catch glimpses of some of the treasures found in the stalls that lined the market walkway, but, at her short height, she mostly viewed people's backs and chests.

"Look!" she cried in excitement, tugging at Finnegan's hand to slow him. "Can we go look at that stall? Please . . ."

"No, I'm sorry, but it's best we get you to the Citadel," he replied, harried. He continued to pull her along behind him, his knuckles starting to go white from squeezing her hand so tightly as he fought to push a path for them through the mass of bodies.

"Ow. You're hurting me," she groaned.

Stella gasped with wonder as a cluster of shimmering jewels caught her eye from a stall to her left. With a determined yank, she broke free from Finnegan's hold and rushed toward the stall. She was quickly swept away like a leaf on a river. Frightened, and realizing her mistake in letting go of him, she called out Finnegan's name. She thought she heard him call back, but by that time she was so disoriented she couldn't be sure where it was coming from or whether it was even the captain.

Stella was carried along with the crowd, in the opposite direction of the wall. She saw a side alley and took advantage of the slight disruption it created in the crowd to scramble away. She found herself off the main walkway and next to a fish stall.

"Are you lost, little girl?" asked the fishmonger, his black apron shimmering with fish scales.

"Yes, I let go of Captain Finnegan's hand and lost him," she said innocently. "Do you know him?"

The fishmonger giggled. "No I don't—sorry." He bent over and lifted a wooden crate. "Perhaps you can stand on this—"

"Great idea! Thanks." She stepped up and looked out over a sea of bobbing heads as the fishmonger turned to help a customer. At last she spied the captain in the crowd. He had made his way closer toward the marble wall, and was looking around desperately, trying to locate Stella. She started waving her arms and yelling his name, trying to get his attention, but he didn't see or hear her. Instead he starting moving further away, likely assuming Stella would be trying to make her way to the gate to rejoin him.

Suddenly from behind, an arm wrapped around her waist, yanking her from the crate, and a large, rough hand clasped over her mouth. Her shock turned to hysteria when a sack was quickly pulled over her head and body and she was flipped upside down and lifted off the ground.

"Hey, what's the idea?" Stella heard the fishmonger's voice, muffled through the thick burlap. "Help! They've got the girl!" he cried out as her abductor hoisted her painfully over one shoulder and took off running. The din of the market quickly faded from Stella's ears as the person carrying her made off down the alley and around bend after bend. Inside the sack, Stella found herself disoriented and nauseated. She could barely take a breath in the position she was being carried in and the air was stifling hot and stunk of seaweed. No matter how much she punched, kicked, and screamed, she couldn't break her captor's hold.

After a while, she heard the hollow clomping of her kidnapper's feet, and then all motion stopped. A metallic clang rang out as she was dropped on her head, and through the ringing in her ears, she heard muffled voices.

"Toss her in with the other prisoners," a commanding voice said. Seconds later, she felt the sack being dragged along the rough boards of a ship's deck and then down a flight of stairs. She was shoved across the floor so violently that she was certain she was about to be beaten. Instead, she heard a door slam shut and then silence. Bruised and terrified, she was surprised when a murmuring of concerned voices filled her ears.

"Open the sack," said an energetic voice.

Stella felt hands grab one end of the sack.

"Who's in there?" a different voice demanded.

Although she wanted to respond, Stella was too shaken up, too frightened. When the sack finally opened and a rush of sweat-scented but cool air greeted her, she breathed in deeply but stayed quiet. She found herself in a dark, dank, and cramped cell, surrounded by a crowd of concerned onlookers, huddling around for a peek at her. The only light came from a porthole on the far side of the room.

"It's a child," a female voice declared, her hands guiding Stella out of the sack. "You poor thing, let's have a look at you." As she examined Stella, she declared, "They certainly didn't take care in collecting you, now, did they? I'm called Rena." Clustered behind Rena, heads bobbed in agreement.

"How are you feeling?" Rena asked with a worried tone. "What's your name, dear?"

Out of nowhere, someone yelled, "Stella!" and a kid squeezed through the tightly packed adults.

Outstretched arms wrapped around Stella, and a familiar mop of black hair tickled her nose. She wriggled away, and a familiar face smiled back at her.

"Sophie?" Incredulous, Stella hugged her tightly. "It's really you?" Sophie was a girl from Viola Island who had always been kind to Stella. Before her abrupt departure, Stella had hoped they would become best friends.

They laughed and finally let go of each other. In utter bewilderment at finding her friend in the bowels of a cargo ship floating in the port of Sentinel Island, Stella reached out to grasp Sophie's hand tightly. "How did you get here?" Stella asked.

"After the fires broke out on Viola Island, soldiers knocked down our door and dragged my parents away. I hid, but they eventually captured me too and I was brought to this ship and thrown in here."

Stella felt the blood draining from her face. She realized that was the night her family had left and that the soldiers had been searching for her.

The dark circles around Sophie's eyes revealed her extreme exhaustion. She added, "I don't know where they took them."

"I'm so sorry about your parents," Stella said, squeezing for her friend's hands in comfort.

"Were your parents taken like mine?" Sophie asked. "How did you end up here too?"

Stella proceeded to tell Sophie all that had occurred since the fires broke out on Viola Island. The other prisoners leaned in, avidly listening to the adventures she'd had.

At that moment the ship lurched, pulling away from the dock, and the two friends clung to one another. "Do you know where they're taking us?" Stella asked.

Sophie shook her head. Fear and worry was etched on every prisoner's face.

Today was Pageant Day and her deadline for getting to the Citadel gate fast approached. A decision had to be made.

Stella squared her shoulders. "We must get off this boat."

"But how?" Sophie asked.

"Yeah—how?" Rena stepped up.

"I'm not sure yet . . . but I think together we can figure something out." Everyone fell silent in thought. Tugging on her golden locks in concentration, Stella studied the cargo hold and her fellow prisoners, trying to work out the problem. Her hand drifted to the universal key beneath her shirt, wishing there was a keyhole on her side of the door. The squawking of sea dunkers and waves hitting the ships hull joined the echoes of the crew working up on deck, indicating they had already made it to open waters beyond the port. They needed to act now.

Think Stella . . . there has to be a way off this ship! I cannot leave this island . . .

"Sea dunkers!" Stella cried out, making Sophie, Rena, and the other prisoners jump.

"What about them?" Sophie tentatively asked Stella.

"We're still close enough to make it to shore. And a ship of this size definitely has lifeboats, so if we can get out of here and up on deck, we can steal them! My parents and I did that on the *Emprezza*," Stella explained.

"Sure, but we'd still need to get out of this cargo hold to use the lifeboats," Rena said with skepticism.

Everyone was looking at Stella now, and she made a sweeping gesture, encompassing the other prisoners. "I have an idea."

The dirty, exhausted people pressed in around Stella to hear what she had to say.

"Okay, hand me your belts and scarves, I'll even take socks." Various articles of clothing started flying at her as she started outlining her plan to escape.

"Ready?" Stella asked, checking that everyone was leaning against the wall on either side of the cell door. Silently, they all nodded or gave her thumbs-ups, and as she pounded on the metal door, they began making a racket, jeering at each other, yelling, sounding as though they were egging people on during a fight.

After a few minutes, the window in the cell door snapped open, and a guard demanded in a gruff voice, "Hey—what's going on in there?"

"Help," Stella pleaded through the window, barely audible over the noise everyone else was making. "They're fighting! Someone's going to get hurt."

"So what? Keeps us from having to beat you ourselves," the guard said and began to turn away.

"I think someone's arm may have been broken, and they're not stopping! One of them already can't walk." She'd figured if they were being taken as prisoners somewhere, it was to be sold as slaves, and that meant they needed healthy prisoners—not battered and broken ones. What if the guard became *too* worried? Would he go get more guards?

The window slammed shut, and the door flew open. The guard stepped in, yelling, "Stop or I'll crack your heads open myself!" The prisoners fell on him, binding him with their belts and scarves. Rena silenced him by stuffing a sock in his mouth.

Stella peered into the hall, and when she saw it was all clear, she waved her fellow prisoners out of the cell. Realizing the layout of ship was similar to that of the *Emprezza*, she led them into the maze of darkened corridors, peeking around corners, sneaking past open doorways, and skirting cold metal walls until they scampered up a staircase that spilled onto the deck. The late afternoon sun stung their eyes after being in the dark cargo hold for so long. Once every prisoner was accounted for, she silently indicated where she hoped the lifeboats would be, and motioned everyone to follow.

With relief, Stella spotted a few covered lifeboats tied up alongside the railing. Their luck held out as no guards appeared while the prisoners huddled up next to one of the boats. Stella said, "Climb in and I'll lower you down—"

"No, you can't," Sophie pleaded, clutching her friend's hand.

"It's too dangerous," Rena whispered.

"It's okay. I promise. I've done this before," Stella reassured them.

Rena crossed her arms over her chest, doubtful, but held her tongue.

"When the boat is safely on the water, I'll climb down." She pointed to a rope ladder hanging from a hook on the railing.

Stella, Rena, and Sophie helped everyone board the small boat, then the two friends assisted Rena aboard.

From inside the boat, Rena stuck out her hand to Sophie. "Come on then, get a move on. We don't have time to waste."

Sophie wrapped Stella in a tight hug. "Promise me you'll climb down as fast as you can once we reach the water," She said breathlessly.

"I promise," she said, pushing her friend toward Rena's waiting hand.

Stella knew full well she would get off this ship . . . she had to . . . even if it meant jumping. After all, she was part mermaid, and, despite never having swum a day in her life, she had to trust that her mermaid instincts would kick in.

The boom bowed and the swivel squeaked as she pushed the lifeboat out from the ship, until it was suspended in midair high above the water. A flock of curious sea dunkers circled around the prisoners in the boat and made a squawking racket. Stella hoped none of the crew got curious about all the noise.

Stella turned the crank handle, and the boat started to slowly descend to the water below, just as her father had done during her family's escape from the *Emprezza*. Periodically, she peeked over the side to see the lifeboat's progress. When it was almost to water, the thump of fast approaching footsteps rang out, warning Stella their luck had run out.

"Hey! What are you doing?" yelled a deckhand.

Stella dashed back to flip the switch on the crank, and the mechanism released with a whir. The rope unwound in a blur and shot out of sight over the railing. The sound of a large splash followed.

As the deckhand lunged for her, Stella bolted toward the railing. She hoisted herself over and plummeted toward the dark waters below.

12

GLOWINDER

The long-forgotten rhythm of an ancient song filled Stella's ears, along with seawater. At first, she held her breath, but as the cold current pulled her away from the cargo ship's hull and down into the frigid depths, Stella thrashed until she could resist no more. Her lungs burned for air. Saltwater seared her nasal cavity and throat like acid as she took in a painful breath of water with a silent, petrified scream. Stella felt a searing pain behind her ears as her skin split open to form gills. But the pain quickly faded as oxygen flooded her system. Each breath she took brought seawater rushing through her new gills, giving her the precious air she needed and calming her panic. But just as quickly, Stella's attention was pulled to another new sensation. With a mix of awe and horror, Stella watched strands of flesh grow out from her legs and start to weave together like a tapestry. Soon, what had been two legs was now a single appendage, and her feet lengthened and flattened to form a large fin. Stunned, Stella just stared in wonder at her shimmering mermaid tail.

Oars breaking the waters surface above her snapped Stella out of her daze and with a swift pump of her tail, she shot the twenty feet to the surface where the silhouette of a lifeboat floated. When her head breached the surface, Stella found the prisoners frantically rowing away from the cargo ship and toward the shore. She called out to get their attention, and once they noticed her, they stopped rowing and started cheering.

Sophie wept openly. "I thought you were dead. That was an extraordinary jump!"

Rena smiled and leaned over the edge of the lifeboat. "Come on now dear, take my hand, let's get you out of the water."

"Nah—that's ok. There isn't really room anyway."

"Nonsense. You can't stay in that cold water." Other prisoners scooted closer to the edge to assist Rena with hauling Stella into the boat, but Stella simply flicked her tail out of the water with a big splash, causing the entire lifeboat to gasp in shock. She noticed that her tail was a dazzling emerald green with a hint of red that appeared when the sun hit her red-tipped scales.

"I'm actually a mermaid, so I'm good—" An unfamiliar survival instinct suddenly hit Stella—an awareness of other sea creatures, approaching fast, flooded her senses. Not her regular senses, but her whole body felt sensitive to all the other beings moving in the water around her, as though her nerve endings could interpret each ripple of water.

To reach the safety of the shore, she'd have to act fast. Recovering from the shock of finding out her friend is a mermaid; Sophie picked up on the change in Stella, the sudden wide-eyed stillness that had settled over her, even as she bobbed up and down in the gentle current. "What is it?" Sophie said in concern.

"Somethings coming. You have to get to shore right away. It's not far. I'll try to lead whatever it is away. Now all of you, row—go!" Stella yelled.

Sophie waved goodbye to Stella as four prisoners took up the oars once more and worked together to swiftly row the boat toward land.

Satisfied her friend and the others were on their way, Stella sunk below the waves to see if she could pinpoint what was coming. *I can sense sharks nearby. They must be coming for me.* As she peered into the depths around where she drifted, she remembered she was wearing her father's bracelet. She almost immediately felt the familiar tingle of electricity up her arm and, to her amazement, a golden globe surrounded her.

Her body instinctively knew what to do, and she swam toward an undersea forest of giant kelp to hide in. The going was difficult, but she clasped onto the long tubes of seaweed and pulled herself along, propelling herself forward with the graceful flapping of her tail. The seafloor rose up, and the water grew shallower. She could see the bottom clearly now. Finally out of the kelp, she felt a current catapult her through a rock crevice, where a wave picked her up like a piece of driftwood and deposited her on a sandy beach. The lifeboat was nowhere to be seen, and Stella hoped that meant Sophie and the others were safe.

As she caught her breath and waited to dry in the late afternoon sun—hoping that was all it would take to transform back—she thought, *Being a mermaid isn't that bad. It's strange how the anticipation of a thing can be far more frightening than the actual doing of it.*

When a song, in a rich baritone voice, wafted down from the cliff, she looked from her place across the beach and saw a soldier dressed neatly in a military uniform emerging from a thicket of elmlock trees. Golden tufted epaulets adorned each of his shoulders, and many star-shaped badges hung from his chest. In one hand, he held a rope leashed to something that appeared to be floating in the air, but it was out of Stella's view.

The soldier stopped singing and, in a gentle voice, said, "To land, Glowinder. Come munch this lovely gruff grass down here." From behind the stand of trees, a flying horse with a radiant silver coat appeared, flapping luminous, white wings and resisting the pull of the rope.

Stella watched Glowinder land soundlessly on the cliff's edge. Folding his wings to his back, he eyed the soldier suspiciously but eventually bent his head to bite off a clump of grass. The soldier looped the rope in his hand and pulled, slowly reeling Glowinder in. The horse was evidently wild, for with each tug on the line, he put up a fight so that the lead remained taut.

"Flap and fight all you want, but I will tame you, Glowinder," the soldier vowed. At last the horse relaxed, allowing the soldier to get close enough to scratch his head. Stella quickly checked herself, being sure that the woven strands of flesh were slowly unraveling into legs as she dried, and her fin was separating into feet. She ran her fingers over her legs, surprised to discover that her skin, though it looked normal in color, was still bumpy with scales. She raised her face toward the cliff and considered the soldier's progress with the horse.

To Glowinder's surprise, as well as Stella's, the soldier kicked his leg up and mounted the horse, who went berserk. Glowinder shrieked like a banshee, then flew off the cliff. Violently flapping and kicking, the creature did his best to unseat the soldier, who appeared to revel in it. Glowinder bucked through the air and then turned sharply and plummeted toward the beach. In twists and fits, the stallion contorted his body into seemingly impossible shapes, repeatedly whipping the soldier with his tail and slamming against the rock cliff in an attempt to knock off his rider.

Having had some experience with horses—though admittedly none of them of the flying variety—Stella knew the soldier was in trouble. Thankfully, her tail had become legs once more and she ran to an open area of the beach, waving her arms overhead at the bucking bronco and his mount. "Here! Over here!" she commanded.

The beautiful horse stopped his aerial spin and, nickering loudly, peered quizzically at Stella. Then, with ears flat against his head, his body dove like a Sentinelian falcon. The soldier grabbed a clump of mane and held on.

Just as Stella was sure they were about to crash onto the beach, Glowinder pulled up with his magnificent wings and gently touched down and trotted toward her. His nostrils flared as he took in her scent, his hot breath moistened her cheek with the smell of sweet pearlgrain and grass. Slowly and gently, she grabbed his reins and rubbed between his eyes.

"Well done," the soldier panted. "You did that like a professional. What are you—some sort of horse whisperer?"

She giggled. "I had some riding experience in the Hollowilds when I was younger, but this is the first flying horse I've ever seen. I didn't even know they really existed outside of fairytales."

Dismounting, the soldier said, "They're called Lializans, and they're very similar to their land relatives. I'm Cavish Awn, and, uh, thanks for your help." When Cavish stepped forward to take the reins from her, Glowinder reared up on his hind legs and nipped at Cavish's hand angrily. "You'd better keep hold of the wild beast," he said, handing Stella the line. "He certainly has taken to you. You're clearly a natural."

Stella shrugged but was pleased. "Thank you." She reached up and rubbed between the animal's eyes again. "He's just so gorgeous."

The soldier cocked his head as he caught sight of her father's bracelet as it slid down her arm. "Oh, how curious! A mermaid with an angel's bracelet."

Surprised, Stella said, "A mermaid?!"

"I saw you swim ashore earlier." He paused and eyed her curiously. "Where would a seafaring fish-child like you come across such a bracelet? And one from Sentinel Island, nonetheless. Curious, very curious indeed. What's your name?"

"I'm supposed to be a new apprentice at the Citadel. I'm Stella Merriss."

"The halfwing daughter of Commander Arago Merriss?" he said, letting out a low whistle when she nodded. "I knew your father well. He was quite the commendable angel before his desertion. How's he doing?"

"He's . . . lost at sea."

Cavish looked only mildly surprised at that. "Well, I'm sure you'll find him soon . . . or he'll find himself. He's too indestructible as a warrior to have succumbed to the water realm. What happened?"

"We were in a lifeboat in a hurricane. When he and Mother went over, we were surrounded by sharks. I-I'm not sure they could've survived." As Stella spoke the words, pain and guilt welled up inside her. But as she considered their going into the water, she thought again of his bracelet and she realized why her father had given it to her—he had sacrificed his own protection for her. Even if he had jumped in on purpose, he'd know she'd be protected. She shuddered at the thought of him knowingly jumping into harm, ready to be attacked by sharks.

Interpreting the shudder for a cold shiver, Cavish took off his jacket and draped it around Stella, saying, "Come now, never let it be said that Cavish Awn allowed the daughter of Commander Arago Merriss to freeze to death. Let's get you to Reslan Josephine and fix you up with some dry clothes."

Dusk started to settle over the island and the silver-gray sky lit the trio's way along the ocean cliff until they came to a gate in the Marble Veil, where a small guardhouse stood. From a window, a guard watched them approach.

"Who's this with you, Grand Master?" said the security guard, rising from his chair.

"Glowinder—he's the Pageant Day parade's main spectacle this evening."

The security guard raised an eyebrow. "Not the equine—the girl."

"Oh, her . . ." Cavish said, his face reddening from embarrassment. "She's just one of this year's new apprentices."

Unimpressed, he held out his hand to Stella. "Papers."

From inside her father's jacket pocket, Stella retrieved her soggy invitation.

His hand retreated. "I don't want wet papers. Dry. Only dry papers."

Stella nervously looked to Cavish for help, wondering if the guard could really reject her entrance past the Marble Veil because of her acceptance letter being wet.

Cavish lost his patience. "Now listen here, soldier, this girl is running out of time to report for angel training at the Citadel. As a ranking officer, I am ordering you to examine her papers."

The soldier shrunk back, his lower lip quivering, he muttered, "Yes sir—"

"Then check her paperwork and let her through, good man!" Cavish's chest puffed with intimidation.

Pinching a soggy corner in distaste, the soldier briefly inspected the letter, then waved them through.

Once inside the Marble Veil, Stella jumped up and down in excitement. "Thank you!" she gushed to Cavish, who simply smiled and gestured down the city street. Stella was one step closer to fulfilling her parents' wish.

As the pair, with Glowinder trotting behind, made their way to the steps of Josephine's Fine Garment Shop, dusk was beginning to fall in earnest. Brilliant sunset pinks streaked across the sky as Cavish tied Glowinder to a post outside the shop. The sign on the door clearly indicated it was closed, but Cavish pounded on the glass until it shook. Finally, the curtain pulled back, and an eye peered through the pane. When the lock jiggled and the door popped open, a little bell rang overhead.

"Cavish, what in the world are you doing here?" Red, curly hair was piled high on the shopkeeper's head. "The parade's about to start. I just closed up to head over there."

Cavish nudged Stella forward, and Josephine stepped aside to let them in.

With a contrite look, Cavish said, "Jo—I need your help. Would you outfit this angel . . . er mermaid—I mean, whatever she is?"

Rubbing her chin, Reslan Josephine turned her attention toward Stella, who was soaked, disheveled, and smelled of seaweed.

"At this hour?" Reslan Josephine protested. "The parade is due to start shortly, and you expect me to clean up a proper mess?"

Stella meekly handed Cavish's jacket back to him and pushed her hair back, and her father's bracelet tumbled down her arm.

"Where did you get that?" the clothier demanded, seizing hold of Stella's wrist to examine it up close. Turning to Cavish, she asked, "Did you see this? It's one from Sentinel Island!"

Stella pulled her arm back gently and answered, "It was my father's—Arago Merriss."

Reslan Josephine gasped. "You're Arago's daughter?" Her azure blue eyes sparkled like glass. Ever so slowly, she reached out her hand and gently caressed Stella's cheek. "I see the resemblance now." She looked back at Cavish. "Where'd she come from?"

Cavish smiled. "She washed up on the sand below Crangston's Crag."

"Washed up? Do you mean from the sea?"

Stella would've said she saved him from his horse.

"Yes. I literally mean she came *from* the sea," Cavish continued. "She's a mermaid."

Reslan Josephine shook her head. "It's against the law. It's . . . My goodness. Arago and a mermaid had a halfwing child?"

"Precisely. She's also a new apprentice."

"Well, the new apprentices are required to be at the Citadel for the welcoming party before the Pageant Day festivities have concluded."

"Hence the hurry," Cavish said.

Reslan Josephine set her hands on her hips and gave Stella a curt nod, but she spoke to Cavish. "Very well. Go on then. Get to the parade. I'll get her dressed."

13

FITTING AND FLIGHT

Reslan Josephine walked to the back of the store and beckoned a reluctant Stella with a bejeweled finger. "Hurry up, dear. The faster you're outfitted, the faster we can head to the parade. I promise you, this isn't something you want to miss."

Stella hurried after her.

Again eyeing the bracelet on Stella's arm, she said, "Your father was so strong and confident. He could fly so gracefully."

Stella felt a pang of sadness. "I never saw him fly."

"You didn't? How could that be? He was a commander in the aerial forces. He flew all the time." She walked into a bathroom, grabbed a towel from a closet, and pulled back the shower curtain with a *whoosh*.

Stella followed behind her. "I had no idea he was a commander or that he was even an angel," Stella said. "My parents kept everything a secret from me. My whole life, we've been running . . . though I never knew why until just recently."

Reslan Josephine cranked open the faucet and let the water run until clouds of steam billowed up. "Take yourself a nice, hot shower while I pick out a few pieces of clothing for you."

The door latch clicked as she left Stella alone.

When Stella got out of the shower, she saw a simple dress Reslan Josephine had laid out on the basin. It had two slits in the back— she guessed it was made for angels, and that was where their wings could unfurl—and it fit perfectly. Stella put the key back around her neck and her father's bracelet on her arm. After wiping the fog from the mirror, Stella studied her reflection. *I don't look any different than usual*, she thought. But inside, she *knew* she was.

Several minutes later, she stepped out of the bathroom and into the bright light of the clothing shop's back room. She called out to Reslan Josephine as she walked through the large room but saw no sign of the shopkeeper and her pile of bright-red hair. The back room was filled with baskets overflowing with fabrics and partially dressed mannequins. Containers of bows and lace, buttons and strings littered the floor. From floor to ceiling, the entire back wall sported shelves stacked with little white boxes.

Stella turned around, checking to see she was still alone, and then pulled one of the boxes from its shelf. Lifting the lid, she saw a brilliant blue jewel, winking as it caught the overhead light. *Are these all jewels? Are they for jewelry or something else? Nothing here is what it seems to be* . . . She slid the box back onto its shelf and took in the sheer number of boxes in front of her, trying to calculate just how many jewels were here.

She leaned back and squinted at the wall. A slight . . . shaking was making the jewels rattle. Was the wall shaking? It didn't seem loud enough for an earthquake. Just a few boxes were rattling. A ladder was leaning against the wall, clearly for retrieval of jewel boxes higher up, and Stella stepped on the first rung, pausing for just a moment to double-check that she was headed toward the box that seemed to be rattling the most. There it was—not quite at the top and over to the right.

She climbed until she was even with the shelf the box sat on and stared. It was as if the box was edging itself off its resting place. Stella reached out to grab it just as it fell. Instinct made her lunge for it, and suddenly she was off the ladder. As she plummeted toward the floor, the lid of the box burst off, and an iridescent blue-green jewel sprouted wings that wrapped themselves around her.

A warmth bloomed between her shoulder blades. The wings slowed her fall and she landed gently just as Reslan Josephine emerged and exclaimed, "What have you done?"

Stella turned around and felt the weight of the wings, now attached to her back firmly. They pushed the air around her—and knocked over a mannequin and a basket of fabric. Of their own accord, the wings stretched to their full span, and she saw they were a dusty blue-green, edged in black.

Reslan Josephine picked up the box and read its label. "Cormorant wings . . . of course. Makes perfect sense," she said. "They're highly unusual because the feathers are not water repellant, meaning they're less buoyant, and will allow you to dive deep in the ocean. It seems your wings have recognized your merfolk nature."

The clothier eyed the girl. "Well, you certainly have a high enough consciousness to manifest wings, but do you have what it takes to put them away? Now, close your eyes. Imagine your wings folding themselves back into the gemstone on your back. Focus . . . see it as clearly as you can in your mind's eye. Imagine what it feels like as your wings fold back into the gem."

Stella felt Josephine's hands on her wings, helping to guide them into the folding motion. "Good dear, keep seeing it. Yes, yes . . . there you go. Well done."

Opening her eyes, Stella felt utterly normal. Having wings didn't feel different at all. Josephine gently patted Stella's back, near the jewel where her wings had just disappeared.

"You'll need lessons before you'll be allowed to fly on your own, and you need to keep in mind that most apprentices don't get their wings before they start at the Citadel. Although you may be tempted to use them to fly, you must assert your willpower to not let them come out. You have to keep these a secret for a while, halfwing."

Stella wriggled her shoulders to get away. By now, Stella had heard the term *halfwing* several times. It made her uncomfortable, and she wasn't sure whether it was meant to be taken positively or negatively. "Since my father was an angel, wouldn't that make me full-fledged angel? More than the landlings who are asked to come?"

"Angels have a prejudice against those who aren't their kind."

"Like landlings?"

"Precisely." Reslan Josephine turned Stella around now that they'd wrestled her wings away, so she could look her in the face. "But if they feel like they're helping another full-fledged angel, they'll give their right wing to do it." She sighed. "In their eyes, because of your mother, you're a halfwing until you *earn* the status of an angel."

Stella shook her head. "I don't understand all this. Why judge someone just because of who their parents are? We can't control that."

"We—angels, mermaids, and landlings—are all essentially the same. We have the same DNA, the same skin, the same minds with similar abilities to think and manifest our thoughts. Each group has simply adapted to their environment—angels in the sky realm, landlings on the land, merfolk in the water. The fear of these differences has divided us. I believe we should focus on our similarities . . . and our common enemies."

Stella thought she knew what Josephine meant, but she had to be sure. "Enemies like Sylvain?"

"Yes." The clothier's eyes narrowed. "So you know about that snake. I met him when he first came to Sentinel Island. He was a recruit a few years after I was."

"You were a recruit?" For some reason, Stella was as surprised that Josephine had been an apprentice as she was that someone as evil and feared as Sylvain had been a normal child, an apprentice like she was.

"Oh yes. I received a notice when I was younger and was tutored in the ways of consciousness. But I didn't have what it takes to become a warrior and manifest as an angel."

"So you're *not* an angel?"

"I quit—or rather, just didn't quite make it through. But the Celestial Council gave me permission to remain on Sentinel Island as apprentice to Reslan Georgette, the Citadel's former garment maker and wing supplier. She recognized my talent with a needle, my flair with fabric, and of course my aptitude for handling the wings. Folks from the land realm like me who are allowed to stay are given the title Reslan to show we are respected landlings in the angel community." She winked at Stella as she said, "Most apprentices need more help than you getting their wings."

Stella cringed. "I'm so sorry. It was all just so . . . It was like I couldn't help myself."

"It's okay, dear. It happens that way sometimes." Reslan Josephine patted Stella's shoulder. "Come on. Let's finish getting you ready. Put one of these on," she said, handing Stella a cloak. "I assume you prefer long sleeves?"

"Yes," Stella said, hiding her arm behind her back.

"What happened to your arm?" Reslan Josephine asked, gently taking hold of it to pull it out from behind Stella and leaning in for a closer look at the half-healed wounds.

"A shark bit me a couple of weeks ago," Stella said.

The clothier stared at her arm for a long moment before softly saying, "These will likely scar, and the lessons of our scars are often underestimated. I have plenty of my own. They make us strong."

Affection flooded through Stella. She felt understood—in a tiny way—like she did with her mother. "Where are your scars?" she asked.

"Mostly on the inside. Many of us have scars you can't see. But scars are scars, no matter where the damage occurred. Always remember—scars are a sign of bravery."

Reslan Josephine picked up a brush and set about untangling Stella's hair, fashioning an angelfish braid and adding a bow. They stood in front of a mirror, so Stella could watch the transformation. "One last thing." She stared into Stella's eyes in the reflection. "I've put some other clothes in a bag for you, including your apprenticeship uniform, but you also have to put your bracelet in the bag."

Stella clutched it. "I don't want to give it up. It's one of the last connections I have to my father."

"Listen," said the clothier, gently spinning the young recruit around to face her, "you don't have to get rid of it, but you must hide it, or the Celestial Council may confiscate it."

"But my father . . ." She stopped and swallowed the lump in her throat. "My father said I need it for protection."

"Sentinel Island is safe. In fact, it's the safest place in the whole universe. Put your father's things in this bag until you really need them."

Stella hesitated before slipping the bracelet off and dropping it into the bag. She also stuffed her father's jacket, with the timepiece hidden in the pocket, into the bag. If the bracelet was an object of interest to the Celestial Council, Stella figured that the timepiece would be of interest too. *Best to keep that hidden for now,* she thought.

"Good. Now let's make our way to the Citadel before the parade is over. The last thing we need is for you to forfeit your chance to become an angel."

14

FIRST CLASS

With the long train journey underway, Dr. Rand Eyvindur could wait no longer to talk with his sponsor.

"Don't do it," Jakin had warned. "She's a different animal than you've encountered before—or ever studied, for that matter. She'll eat you alive and do it with a smile."

Rand knew his guardian was right, but he wouldn't be able to live with himself if he failed to speak for the animals. *If I can just discourage her from starting her Fashion Farm*, he thought, chewing his lip. *Then my animals would be safe.*

A rolled-up magazine from the Ilya station featuring an article about Meenah spurred him on. "The Life and Times of Meenah Battelle" painted a vivid picture of his sponsor. She was the daughter of a South Vilunian goatherd but ran away from the farm at a young age with a desire for a career that could only be found in the big city. Eventually she turned her attention to fashion. Her clothing line, *Meenah!*, with its faux animal print signature look, had been a smashing success—although she ultimately began to use actual furs and hides. Not long after, she sold her clothing brand for a small fortune; however, she never lost her lust for the spotlight.

Wiping his sweaty palms on his pant legs, Rand murmured to himself, "Here goes nothing," and then began his slow march through the cars. *I'll just tell her about the need to treat all animals with dignity and respect in much the same way that her father must treat his goats*, Rand thought.

Surveying the spacious layout of the first-class dining car, he took in elegant elmlock tables, shiny silver cutlery, hand-blown crystal stemware, and plush booths upholstered in red leather— an archaic animal-exploiting tradition banned eons ago. Beside a booth toward the middle of the car, Rand spied Meenah's lion skin coat draped over a stand for all passersby to admire as though it were a famous sculpture in the Ilya Museum of Antiquities. Seeing it strengthened his resolve, and he approached the booth. He took a moment to collect his thoughts and muster his courage.

As he stepped up to them, his sudden appearance startled Meenah and she splashed her tea across the table. Hort, who'd been gossiping with her, now had tea dripping down his jacket. "You've ruined my suede," he exploded at Rand, even though it had been Meenah who'd splashed him with her drink. Hort dabbed at the dappled suede with his yellow linen serviette. In a huff, Hort clambered to his feet, as he continued to dab at the suede, muttering "you klutz."

As Hort fled the booth, Meenah turned to Rand, narrowing her devilish eyes thick with charcoal eyeliner. "Excuse me, but we were having a private conversation."

As she mopped at the puddle of tea in an attempt to keep her own dining ensemble pristine, Rand slid onto the bench opposite her. "Since I have your attention, there are a few things I'd like to discuss with you."

Meenah hissed through her teeth. "You've some nerve barging into first class—it's exclusive!" She carefully slipped from the booth so as not to get tea on herself and then stood, her face purpled with vexation and strongly resembling a big, fat beet. Rand followed suit.

Undeterred, Rand held the magazine out to her. "Have you seen this?" he asked. "It's about *you*."

She snatched it from his hand and leafed through it until she found the exposé. In a huff, she ripped out the pages, shredding them into tiny bits, which she tossed into the air like confetti. "Lies."

"Which part?" Rand asked, hoping he had read her wrong.

"The goatherd . . . I haven't seen my fa—I mean, that goatherd in decades." Her face flushed at the admission.

"At least you have a father," Rand said quietly. "I don't. But being an orphan doesn't embarrass me."

"I would rather have been an orphan than had the parents I did," Meenah shot back. "They are . . . more common even than you."

"But I bet they have good hearts," Rand reasoned with her. "They love their goats. Surely some of that love must've rubbed off on you."

"No, it actually had the opposite effect. I despise them."

"Goats or your parents?"

She gave Rand a look that would have frightened an attacking Aridian lion. "Both!"

He gave a single nod, as if that was the confirmation he'd been waiting for. "I came to ask you not to sponsor me. If your only intent is to kill my animals, then you can't be involved."

"Too late." A wicked smile spread across her face. "We're partners now—you cashed the check. Your job is to catch that little horse and hand it over to me. Imagine, this will only be the first in a string of discoveries I will pay for. And I always get what I pay for, one way or another."

"Then I'll give the money back. You can't have the animals—not on your Fashion Farm. You'll slaughter them for their hides."

Meenah sneered at Rand. "I'll show you how things work in the real world, young fool." Her bony finger wagged wildly in his face. "I control you now. We have a binding agreement, and if you break it, I will destroy you."

When it came to difficult individuals, Rand had learned early on from his time at the orphanage that there was always a way to avoid their tricks. "My name is Dr. Rand Eyvindur," he said calmly. "My job is to protect the animals I discover, no matter the cost or consequences."

"Did you say consequences?" Meenah growled, narrowing her eyes. "I can arrange substantial consequences for you if you don't deliver that horse to me."

"How many times do I have to tell you? It's not a horse. And you can't ride it."

"Oh yes, I can."

"Don't be ridiculous. It couldn't hold your weight. You'd crush it."

"I will crush *you*, Dr. Rand Eyvindur. You'll pay dearly if you cross me. Not only will you never be taken seriously again, but you will also leave me no choice but to hunt down these beasts myself."

15

THE PAGEANT DAY PARADE

Reslan Josephine led Stella through the dark streets to the Pageant Day Parade route. Stella tried not to stare in awe at the ornate pink granite buildings with red tile roofs that lined the Avenue of Angels. As she hurried to keep up, Stella recognized the Marble Veil peeking between buildings every now and then.

They squeezed into a space in the crowd. Streetlights flashed and trumpets sounded the commencement of the parade. A marching band kicked things off with a loud rendition of what Josephine explained was the sky realm's anthem. The crowd cheered enthusiastically.

Abruptly, everything darkened and the music stopped. Everyone looked up expectantly. As music of heavenly proportions erupted from the band on the ground, beams of light exploded across the heavens like shooting stars. Watching them dance in an intense burst of color, Stella gasped, along with the rest of the crowd. Electrical energy as bright as lightning illuminated the sky, and the audience roared its approval.

The percussive beat of synchronized steps clip-clopping on the cobblestones preceded the infantry, outfitted in dazzling blue-and-white uniforms. On the heels of the infantry, a troop of flag bearers held their staffs aloft, waving their banners in unison as they advanced in a march of intricate footwork. As the flags passed and Stella's attention shifted to the blue-and-white banners, she recognized the insignia as the same design that decorated her father's bracelet.

Reslan Josephine noticed her interest and said, "The winged sword is the crest of Sentinel Island."

A squadron of soldiers followed behind the flag bearers, marching in five-by-five formations. Fringed with gold, their polished metallic armor shimmered in the lamplight. Dangling from thick, black leather belts, swords encased in emerald-encrusted sheaths swayed in time with their steps. Luminescent verdant capes flowed from the soldiers' shoulders to their calves, while their knee-high metal boots tapped out a rhythm on the street's surface.

"Who are they?" Stella asked, enthralled by their splendor.

"The aerial forces of the sky realm," the clothier whispered. "Their job is to protect the angelic territories. At one time, your father was their commander."

Stella felt overwhelming pride in her father. The attendees thundered with delight as the spectacle of strength passed before them, and she found herself clapping along with them. It was a sight like nothing she had ever seen.

The squadron halted, and a flock of riderless Lializans appeared overhead, flying. They swooped and dove, their wings flapping in sync.

When the aerial forces shouted, "To land," the equines plunged toward the ground impossibly fast. Shrieks went up, but at the last moment, they pulled up and gently landed near their riders. Half of the squadron stepped up to the horses and seized their reins. Each equine dropped to its knees and extended its left wing, so the soldiers could easily mount them. The Lializans expanded their wings and took off, their manes dancing in the wind. Cheers echoed off the buildings as the remainder of the squadron stood motionless on the street. Then, manifesting wings of their own, the remaining soldiers took flight as well. Trailing in the equines' wake, they rose higher and higher until the entire squadron disappeared into the clouds, only to swoop back down several times, dazzling the exultant crowd.

"They're beautiful," Stella said, mesmerized.

"Yes, the Lializans—the flying horses of Lialia," Reslan Josephine said leaning over and speaking softly out of the side of her mouth.

Puzzled, Stella said, "I once lived in Lialia, but I never saw flying horses."

"That's because Lializans are bred high in the mountains out of the sight of landlings. Their existence is protected by angelic cloaking technology—Oh! Here comes five of their stable masters." Her bejeweled finger pointed toward five riders astride magnificent equines, each fitted with a silver saddle and bridle and prancing with the precision of a dance troop. "But Grand Master Cavish will show up with Glowinder near the end of the parade. Glowinder's the main event. Don't tell anyone—it's a surprise." Stella giggled at the notion. She was a stranger to Sentinel Island and know no one. Who was she going to tell?

The entire venue began to shake—to Stella it felt like an energy vibration not unlike that from the electricity of her father's bracelet but on a much larger scale. One by one, a variety of new models of convertible hovercraft, their tops down, floated into view. Though their occupants waved to the parade-goers, the crowd's enthusiasm died down markedly.

"That's the Celestial Council," Reslan Josephine said, sucking her teeth in distaste. "They're not popular. A majority are unhappy with how they're governing the realm. For example, there's a law called the Species Separation Act the Council passed many years ago. You may hear it called the SSA. It's not a universal law but an angel-made law meant to keep the three realms separated."

Stella felt an icy rush. Her parents had probably violated that law when they fell in love and had her.

When the hovercraft halted, a few boos were heard from parade-goers. As angel guards descended from the rooftops to surround the hovercraft, the Councilors rose to their feet and waved.

All at once, the streetlights went off. A faint glow could be seen moving slowly below the hovercraft. Then the main attraction was unveiled. The phosphorescent light from Glowinder's coat shattered the darkness. Gasps filled the air, followed by loud applause, whistles and whoops. The noise made Glowinder rear up.

Stretching his wings, Glowinder bolted skyward, kicking his way to the end of his rope until all its slack was gone. With bucks and brays, dodges and lurches, the phosphorescent Lializan made a show of it. That he was unbroken added to the excitement, especially for the angel who had unveiled him and now wrestled to keep hold of the rope. Seeing that the horse's behavior wasn't any different from how it had been on the beach, Stella looked around, her eyes wide, trying to find Cavish somewhere in the crowd. She needed to help. Glowinder listened to her.

Without thinking about it, Stella dropped the bag Reslan Josephine had given her. She ran to the angel holding Glowinder and grabbed part of the rope as well. "To land, Glowinder, to land," she commanded, her tone assertive and confident.

Glowinder stopped bucking and rushed landward. As gracefully as he'd done on the beach, he came to rest directly in front of her. She smiled, but that feeling dimmed when she caught sight of the Celestial Council. The sour looks on their faces said they were unimpressed—and perhaps knew who she was and didn't like that much either.

As most of the crowd applauded, a faint chanting rose up. Stella looked around and saw signs appearing in the crowd: *Down with the Councilors*, some read. *Say NO to the Species Separation Act*, others urged. *Angels for Landling and Merfolk Equality*, several declared. There were dozens that proclaimed, *Landlings for Liberty*. The crowd was clearly becoming restless, and Stella couldn't tell if the protesters were shoving their way to the road or the parade watchers were trying to jostle the protesters out of the way, but it was clear that there were suddenly factions.

Shouts could be heard everywhere as the roofs on the Councilors' hovercrafts began closing. Glowinder was dancing in place, not spooked again yet, but clearly anxious from all the noise and rowdy crowds.

Cavish appeared at her side, another beautiful horse in tow. "We're going to have to get out of here before things get worse," he said grimly. "I'm afraid this crowd is going to riot. Easiest way is to ride out. I'll boost you up, and then, it's simple: hold on."

Stella put her foot in his laced-together hands, and he boosted her onto the horse's back. She tried to calm her nerves by redirecting her thoughts. "What about Reslan Josephine?"

He flashed her a grin. "If anyone knows how to take care of herself, it's Jo. I'll be on this horse"—Cavish patted the one he'd arrived with—"called Moonglow. She's Glowinder's mother, so he'll follow her."

Stella wanted to ask a million other questions—especially if riding Glowinder solo was really such a good idea—when Cavish commanded, "To flight."

Stella felt herself rise above the parade and held tight to Glowinder's mane, her feet tucked neatly under his wings as she'd seen the soldiers at the parade do. Below her, guards were closing in on the protesters, seizing their signs, although their chanting went undiminished.

As she and Glowinder rose, the cold rush of air caused her squinted eyes to leak tears. The higher they went, the lower the temperature dropped, until Stella's skin prickled. Teeth chattering, she looked over at Cavish, who was a tight ball on top of Moonglow, his head ducked so his face was practically buried in the horse's mane, his knees nearly touching his chest. Stella tucked smaller too, trying to stay warmer as well, just as fireworks exploded all around them. Clouds of burnt sulfur tickled her nose.

This time, Glowinder didn't seem bothered. Instead, he calmly beat his wings in time with Moonglow's, as far below, the parade, the Avenue of Angels, and the Marble Veil, shrank.

A rush of exhilaration surged through Stella like an electric current.

She was flying.

16

ARRIVAL OF THE EIGHT

Cavish led Stella to the Citadel, where she was to be before the parade officially ended. With the wind brisk against her cheeks, she felt a freedom unlike anything she had ever known.

"Wow," Stella exclaimed, pointing to the monumental structure that topped the island like a crown. She had seen it before, of course, as it dominated the landscape. But being so close gave her a new appreciation for its exquisite architecture. Pointy turrets and jutting chimneys pierced the sky. On its tallest spire, a weathervane in the shape of the winged sword insignia of Sentinel Island turned in the breeze. A thick rock wall not unlike the Marble Veil encircled the building, closing it off from the outside world.

Cavish descended directly in front of the structure, and Stella followed. They both touched down with the clatter of hooves on cobblestones, and Stella patted Glowinder on the neck before swinging her leg over his withers and jumping off. "Thank you for the great ride," she said. "I hope we can do it again sometime. You're an excellent flyer." His neigh made her think he understood.

"Here we are—the Citadel," Cavish said, grabbing Glowinder's reins. "This is the military outpost and administrative center for the sky realm. It's an honor to be invited here."

Fireworks burst overhead, and Cavish looked up. "The grand finale. You don't want to be late."

"When will I see you again?" Stella asked.

He gave her a small smile. "I'll be around." They approached the gate where a guard stood at attention. Seeing Cavish, the guard saluted. "Grand Master," he said formally.

"At ease, soldier," Cavish said. "I'm delivering one of this year's recruits."

The guard relaxed a bit and lifted his clipboard. "I don't see your name on the list of recruiters, sir."

"Do you have Stella Merriss on your list?"

"Yes, sir."

"I'll sign for her and you can take her into your charge as you've done with the others." Cavish motioned with his head for her to approach the Citadel's gate as he hopped back on Moonglow and took to the sky again with Glowinder in tow. Seven kids who looked about Stella's age stood at the iron gate, all wearing clothing from various regions of the land realm—and all staring at her with mouths agape. She instantly regretted arriving on a glowing, flying horse. She wasn't sure what they thought of it, as no one made a peep, though they could have all simply been as nervous as she was.

Each held a different type of suitcase, pack, or bundle, their one commonality being that they all had a Josephine's Fine Garment Shop bag—her bag! Stella had dropped it to help soothe Glowinder. And her father's bracelet, timepiece, and jacket! She turned to ask Cavish for help finding her bag, but he was already gone. What was she going to do? According to her letter, uniforms were required. More importantly, her father's things were all she had left of her life with her parents. Her insides twisted into knots at the thought of losing them. Hopefully, she would get some help retrieving it, as she had no idea how to do it herself.

Stairs led from the gate to a large veranda illuminated by a porch light. When the door to the veranda opened, a figure sporting black-rimmed glasses and nut-brown curly hair stepped out. Her attention was so focused on a flat piece of technology she held that she scarcely noticed Stella and the other children in the square. As her fingers tapped on her device, holographic images of the group of eight children sprang out. Her white gown glinted, and sliding her glasses up the bridge of her nose, she finally looked away from her holograms and saw the children at the gate itself. A toothy smile spread across her face, and as she lowered the technology, the holograms disappeared.

"I am Orica Astras, recruit coordinator," she said from the top of the stairs, "and I welcome you to Sentinel Island. I see you all made it safely, although one of you did leave it until the very last minute to arrive, forcing us to wait for you." Orica's eyes bore into Stella. The others turned to stare at her again as well.

Guilt and shame reddened Stella's cheeks. "Sorry, I . . ." She stopped, keenly aware that the fireworks hadn't ended until after she'd arrived, so technically she hadn't been late. She wasn't going to point that out, though. Apparently, she'd already upset one of her new teachers.

"Step forward to be scanned when I call your name. Only those who have the potential for higher consciousness will be allowed to enter the grounds of the Citadel. For those who don't, your recruiter will be summoned to escort you home."

Orica proceeded gracefully down the stairs and unlocked the gate. Stella wondered whether the universal key around her neck would open a lock as big as this one and reached up to assure herself she still wore it.

Just inside the gate, Orica again raised the tech, and a hologram appeared. Clad in the colorful clothing of South Vilun, the image danced and waved her arms overhead. "Vara Tiko," Orica called out. A beautiful figure with amber skin and long black hair stepped forward; dangling earrings jingled softly and a stud glittered in her nose.

Orica held out the electronic equipment and said, "Hand, please." Vara placed her hand on it, and the machine made a chiming noise. With a nod of approval, Orica stepped aside to allow Vara to enter the grounds of the Citadel.

A new holographic image appeared, this one of someone standing on the back of a Lializan who then dismounted with a backflip. "Fen Yanting," Orica called out.

Fen put her hand on Orica's pad, and after it chimed, Orica stepped aside for her too.

Next was Akila Lily, whose hologram showed a figure with mahogany skin and the beaded braids of the Hollowilds region. Callum Cardiff's hologram depicted him lifting a boulder above his head, competing in a Vast Bog throwing competition. Daith Fiveton's image showed him with fists clenched in a combative stance of the Five Isles. The hologram of Reginal Webb clutched an armful of books and scrolls, illustrating the Dragonkirk propensity toward the gathering of knowledge. The image of Lasker Marlow revealed him wearing a finely crafted belt with intricately inlaid metal work clearly from the mountain bluffs of Arid.

Orica stepped aside for one recruit after another, until finally it was Stella's turn. As the eighth and final image rose up gracefully from Orica's handheld device, Stella looked at the image of herself standing waist-deep in the ocean with a faint breeze stirring her hair. Orica announced, "Stella Merriss."

Stella's stomach was aflutter. She owed her arrival here to a series of unforeseeable events that arose from unpredictable circumstances and the actions of several people: Magnus, Esmi, Captain Finnegan, Sophie, Cavish, Reslan Josephine, and her parents. Her heart filled with happiness and—

"Are you planning on standing there all night, or do you just like making me wait?" Orica demanded, tapping her foot impatiently. Sensing that the apprentice coordinator didn't much like her, Stella rushed up to her and held out her hand.

Orica grabbed it roughly, slapped it on the device, and snapped, "Well, go on then. Join the others—we've waited long enough for you."

Stella ran to join the group, wondering why the apprentice coordinator seemed to have it out for her.

The hinges on the iron gate creaked as Orica closed it with a thud and locked it. "Follow me," she instructed, marching up the front steps ahead of them.

Once on the veranda, she said, "Now that you're inside the gates of the Citadel, your future has taken a turn for the better. Your life will be beyond your wildest imaginings. Say good-bye to your past."

PART TWO

BASIC ENLIGHTENMENT

17

NEW HOME

The young recruits followed Orica to the entryway, where the winged sword insignia of Sentinel Island was etched into the wood of the front door. A shiver ran down Stella's spine as she crossed the threshold. She imagined how her father had passed through these very doors at one time, and the thought somehow made her feel less apprehensive.

Inside the foyer, a thousand twinkling crystal wings dangled from a chandelier in the vast space above their heads. Its light illuminated the wood that paneled the walls, on which hung oil paintings of angels. Joyful music from a choir echoed through the corridors, and the deep, somber tones of a pipe organ could be heard playing in the distance.

Sweeping her arms in a grand gesture, Orica said, "Congratulations on being offered apprenticeship at the Citadel." She looked at each of them in turn. "The Citadel is a place of great secrecy. Inside its walls are universal treasures and truths, which need special care and protection. You're among an exclusive group of landlings selected to apprentice in the ways of the angels."

"Yes, angels are real, as your recruiter has informed you. You were all chosen because your minds have an innate higher consciousness and the capacity for developing to the same level as the superior minds of the angels." She paused briefly, giving them a few seconds to adjust to their new reality; then she went on.

"This will take considerable effort on your part, requiring you to focus your mental faculties—memory, reason, perception, intuition, imagination, and will. You were all chosen because you have demonstrated the use of one or more of them competently."

"How do you know?" Stella asked, curious.

"We have our ways," Orica answered, looking down her nose at Stella with annoyance. It wasn't clear if she was irritated with Stella or just being matter-of-fact, but Stella caught a glare before Orica whipped around and took off down a long corridor. "On Sentinel Island," she called back to her charges hurrying along behind her, "there are many matters you won't understand at first, so your tendency may be to think they are supernatural in nature. Oftentimes they can only be understood when they are explained. For example . . ." Two wings unfurled from her back as she continued down the hall.

Stella's own shoulder blades prickled, and something warm bloomed down her spine. She took a deep breath and assured herself: *This is normal. This is fine. Your wings do not need to come out now, not in front of Orica.* The prickling eased, and as Orica's wings tucked away into her back and disappeared, the warmth on Stella's back finally abated as well.

"The fact that I have wings and can fly no doubt seems magical to you," she said, "but there is no magic to what we do here.

In reality, it's just what we do when we manifest as angels—we fly."

Pulling up a sleeve, she revealed her bracelet. "As a token of our mastery, a bracelet is given to everyone whose consciousness rises to the point where they can manifest wings. Many believe their bracelet gives them special protection, and it does, but that's a side effect. In reality, it's an energy booster that magnifies and focuses the power one already possesses."

With an energetic boom, Orica was engulfed in a globe of light exactly like the one that came from Stella's father's bracelet. "The power isn't derived from the bracelet," she said. "It comes from inside your heart. The truly magical thing is learning to use your mind properly. That's what you will concentrate on while you're under our tutelage." Fear rose in Stella again as she thought about her father's bracelet—lost in her bag along with his jacket and timepiece and her apprentice clothing.

"Along with your notice of apprenticeship, you received a packet." Orica came to a stop and swung around. "By now you have hopefully familiarized yourselves with its contents, especially the maps of the facilities as well as the Laws of the Universe, which were printed on the backs of your notices. We'll also need your signed form."

Stella tensed. Not only had she lost her bag, but she didn't have a packet, and no one had signed anything. Looking up, she saw Orica's gaze move from face to face before fixing on Akila, whose lower lip quivered. Akila wiped her tears with the back of her hand.

"You're a baby," Daith whispered to her.

Stella stepped between them. "Don't talk to her like that."

A few of the kids gasped, but she stood her ground as Daith locked eyes with her, clenching his jaw and daring her to fight. As they stared one another down, Orica interrupted, her voice commanding. "I beg your pardon, Miss Merriss. It is not your place to discipline your peers. Focusing on keeping your own behavior in check would be advisable."

Taken aback, Stella sputtered, "But he's bullying someone half his size. Why am I the one who gets in trouble?"

Orica's eyes narrowed. "I believe an apology on your part is in order."

"Who should I apologize to? Akila, because no one else stepped in? Or you for doing what you should have done?"

"So far," Orica boomed, "I've seen inappropriate behavior from you twice, Stella Merriss." She spat out her name like a dirty word. "First, when you showed up late and just now when you were so insensitive to Daith. The law of cause and effect states that every action or thought has a consequence. Do you want consequences for your disrespectful and thoughtless actions? Because if you do, I can arrange that. I have the entire angelic army at my disposal."

Orica's directness startled all the recruits, but no one was more rattled than Stella. Her face flushed red. "No," she said quietly.

"Good," Orica said. "Only you are in charge of you. Remember that there are always consequences for your actions." Then, turning her attention back to Akila, she asked with surprising tenderness, "Is this your first time away from home, dear?"

"Yes," Akila squeaked.

"Well, don't fret. We'll make the transition easy for you." Orica's tone was soothing now. "When I was your age, I did my apprenticeship here. I sniffled like you, but I survived just fine, and you will too. The first few weeks are the toughest, but I promise it'll pass."

Orica reached out to give Akila's shoulder a little squeeze, then she faced all the recruits. "I know that not seeing or communicating with your families until next summer might seem like a long time, but we've found that full immersion into the angelic way of life will help you adapt more quickly to our ways. Besides, we'll keep you so busy that summer will be here before you know it."

Orica's words may have soothed Akila and the others, but Stella once again remembered her mother standing in the boat and being swept overboard, and then waking up to find both of her parents missing. What if her parents really were gone forever? Could she go back to the lighthouse for the summer? Or to her grandparents in Abalonia? *Forget it*, she told herself, shaking away the memory. *Be strong.*

"Take out your packets and turn to the maps section," Orica instructed.

Everyone pulled out a packet except for Stella.

"Miss Merriss, where's your packet?" Orica asked.

Stella cleared her throat. "I never got one."

"I know one was sent to you because I mailed it myself."

"Maybe it was in my father's knapsack, which got lost when the sharks attacked." She cringed as the words escaped her mouth. They sounded made up, and she flushed with humiliation.

"Or maybe your goldfish ate it," Daith scoffed.

Some of the others chuckled, and she felt herself flush again. Akila leaned over and said, "You can share with me."

Orica's lips tightened into a stiff line. "I'll allow it for now, but understand that it is not guaranteed that you will be permitted to stay on at the Citadel if you didn't receive your packet and do not have your permission slip. Do you have it? Unless your fallen angel father signed it—"

"My dad is missing . . . probably dead," Stella said softly in despair.

Orica looked as though she'd been punched, her head jerking back and a rasping sound escaped her throat.

No one knew what to say or do. A tense hush fell over the group.

Orica shook off her shock and simply said, "Well," as she stared fiercely at Stella. She cleared her throat and continued, "Let's proceed to the dorms so you can change into your garments, assuming everyone picked them up from Reslan Josephine." When she glared at Stella, evidently expecting her to say she hadn't visited Reslan Josephine's yet, Stella looked at her feet—anything to avoid more scorn.

Orica threw one last disgusted look at Stella before indicating with a jerk of her head that the kids should follow her up the stairs. As the recruits trailed behind her, Stella stared at Orica's nut-brown curls and just knew she'd somehow already made an enemy of one of her new teachers. There was nothing to be done about it now but to move forward. Outwardly, Stella portrayed the picture of confidence, but internally, she was a mess. Would having no uniform, as well as no permission slip, give Orica the ammunition to kick Stella out of the training program? Where would she go if she were asked to leave the Citadel? Maybe back to Magnus's lighthouse, or she could go to her aunt Esmi and grandparents in Abalonia. With resolve, Stella decided then and there that it was no use worrying about what might happen. She'd figure something out about the missing clothes. But she still couldn't shake the worry over possibly losing her father's bracelet, timepiece, and jacket.

At the top of the staircase, a figure stood waiting for the recruits. "This is your angelic advisor, Baribur," Orica announced, as she turned to face the kids. "He'll be taking over from here. I must call an emergency meeting to address the matter of the applicant who showed up unprepared."

18

ANGELIC ADVISOR

Stella tried to focus on the immediate issues at hand: the tour with Baribur and her lack of uniform. She couldn't do anything about what Orica was saying in the emergency meeting, but she could make things better by figuring out her uniform situation as soon as possible. She followed Baribur, with the rest of the recruits, into a spacious room with a table, chairs, and an exquisite silk Vilunian rug woven in bright colors and geometric patterns. Wall sconces glowed softly adding golden light to the otherwise darkened room. Once everyone was inside, Baribur inspected his new charges. "Kindly line up in front of me, candidates."

With his hands on his hips and his prominent chin tilted high, Baribur exuded strength and competence, though a twinkle in his brown eyes pointed to a mischievous side. A halo of sapphires rested on his head and shimmered the same color as the cape that swept down his back from his golden epaulets. Scrunching up his nose, Lasker asked, "What's a candidate?"

"You are," Baribur answered. "You became candidates when you passed the consciousness scanner detection test with Orica. Before entering the Citadel, you were merely recruits, but you've already ascended in rank. Over the course of the next nine months, it is my job as your angelic advisor to prepare you for your ascendancy exams. After three months of candidacy, you will take an exam to become cadets. Providing you pass, you will then work for the rest of the training year toward becoming angel apprentices. With hard work and determination, you will all ascend on Sentinel Day."

Lasker looked as if he was going to speak again, but before he could, Baribur continued. "Sentinel Day is a holiday celebrating our beloved sentinels and the peace they have kept throughout the realm. Because the ultimate goal for each of you is to become sentinels yourselves, we correspond the start of your official apprenticeship with Sentinel Day. As part of the celebration, you will perform as a choir." A few of the candidates groaned. "But you'll learn more about that later.

"During your time with us, our job is to strip you of the behavior taught to you by each of your cultures, so that you become blank canvases."

"Does that mean I won't be able to wear my silks anymore?" asked Vara, pouting as she twirled to model her colorful garments.

"That's correct," Baribur responded. "We require you to dress in the simple uniforms Reslan Josephine has provided. We expect a certain homogeneity among our new additions here at the Citadel.

"In exchange, you will learn how to use your sixth sense—your creative imagination. When this is tapped into, you step beyond the limits of your own experience and access an infinite storehouse of unlimited knowledge. Everything that ever was, is, and ever will be becomes available to you."

Stella scratched her head at this. She was going to be able to tap into *all knowledge* that ever was or would be? That seemed . . . overwhelming—but also pretty cool.

"Please understand, you will be *completely* changed," Baribur said. "We're going to raise your consciousness and your awareness of who you are. Each of you has infinite power within, but you must learn to conform to the rules of the Citadel. We demand you release your former sense of self and adhere to the angelic way of doing things.

"Boys, your dorm is on the right. Girls, you're on the left," he said, gesturing vaguely to each side as he did so. "Please arrange your things and change into your new garments and return here. Then I'll explain more house rules. You will find your Laws of the Universe primers in your closets. Please carry them with you at all times."

In the shared common room between the dorms, there was a small study area with a few comfy but practical chairs and a table, near a fireplace. Inside her dorm, Stella saw doors in one wall with their names written on them. Beds lined two other walls, the foot of each bed marked with a name. All of the linens were white, all of the wood—from the floor to the bedframes—a light elmlock. It felt sleek and minimal but also cozy somehow, helped by the plush bed linens and the sumptuous rugs.

Stella's closet was on the end, next to Akila's, and when she opened it, her knees buckled—she saw her Josephine's Fine Garment Shop bag inside. She didn't know how the clothier had managed it, but she'd saved Stella. Stella opened the bag and first removed an everyday tunic and leggings as well as sturdy boots and a pair of simple white shoes. Next she found a dress-up gown, halo, and silver slippers, which she put away neatly into the closet, along with sleeping clothes. She then extracted her father's bracelet, which she hid behind the slippers at the back of the closet.

Stuffed down at the bottom of her bag was her father's jacket, damp and stained with lines of salt. She pulled it out, buried her nose in it, and, for a brief moment, she was sure she could still sense her father's musky scent. She carefully removed his special timepiece and her mother's letter—so water damaged it was barely readable—and hid them with the bracelet at the back of her closet.

Akila shut her closet door a little too hard and let out a tiny squeak that pulled Stella back to her senses. The others had finished putting away their clothes and belongings, had changed into their uniforms, and were apparently waiting for her. She changed quickly out of the cloak and dress Josephine had given her for the pageant, and put her new uniform on. Stella snatched up her Laws of the Universe primer—*LOU*, it said on the cover—and hurried to join the others in the common room where Baribur was waiting.

"You may have noticed the laundry chutes in your rooms. Just drop your dirty clothes into them, and cherubs will wash, press, and fold everything before returning them to your closets, though you'll find angelic clothing more sturdy than landling clothes."

A few of the apprentices looked at one another. "What's a cherub?" Vara asked.

"Cherubs are highly intelligent beings who choose to pursue higher consciousness through acts of service," Baribur clarified.

"They look quite young, but they're not children. We ask you to give them the utmost respect, as you would any trainer or adult here."

"So where are angel children, then?" Lasker asked. "We're all"—here he paused and said it carefully—"landlings, right?"

"Yes. Angel children who are called to military service go through different training. They are not born with wings either, but they are born with the advantage of growing up among beings of higher consciousness—we angels—so they're trained differently at least for the first year. Once you've earned your wings, the angel and landling cadets are combined into a single class."

He pointed to a door in the common room that was between two bookcases. "That is my room. If you ever need anything, and can't find me, please knock." They all bobbed their heads in agreement.

Baribur indicated they could investigate the common room for a bit and get to know each other. While the others looked around and sat on the couches chatting, Stella noticed they were all dressed in white leggings, white shirts, and white shoes. Their uniforms weren't exactly stylish, but then, she supposed they all probably had very different ideas about what that meant. More than anything else, she was worried she'd spill stuff on her pristine white garments and always look dirty.

After a time, Baribur called everyone to attention. "One final note of welcome to our newest candidates: remember that today you left your previous life and way of thinking where it belongs, behind you. Tomorrow, you each will turn your attention to the future—to a new you. Where you came from matters less than where you are going. Ok now, it's nearly midnight, so off to bed. You all have a big day tomorrow."

After returning to their respective dorm rooms, the girls quickly changed into sleeping clothes, and made their way to their beds. A sliver of moonlight sliced through the room as Stella fell into her bed exhausted. Stella quickly found herself in a vivid dream. Her father materialized in the ashy smoke of a bonfire—like one of those holograms leaping from Orica's device. He seemed to be cheering Stella on, encouraging her to move forward, to live this new life. As quickly as he'd appeared, he was gone, and Stella drifted off into a dreamless slumber.

19

THE TREE OF LIFE

When Stella woke the next morning, she stretched and yawned, uncertain of the time. Her bed had been even more comfortable than it looked. She noticed her dorm mates had begun to stir. Akila, whose bed was next to Stella's, bounded from her bunk, clearly chipper and excited, and, socks on shiny, marble floor, nearly had her feet go out from under her. She flung her upper body onto her mattress and grabbed the foot of the bed to stop herself from going all the way down.

"Yeesh," Akila said, rubbing her neck and scrambling to stand upright. "Me and my clumsy ways."

Giggling with her, Stella said, "No worries—I bet we're all going to flop a few times before we've earned our wings." They grinned at each other at the prospect.

"I've been waiting forever for you to wake up, so I could thank you for standing up for me to Daith yesterday," Akila said. "He's so mean."

"It's not a problem," Stella said as she rose from the warm comfort of her bed and readied herself for the day. "I'm still trying to figure out how *I* was disrespectful but Daith wasn't."

Akila shook her head. "I know. It was really unfair, what Orica said, but I just wanted to be sure you knew how much *I* appreciated it."

Everyone gathered in the common room to find a tray of simple fruit pastries and a note from Baribur instructing them to study their LOU primers on their own for the morning and that there was to be no wandering, rough-housing, or horsing around. At lunch time, Baribur marched them down to the cafeteria. Inside, rows of tables were occupied by individuals of all ages, some wearing what looked like military uniforms, others in what could have been civilian clothes, and all in a variety of colors. Each sported a bracelet, and many wore belts with swords attached to them. Stella noticed that the Sentinel Island insignia appeared to be engraved on everything, even the dishes.

Baribur grabbed a plate. He ushered the candidates past bubbling pans of buttertail casserole, steaming pots of creamed shimmer cress, and overflowing dessert trays piled with scrumptious-smelling pastries (all of which made Stella's mouth water). He stepped up to a stout-looking cook wearing a white apron smudged with all the colors of the rainbow. "I'd like to introduce Reslan Belja Burnum," Baribur said, smiling. "She's our head chef. Belja, please tell our new arrivals about the food you've prepared today."

She wiped her hands on her apron and said pleasantly, "Over here we've got all the fixings to make yourself a piney." She indicated platters of flatbreads, chopped vegetables, seaweed, sausages, shellfish, chunks of a pungent cheese and bowls of colorful sauces. "A piney is an angelic delicacy. I'll show you how it's done."

She grabbed a piece of flatbread, slathered it with a purple sauce, and then layered on sausage and scallops. A layer of greens came next, along with a dollop of seaweed and a few hunks of cheese. "Oh, you mustn't forget the pine needle powder," she said. After pointing at a bowl of green grit set out at the end of the display, she sprinkled a light dusting on the concoction. "Pine needles give the dish its name, of course. Most of the ingredients in a piney come from the land and water realms."

As she took a bite, she closed her eyes and groaned. When the purple sauce oozed out everywhere, she casually switched the piney to her other hand, so she could wipe the sauce on her smock.

The candidates somewhat hesitantly picked up plates and began making their own pineys. After assembling their meals, Baribur waved to a corner table, so they all trooped that way. They pulled out their chairs and sat down, but Akila, who was clearly distracted by the other diners and everything going on, missed her chair and ended up with her behind planted on the floor. Lasker reached out and grabbed her plate, which had caught the edge of the table as she'd gone down and was teetering.

Daith elbowed Callum and pointed at Akila. As Akila scrambled to take her seat, Daith said in a low voice, "What an idiot."

"Don't worry," Lasker reassured Akila as he handed her the plate of food he'd saved. "It happens to me sometimes too."

She nodded gratefully.

At each place setting was a glass of purple juice. Calling attention to it, Baribur asked, "Have any of you ever tried zochi berry juice?" When no one said anything, he went on. "Give it a try.

Zochi berries come from the Tree of Life, which you'll observe later on. Their juice is a staple of those who enjoy an angelic level of awareness. You might especially benefit from it, Akila," he winked kindly at her. "It helps with awareness and coordination."

After sampling the purple beverage, all the candidates agreed that it was delicious, but then their expressions changed. Some looked confused, others in awe, and a few a bit stunned.

"*Everything* is purple." Lasker's voice cracked with a note of panic. "Is anybody else seeing this?"

"I am," said Vara, fluttering her eyelashes. "It's beautiful."

"The purple flash is a side effect of zochi berries that wears off quickly, whether you eat the whole berry or drink the juice," Baribur explained.

Surveying the different tables scattered throughout the cafeteria, Lasker asked, "Who are all these people? Are they in training too?"

"Most of them work here at the Citadel, keeping all functions of the sky realm operating," Baribur said. "But some of them are in training just like you."

"Will we be studying with any of them?" Akila asked.

"Not until you officially graduate to apprentices. Until then, the cafeteria is the only place you will encounter them until you earn your wings," Baribur said.

Once everyone had finished eating, Baribur led them through the corridors again, showing them the Citadel so they'd know their way around. The candidates rounded a corner and nearly tripped over one another as they came to a halt where a suit of armor stood at the base of a huge flight of stairs.

"Look how shiny it is," Akila remarked. "I've read about knights in shining armor before, but I've never seen one in real life."

In the center of the breastplate, a golden, embossed, winged sword contrasted with the gleaming silver of the rest of the armor. The helmet's visor was closed, and knee-high metal boots ended where the leg coverings began. A green cape cascaded down the back. The armor was showy, reminiscent of what the angelic forces of the sky realm had worn at the Pageant Day Parade.

Akila reached out to touch the armor.

"Excuse me," boomed a voice from within it. "Don't smudge the metal."

Startled, Akila jumped back, bumping into Daith, who snapped, "Hey! Watch where you're going, you dimwit." He shoved her away, knocking her into Fen and Stella; all three crashed into the knight.

Stella marveled that it was like running into a brick wall as she, Akila, and Fen fairly bounced off of him and toppled into a heap on the floor. Daith, Callum, and Vara laughed hysterically as Lasker and Reginal rushed to help them to their feet.

"Kindly control yourselves!" Baribur called out above the hubbub. Turning to the knight, he apologized, "Sorry about that, Sebastian. This year's candidates arrived last night."

The knight continued to lean on his great sword. Shifting his weight, his metal joints creaking as he did so, he remarked casually, "Not to worry. It's the same every year."

Stella eyed the suit of armor—or rather, the *knight* in the shiny armor—carefully as Akila asked, "What exactly do you do, Sebastian—guard the stairs?"

"I am the protector of the Timekeepers, the stewards of destiny," said Sebastian, his voice echoing deeply from inside the helmet. "They're the whole reason the Citadel exists."

"Yes, and he does a fine job—most of the time," said Baribur, though the last part was a little under his breath. "Onward, young recruits. We're on a tight schedule." Up the stairs they went, though Stella kept glancing back at Sebastian, waiting for the suit of armor's head to turn and watch them as they left.

Soon, however, they were down a corridor where they came to a glass door. Baribur opened the door. An enclosed courtyard lay beyond. He began handing out baskets from a stack just outside the door.

The enclosure was dominated by a large tree with deep grooves of dark-brown bark meandering along its fat trunk. Knots seeped a sticky, bloodred sap that pooled in its furrows and crags. Long branches stretched out, reaching toward the glass dome above as though in praise, covered in heart-shaped, jade-colored leaves. Hanging clusters of misshapen purple berries drooped from branches; occasionally individual berries dropped and landed gently on the soft grass, blanketing it with a velvety carpet of violet.

"Wow! Look how big that tree is!" Daith exclaimed. "I bet you'd score twenty cords of firewood out of it. My father's a lumberjack. He'd love to chop down a tree like that."

"Daith Fiveton!" said Baribur, spinning around so angrily that all the candidates shrunk back, frightened. "Never, I repeat, *NEVER*, speak disrespectfully about the Tree of Life again." His reaction stunned the candidates, but none more than Daith. Stella was happy to see Daith finally reprimanded for something.

After a moment, Baribur cleared his throat. "Listen, the centerpiece of our courtyard is the Tree of Life. A rare species of zochiwood—the last of its kind. As stewards of this beloved tree, it's our collective responsibility to ensure no harm comes to it." He looked upon the tree with rather dewy eyes.

"Every day, zochi berries fall in a purple hail." He scooped up a few berries and pinched one, juice dribbling down his hand from the nodules that bulged unevenly from its center. "Give it a try," he urged, encouraging everyone to take one.

"They're lumpy," Lasker said.

"Yeah," Daith chimed in, "and sorta weird looking."

Baribur chuckled. "When you bite into one, you'll notice a purple flash similar to the one you got from the juice at breakfast, but with the berries, it only lasts a second."

"Why does it flash purple?" asked Fen.

"No one is quite certain what causes the purple flash, but scientific studies have shown that the chemical composition of the berries opens up the mind, allowing us to attain higher levels of consciousness with less effort. For this reason, zochi berries are highly prized in the sky realm."

They all popped berries into their mouths.

"It tastes like the Vilunian blue bechewi fruit," Vara moaned. "I remember how my grandmother made the best blue bechewi fruit pies."

"It's sorta like the famous Boggers peat-pears. I hold the peat-pear throwing record," Callum declared, proudly beating his chest.

"Everyone will find their own interpretation of the flavor. Because the berry helps open your minds, there's a connection to your memories as well. For that reason, each person connects the taste to something different," Baribur said. "Normally it's the cherubs' job to collect the berries, but today, it's yours. You'll be competing to see who becomes the Guardian of the Well of Life."

Stella looked at the deep-purple berries carpeting the ground. If any of them popped, their white outfits wouldn't stay white long. *Maybe they have some kind of magic soap that gets out zochi berry juice stains . . .*

Behind a desk, away from the canopy of the tree, Orica was perched on the edge of a chair. She stood and approached the group. "Hello again, recruits. You'll be collecting the berries in the baskets provided. Each basketful must weigh five pounds—no more, no less. If you bring me a basket that weighs less, you'll be sent to finish filling it. If a basket weighs more, I'll dump the excess in a fresh basket. The candidate who collects the most baskets in the allotted time wins. No fighting, pushing, or name-calling. The winner will be crowned Guardian of the Well of Life."

Pointing to a round, waist-high rock wall standing on the far side of the Tree of Life, she said, "The winner will need to be up early every morning to collect elixir from the well. Being a well keeper comes with tremendous responsibility, but it is also a tremendous honor."

The candidates quickly lined up shoulder to shoulder, baskets in hand, and when Orica said, "Go!" they all dropped to the ground and started picking up berries. Everyone was frantically collecting berries and running up to Orica to get their basket weighed. When Stella took her first basket up, Orica appeared to accidentally knock it over, and more than half the berries spilled out. "Whoops . . . your basket isn't full," she declared with a dismissive flick of the wrist. "Back to work you go."

Stella had tried to give the coordinator the benefit of the doubt. She knew her father had probably upset a lot of people when he ran away with her mother, but she had no idea what Orica had against Stella herself. Now it was clear Orica had it out for her. Shaking her head at the ridiculousness of it, Stella returned to picking.

Out of the corner of her eye, she caught a movement in the underbrush at the edge of the courtyard. Upon closer inspection, she saw three little creatures. No taller than her shins, they were clearly cherubs. They wore orange puffy jerseys with baggy pants tucked into leather boots. From their backs sprouted iridescent, insect-like wings. Stella walked over to investigate.

"Are you the cherubs who normally pick the zochi berries?" Stella asked.

"Indeed we are," squeaked one of the cherubs in a high-pitched voice.

"Can you give me any pointers on how to pick them faster?"

"We can show you how we do it," said the second.

"That's very nice of you to offer, but is that allowed?" Stella asked, glancing over to where Orica was weighing the other candidate's baskets.

"I didn't hear Orica say we couldn't," said the third, "so I suppose it's within the guidelines."

The three cherubs stepped out from beneath the underbrush and filled Stella's basket at an astonishing speed. Daith must've noticed the cherubs helping to fill her basket, because his whiny voice soon sounded across the courtyard. "Stella's cheating!"

Everyone paused in picking the delicate berries from the ground to look over at her in curiosity. With cupped hands, Orica yelled, "Soliciting help is against the rules Miss Merriss!"

From across the courtyard, Stella boldly cupped her hands to her mouth. "Not according to the cherubs," she yelled back. Stella turned to Baribur who stood nearby supervising and asked, "If this rule wasn't stated before we started, it's okay, isn't it?"

Baribur simply grinned at her brazenness and looked over at a scowling Orica. After what appeared to be a silent debate between the angels, Baribur turned back to Stella with a good-natured shrug and indicated to follow him to the weighing table where Orica presided. Stella grabbed her filled basket and hurried over.

"It's true—nothing was specifically said about help from the cherubs," he confirmed. "In fact," he smiled at Orica who just continued to glare coldly at Stella. "It might be seen as showing great initiative. You're free to carry on, Stella. Have Orica weigh your first basket."

Orica grabbed Stella's basket out of her arms, and threw it onto the scale. It of course weighed a perfect five pounds, which seemed to irritate Orica even more.

Daith had wandered over during the exchange, clearly irked that someone might be doing a better job than he was. "Then I want cherub help—" Daith cried out, trying to appeal to Orica for help.

"Find your own cherubs," Stella replied. She reached for an empty basket to head back to berry picking but then paused and snatched up another basket. "On second thought, I'd better take two. They're quite fast, you know." Stella smugly smiled at Daith before turning to hurry back to her new cherub friends.

When Stella returned to the cherubs, their shirttails—which they had pulled up to use like baskets—were overstuffed with berries. They promptly dumped the berries into the baskets she carried. Stella was immediately on her way back to Orica, who begrudgingly marked her second and third basketful on the score sheet. Snatching up two more empty baskets, Stella headed back to where the cherubs waited for her. She noticed that the berries left no stains on the cherubs' clothing. Looking down, she realized her own white clothes were also clean, even though her hands were stained with zochi berry juice. She briefly wondered if she'd ever stop being amazed at angelic advances like nonstaining cloth. Before long, she was racing back and forth between Orica's table and the cherubs, barely able to keep up with the pace of their picking.

When there were no more berries on the ground, Orica announced, "Time's up." She clenched her teeth as she viewed the final basket tally on her score sheet, and then she said, "Stella Merriss is the winner." Baribur added, "She's the one with the most baskets, but I'd also like to point out she completed this task successfully through the creative problem-solving she showed by asking the cherubs for help."

Stella beamed, but also snickered to herself as Orica stacked the baskets, gathered her tally book, and tramped off in a huff.

Most of her fellow candidates congratulated Stella on a job well done, except for Daith, who got so close that his nose practically touched hers and hissed, "You're nothing but a cheater." As Daith stormed off, Stella wondered what his problem really was. It couldn't possibly be her or even Akila, because neither of them had known him long enough for it to be something they'd done, but that didn't matter if they were the ones getting picked on.

Baribur said, "You have half an hour of free time." As the candidates dispersed throughout the courtyard, Baribur pulled Stella aside. His tone was grave. "With no signed release form, it seems the Celestial Council is not inclined to have you stay. They aren't making you leave quite yet, and by claiming the title of Guardian of the Well, you've helped your cause considerably. Be patient, work hard, and hopefully there will be some good news soon." Stella nodded miserably.

Once Stella was by herself, Akila and Lasker rushed over to congratulate her again. "Wow, great job Stella! I never would've thought to ask the cherubs for help," Lasker said.

"Thanks."

They were interrupted by the cherubs, who had reappeared to introduce themselves, since they'd been too busy helping her. Stella and her new friends found out the cherubs were named Grunz, Maslo, and Larkin, and they lived in the garden, their service to others being to gather the berries.

They chatted, and Stella thanked them again—for their service in general and for helping her specifically, especially as she now knew she may need the responsibility of the Guardian of the Well to keep her at the Citadel. The half hour passed quickly, and soon, they were getting ready to begin touring the facilities again, but Orica beckoned Stella over.

"Tomorrow, your duties as Guardian of the Well begin. Meet me at the courtyard door at 4:00 AM. And don't be late like you were arriving at the Citadel."

Stella wanted to protest but was afraid it would only exacerbate Orica's dislike of her. Instead, she paid close attention as they continued touring the Citadel. It was a maze of corridors, hallways, and stairways big enough for anyone to easily become lost, and she refused to be late in the morning. She wouldn't give Orica a reason to kick her out.

As they got their bearings, Stella realized there were a number of departments and angels who oversaw them: an information department—where the candidates watched a room full of headset-wearing angels tap away on devices updating everyone of the goings-on in the sky realm; an infantry training area—where they observed a squadron of angel warriors perform aerial loop-the-loops while lobbing what looked like water balloons at an army of life-sized soldier figurines on the ground; and a technology section—where they saw researchers in lab coats zap gemstones with lasers to make them sprout a variety of holographic wings and fly (the giant wasp wings were Stella's favorite, even though they fell off mid-flight, making the scientists scatter to avoid any fallout).

The familiar scent of horses hit Stella well before she could see the stables, and excitement coursed through her when she saw Moonglow, the horse Cavish had ridden the night before, as well as Glowinder himself.

Grand Master Cavish entered the barn and introduced himself. He explained his duties and the Lializan horses and their training. Stella nearly burst with happiness at seeing him but stayed quiet. She didn't want to remind anyone about her "improper" landing in the square or that she may have a head start when it came to training. She sensed Lasker and Akila wouldn't care, but she wasn't sure about the others—except for Daith, whom she knew would hate it.

It was easy enough to keep quiet and not draw attention. Between her foreknowledge of angels and Lializans, her illegal early wings, and her parentage, she was hiding enough from everyone.

20

ANIMAL QUEST

The train stopped at Dragon's Den, a long-forgotten station on the railway, which was the starting point of the portion of the trek to be undertaken on foot. Rain drenched the crew as they unloaded their gear. Watching from the dry platform, Meenah shuffled her feet impatiently, while Hort fidgeted with his hairdo. This next leg of the journey was going to cause some serious problems for the two of them.

Once the train pulled away, Rand spread out the laminated map on the ground, crouched over it, and ran his finger along the indicated route. "We'll climb along the Maidenclaw River canyon until we reach Cloudridge, where we'll set up camp for the night. Tomorrow, we'll follow the ridge to the tree line. We'll have to ford several rivers along the way, but after that, the hike should become easier."

Jakin jumped in. "The area is known for its nearly constant rain, so wear your waterproofs from here on. In fact, plan on it being wet for the rest of the trip." While the crew of six slipped on their rain gear, Meenah turned around and stuck her arms out, seemingly in expectation that someone would dress her in the appropriate gear. When neither help nor a jacket came, she spun around.

"Where's my jacket?" she demanded, her shrill voice rising an octave above normal.

"You're wearing it, aren't you?" Rand asked.

"Very funny. Everybody knows you can't wear a lion skin coat in the rain."

"We set aside necessities for you when we picked up our gear, and we sent you a message about it. You just needed to pick it up. Surely you received my note and grabbed your things?" Jakin said, swallowing nervously.

Meenah turned to Hort, who looked at Jakin defiantly. "I did, and if you think *the* Meenah—or I, for that matter—would be caught dead in any of that *plastic*, you're crazy." He sniffed and looked at his boss for backup.

Unfortunately, he was on his own. Through clenched teeth, Meenah spoke slowly. "Your only job is to take care of me!"

Like a whipped puppy, Hort turned to Rand. "You wouldn't happen to have a spare raincoat for Meenah, would you?"

Before Rand could yell at the two of them for being so thoughtless, Jakin stepped in. "Don't worry. We'll find something for you both."

"No," Meenah said. "Hort doesn't deserve a jacket. If he failed to pack properly for the trip, he should suffer the consequences."

"He won't survive without protection from the elements," Rand said.

"Proper planning prevents poor performance. No preparation, no protection. He should've predicted this outcome before neglecting *my* needs."

Rand shook his head. "The same could be said for you, Meenah. If you didn't verify his work, then you didn't properly plan either."

"How dare you point a finger at me," Meenah said, her nostrils flaring.

Then, surprising everyone, Rand pulled out two raincoats that had been folded into their own carrying pouches from his backpack. "I thought this might happen." After handing one to Meenah and the other to Hort, Rand jammed his arms through the straps of his backpack, vaulted from the platform, and disappeared into the thick jungle, his crew close on his heels.

Meenah and Hort found themselves alone in the abandoned train station, struggling to pull the jackets out of their pouches and to put them on over their expensive and ridiculous clothing. Finally, Meenah stomped off to catch the others, leaving Hort to scramble after her.

Rand and his crew followed the rocky trail as it snaked through Maidenclaw canyon. Sheer cliffs jutted up both sides and disappeared into clouds. Waterfalls cascaded down the rocky crags, splashing into the river below. In several places, the river filled the canyon, forcing the team to trudge through high water until the shoreline reappeared. The exhilaration of starting a new adventure faded quickly, replaced by the reality of the physical effort required to hike an ever-steepening trail in a downpour.

From the back of the group, Meenah's grumbling echoed off the canyon walls. Rand quickened his pace, hoping to put some distance between them. His one desire was to capture a dahu quickly so he could be rid of his horrible sponsor and her sorry assistant as fast as possible.

By late afternoon, the team had reached Cloudridge, where the rain mingled with thick mist. Dropping their gear, they set up camp under a ledge. While Rand again got out his map and began studying it, Jakin and the rest of the crew gathered what dry wood they could find and built a fire. When darkness fell, there was still no sign of Hort and Meenah.

One by one, the crew members fell asleep, and Rand became more and more worried he'd set a pace that had endangered his "benefactor." Then, as Jakin was hoisting their provisions into trees to keep the water panthers from getting to them, Meenah and Hort stumbled into camp, sopping wet and barely upright. Meenah practically collapsed in the fire, she was so anxious to warm herself and dry out.

"Where have you been?" Rand asked.

"Lost because of this fool," Meenah said, pointing at Hort, who had slumped on the ground.

"There's roasted jungle grouse and some beans if you're interested," Jakin said.

When he offered her a jug, Meenah took it and gulped a mouthful. Coughing, she immediately spat it out. "That's disgusting," she said, scowling. "You could've warned me you were giving me rat bile."

"It's shimmer cress tea, actually, and I brewed it myself."

A loud sound, part cry and part howl, ripped through the camp, causing Meenah and Hort to jump.

"What was that?" Meenah barked like she did everything else, but Rand could see the fear in her eyes as she glanced into the darkness of the jungle.

"Water panther," Jakin said. "A nocturnal nuisance, most likely planning their raid on the camp later tonight. I'm turning in, so I suggest you climb into your tent as soon as possible." Walking to his tent, he pulled back the flap and crawled inside.

"But I didn't bring a tent," Meenah called after him, shooting a look of disdain at Hort, who was still shivering on the ground next to the fire.

"Jakin and I are doubling up," Rand announced, "so you and Hort can use mine. I've also set up a sleep sack for the two of you to share."

Pointing at Hort, Meenah exploded, "I am not sharing with *him*."

"Whatever." Rand was tired of arguing. He jumped up and stuffed the map into his backpack. He stoked the fire one last time and, going to join Jakin in the tent, called over his shoulder, "As long as you're up, keep the fire going . . . unless you want visitors."

When he threw back the tent flap the following morning, Rand found Meenah curled up next to a blazing fire. Hearing him moving about, she awoke with a groan. "I gave Hort the tent," she said. "The last thing I wanted was one of those water panthers tearing me to shreds, and I didn't feel I could trust him to keep the fire going."

Jakin, who had followed Rand out of the tent, exchanged a glance with Rand, and they burst out laughing. "Water panthers are harmless," Jakin said. "Their only goal in life is to eat—and they can't eat you. Look, there's one now." He pointed at what looked like a tuft of hair with legs scurrying into camp. The tiny thing ran to the fire, nabbed a roasted grouse bone, and tore off into the underbrush. Once out of sight, the creature let out a ferocious roar that sounded like it came from a much larger and more vicious beast.

"You mean to tell me I stayed awake all night, scared half to death, trying to keep this fire going because of a fluffy little grease sack?" Meenah sat bolt upright at this. "Laugh now," she growled, letting whatever threat she was going to make hang there. As she traipsed off, mumbling to herself, Hort tore out of his tent and after her, fumbling with his jacket.

That day's hike put the group in largely uncharted territory, and Cloudridge wasn't nearly as close to the tree line as Rand's map indicated. As the fog increased and they were scarcely visible to each other, Rand called for a stop to reassess.

"There's still a full day's hike ahead of us, and this fog is unlikely to lift. Better strap on your fog lamps."

As expected, Meenah's grating voice bellowed, "Where's mine?" When Jakin presented her with a handheld flashlight, she snatched it from him without so much as a nod of gratitude.

For the remainder of the day, the trek was uphill through dense jungle. Wielding machetes, the crew hacked through the thick vegetation to create a trail. Although it was still daytime, their surroundings darkened as if it were dusk. Meenah and Hort stayed closer to the team, who had to listen to the frequent insults Meenah lobbed at Hort. She blamed him for everything, including a rogue tree branch that whacked her across the face.

Long after nightfall, they finally came to a clearing where they set up their tents in a steady rain. They gobbled down canned beans before turning in. Hort begged Meenah to be allowed to share the tent, but she refused. Instead, he hunkered down in the open air, his rain jacket draped over a stick he shoved in the ground, so it at least protected his face from the downpour.

On the second morning, the clouds had lifted sufficiently to afford them a view of the three snow-covered Dragonspurs and the lake at their base. As Jakin stoked the fire, Rand looked for Hort, eventually peeking into Meenah's tent and realizing he'd either snuck in or made his case in the night to be afforded some measure of shelter.

The team ate, packed their gear, and even sent out scouts— who found cloven hoof tracks—before Meenah and Hort emerged from the tent with disheveled hair, rumpled clothes covered in dried mud, and forlorn faces.

"Tracks, possibly of a dahu, have been found. We're going to begin following them. After you break camp, join us, but be sure to be quiet, so as not to frighten the animal should we come upon it unexpectedly. We left you some mushroom gruel."

"Gruel?" Meenah screeched loud enough to scare any wildlife within a hundred-mile radius. She walked over to the pan and gave it a swift kick, spraying mushrooms and grain across what remained of the encampment.

"I can't take this anymore," she said, her eyes wild. "I've got to get out of here." She began hurling things—rocks, sticks, whatever she could latch on to.

Rand and Jakin watched her meltdown, incredulous.

"I am *Meenah*!" she shrieked. "I don't eat *gruel*."

Hort touched her lightly on the shoulder, and she spun around, nearly taking off his head with the branch she had in her hand.

"Don't sneak up on me like that!"

Without saying a word, he pointed toward the lake. She wheeled around and saw it—a village nestled on the banks of the lake. It wasn't as large as Ilya, but it meant hot food, dry clothes, warm sheets, and an escape from this nightmare. Her eyes lit up. "If I wasn't so mad at you, I'd kiss you."

Turning back to the members of the expedition, she announced, "Hort and I will be departing for the lakeside village immediately."

While Rand was relieved, Jakin panicked. "You can't leave!" he said. "What about the dahu?"

"Coming on this expedition was a terrible error in judgment on Hort's part," Meenah said. "We'll join you back in Ilya when you return. We can induct the dahorse into the Fashion Farm then."

"It's a dahu, not a dahorse," Rand said, sighing with frustration.

"Whatever." Meenah took a deep, calming breath and brushed the grit from her jodhpurs. She scooped up a machete that was lying on the ground and disappeared into the dense vegetation. Hort scurried after her.

Rand broke the silence. "I'd like to follow the tracks we spotted this morning. Shall we pack up?" He gestured at his tent, which Hort and Meenah had used, and the pan she'd kicked.

The team broke camp and doused the embers of the fire. Then Rand led the way up the side of one of the volcanoes.

21

SEAT OF POWER

Sylvain had things on his mind—his foothold in the water realm and his lack of loyal and competent generals being just two of them—but he could hear some of his minions outside the door.

"Enter," he told them.

As Red Eye guards shoved their captives into his chamber, he considered imprisoning one or maybe even killing one, just to make a point, but a voice he didn't recognize cut into his thoughts.

"Hey, not so rough," the shrieking voice chastised.

"Lord, sorry to disturb you. More prisoners. Rogue villagers." At least his Red Eyes didn't go on with too much unnecessary talking.

Before Sylvain could answer, the incensed prisoner interjected. "I'm no rogue villager, and I won't tolerate being treated like one. Now take your filthy claws off me." She wriggled, trying to break free as Sylvain watched, amused by her spunkiness. "Do you have any idea who I am?"

His voice was icy as he said, "Go on then—tell me."

She straightened her spine, tugging her wrist free to stand as tall as she could, but Sylvain could practically smell the fear on her. "I am Meenah Battelle from Ilya."

He rose from his chair and slowly, ever so slowly, manifested and expanded his wings to their full span. Meenah gasped, her legs shaking as she took in the magnificent sight of the fallen angel. The other prisoner who had been brought in with this Meenah character fainted.

With a single flap of his wings, Sylvain lifted off the ground, and then he rushed at her, stopping to hover nose to nose. "And do you know who *I* am?"

"N-no, I'm afraid I don't."

Sylvain moved into the firelight so she could clearly see the dragon and viper tattoos scurrying just below the surface of his face. "I am Lord Sylvain, soon to be the absolute ruler of everything and everyone."

At each of his declarations, she trembled, but she did her best to pretend she was unaffected. "I've never heard of you," she said, though her voice wavered a touch.

"Bold, aren't we?" Sylvain retorted. At the snap of his fingers, his numbats descended from the ceiling, screeching loudly, but when they circled her head and landed on her, cooing instead of tearing at her skin, the lord raised his eyebrows, perplexed.

Meenah preened at the attention from the animals, and her eyes flashed as she looked at Sylvain. "If you are looking to rule, you need the powerful and influential by your side. I am powerful and influential—and I have plenty of friends who are as well." Again, her voice shook, but she had a haughty tilt to her head as she was surrounded by his pets, making him think there may be more to this loud creature than he'd originally thought. Maybe his day had taken a turn for the better.

Sylvain drifted to the floor and retracted his wings into the jewel on his back. He limped to his chair and peered at this stranger who had enchanted his numbats. The Red Eyes who'd brought her here were standing at attention, still waiting for orders. "Be gone," he ordered, flicking a quick glance at his subordinates.

"Yes, my lord," they said in unison, bowing and shrinking back.

One Red Eye pulled a sniveling Hort up from the floor. "And her companion?"

"Since he's your friend, Miss Powerful and Influential," Sylvain mocked, "what do you propose I do with him?"

Meenah cast her glance over Hort and only took a second to look back at Sylvain and say, "He's dismissed."

When the Red Eyes yanked Hort from the room, his screams echoed off the walls.

Sylvain smiled and looked curiously at this creature who'd just calmly handed great suffering to her associate. His mouth turned up in a diabolical grin. "So, let's discuss your landling connections."

22

GRUEL AND VIZIOSCOPES

When Stella sleepily stumbled into the common room at 3:50 AM, dressed and ready for her new duties, she found no one else awake, and she certainly wasn't surprised. She wouldn't have been awake either, except she didn't want to get kicked out, and she was not going to give anyone any reason to.

The only other person she encountered on her way to the courtyard was Sebastian, whom she waved to, managing a quiet "Good morning" as she did.

Cool and fresh, the air outside smelled of starcresters, and sconces shed the only light on the courtyard. Startlingly, the Tree of Life stood seemingly lifeless—no leaves, no berries, and, to Stella's disappointment, no cherubs.

Orica entered the courtyard without saying hello and marched past the tree on her way to the Well of Life. Beside its wall lay a coiled rope and a bucket. Without a word, she demonstrated how to tie a barrel knot. After doing it a few times, she let Stella try.

"If tied correctly, the barrel knot will hold the bucket," she said in a voice that was soft and reverent. It was the nicest Orica had been to her since she'd arrived at the Citadel, and it felt good to be spoken to in this way, though she didn't expect it to last. "The rope should be tight, so the bucket won't flip."

After several tries, Stella succeeded in tying the knot correctly. Orica then opened a tiny door nestled in the well's wall and took out a piece of technology Stella had never seen before. Orica attached it to the bucket and powered on the device. A hologram of the well jumped into the air. "This sensor reads the elixir's level," she said. "Any changes will show on the screen. But I wouldn't worry about this too much since the well's level fluctuates a small amount normally anyway." When she pressed a button, the hologram showed a graph with relatively constant elixir level over the last five years. "See? Only very small changes. Once you've extracted the elixir, remove the sensor from the bucket and put it back in its cubby, and pop the lid on the bucket so none of the precious liquid spills out in transit."

While Stella looked on, Orica demonstrated the whole procedure. Hand over hand, she lowered the empty bucket. Moments later, she pulled it up, full of a swirling, greenish-blue liquid with emerald mist dancing off it like steam. With agile hands, she loosened the sensor and the rope before snapping the lid in place. Glancing at Stella, she said, "If you think you've got it, tomorrow you will be on your own. After you check the elixir levels and collect it, your only other well-keeping responsibility is to carry the bucket to the door, where I'll take it from you. After that, you can return to bed, read, or eat rocks, for all I care." Her attitude was back, as Stella had suspected it would be. "Tomorrow, just show up on time again. Any questions?"

"What's the elixir for?" Stella asked.

"You'll learn that in the course of your studies."

Stella had more questions but didn't ask. She didn't know if Orica was keeping things from her because of whatever issue she had with Stella or was being truthful that Stella would learn in time, but regardless, Stella realized it was useless to ask. So she followed Orica back inside where, in the hallway, they parted ways.

She sat alone in the common room, waiting for the others to wake up, and when they did, they all made their way to breakfast.

The diners who were already present eyed the new candidates as they walked to their corner table. Baribur presented their breakfast, which was already waiting for them. A bowl of gloppy, gray pearlgrain gruel steamed at each place setting.

"Until you become cadets, it's pearlgrain gruel," Baribur said.

"For breakfast?" Fen asked.

"For *every* meal."

Stella was briefly confused, but she quickly realized yesterday had been a treat, a "welcome to the Citadel" day, and she wasn't surprised when a few kids groaned. Snickers could be heard throughout the cafeteria.

"Of course, you'll also receive a cup of zochi berry juice with each meal," Baribur said.

"That's just cruel," Callum said, crossing his arms over his chest and pouting. "My heart was set on pastries."

Once everyone had finished choking down their cruel gruel, a term Lasker coined after Callum's rant, Baribur led the candidates out of the cafeteria and into the gymnasium next door. "Quiet please," he said, clapping his hands. Then, without explanation, he closed and locked the door, leaving the candidates alone in the empty room . . . or so it appeared.

Stella scanned her surroundings—there were eight insignias of the winged sword on the floor, there was a rack of swords to the left of the locked door, and a dark figure was standing alone in the shadows on the far side of the room. Dressed in the angelic warrior garb of white combat pants, a form-fitting white breastplate, leather gloves, knee-high boots with metallic greaves, and a helmet fabricated with swirls of Aridian gold, he remained completely motionless.

While some of the candidates stood around yakking and goofing off, Stella tried to put it all together like a puzzle. Eventually she moved to the rack of swords, took one, and walked over to stand on one of the insignias on the floor, mimicking the figure's stance. She carefully placed her hands and the sword's tip in the exact same position as the figure.

All eyes turned to Stella. One by one, they followed her lead. After all of the candidates were finally standing, swords in hand, each on one of the symbols, the figure unfurled its wings and took to the air.

Landing in the center of the circle, he said, "I'm Thaddeus, your combat instructor. You just finished your first lesson: Understanding your opponent through observation. Class dismissed."

As the days passed, Stella decided that easily the most taxing part of the day was calisthenics with Bartholomew—an athletic combat soldier who was always barking out orders in a gruff voice. The twice-daily activity took place outside on a grass field. Before each session, Bartholomew had the candidates warm up with sprints, and during the following twenty minutes, he obliterated them with a rigorous routine. Every exercise had an accompanying affirmation that the candidates were required to repeat out loud vigorously:

Push-ups—Develop stamina by training your body to a higher level of fitness.

Jumping jacks—Endurance and strength are essential for your future.

Pull-ups—You must develop resilience.

Sit-ups—Mind over matter.

Stella thought the whole thing a bit ridiculous, but she knew she would enjoy getting stronger and more agile as the training went on. She could've done without the pull-ups, though, even if she was certain she'd eventually be able to do them.

Although Bartholomew could be demanding and surly, Stella also found him to be quite pleasant. "Angel warriors exercise every day," he said. "In fact, they train three times harder than your average angel, with more demanding workouts on account of needing to maintain the strength of their wing muscles to fight. Rising to a high level of consciousness requires discipline, and exercise helps develop that discipline."

Every other afternoon, choir practice was conducted in a rehearsal hall filled with music stands, various instruments, and shelves and shelves of sheet music that lined the walls. The room was shaped like a clamshell, a design meant to maximize acoustics, but everyone thought their voices sounded like toads with bronchitis. The choir director, a middle-aged landling with long blonde braids called Reslan Harmona, must've agreed, because she'd frequently stop the budding songsters by flailing her arms overhead like noodles, point at the sheet music, and have them start again from the top. With such slow going, it wasn't clear how they'd ever have their song performance-ready by Sentinel Day.

On alternate days, Baribur taught them angelic history, including the hierarchy of angels.

"Archsentinels are the highest-ranking angels, followed by archangels," said Baribur. "As archsentinel, Michael holds the highest rank of all angels, followed by Theophilus, Dodovah, and Gilda. Then we have high-ranking archangels Wunsch, Fresenius, Jehoram, Malkiel, and Parmenius. Does anyone know whether the sentinels ever change rank?"

Akila raised her hand. "Michael, Theophilus, Dodovah, and Gilda hold permanent positions as archsentinels. As for the others, I believe their posts change."

"That's correct, you've obviously been reading ahead in your primer, Akila," Baribur said approvingly. "The four highest-ranking angels have lifetime appointments, while archangels, who are also appointed by the Celestial Council, hold their posts for five-year terms. Can anyone name any previous angels who've held archangel positions?"

Again, Akila's hand shot into the air, and looked around to see if she was the only one, "Yes, the archangels are—"

"You need to learn not to talk out of turn," Baribur interrupted. His tone wasn't harsh like it had been when Daith made the comment about chopping down the Tree of Life, but it was certainly one Stella wouldn't want to argue with.

"Each of us must learn to restrain our impulses, even when we know we are right," he explained to the class. "The thing that differentiates higher beings like us from all the little creatures of the realms is that we have learned to be aware of our behavior and the impact it has on others. We rein in our impulses, instead of succumbing to them."

He looked at Akila. "I have been wanting to bring this lesson up because I've seen this behavior from each of you. Thank you for giving me the opportunity to teach such an important lesson, Akila. Anyone who doesn't abide by the Laws of the Universe sets themselves up to be seduced by negative forces. One reason we do our calisthenics is to learn discipline so that we can exercise self-control when it's required, even if it's uncomfortable."

Akila, who had at first shrunk sheepishly into her chair at his criticism, sat up straighter at this.

Baribur lowered himself into his chair before continuing. "Discipline isn't just about keeping our bodies fit and strong but also about retaining mental sharpness. The temptation to let our emotions run us is the same in all of us—except that because we are aware, we choose the right instead of the wrong. Our awareness empowers us to act wisely, instead of reacting without thinking. It's about *using* your head instead of *losing* it."

Lasker raised his hand. "So, we're all landling candidates, and the angel candidates are in a different course. But I still don't understand why. Are we any different than those who have two angel parents?"

"Angels, merfolk, and landlings are all, essentially, alike," Baribur began. "The primary difference is an evolving consciousness. Most landlings have not opened their minds and raised their consciousness to a level where they can manifest as anything but, well, landlings. Merfolk have evolved consciousness that have helped them adapt to where and how they live—unlike landlings, they know about angels; they know other creatures exist; they know they essentially manifest as merfolk and can manifest as landlings; so their consciousness is at a higher level than landlings' but not quite as high as the level of angels. On a biological level, we're all the same; it's our minds—our evolved consciousness—that sets us apart."

Everyone took a few moments to digest this, and Stella finally asked, "How is it that the consciousness requirements for merfolk to manifest tails is not as high as it is for angels to manifest wings?"

Baribur's expression jolted Stella. The angelic advisor could be a bit pompous when describing life in the sky realm, but she'd never seen him like this. He looked like he had a very weak handle on his anger, and his face was turning red.

"The Celestial Council has deemed them monsters, which is why they cut all ties with them."

Stella became shaking mad at his comment. "They are not monsters!" As she looked around, she noticed how the other candidates were staring in shock, but she couldn't help it—that was her *family*, her school, as Esmi had called it, he was talking about, even if she didn't know them all. "I've met merfolk, and they were not bad people or . . . or *beasts*."

"Angels," Baribur thundered, leaping out of his seat, "are legitimately high-conscious beings who have elevated themselves to higher planes of existence through work—deep personal work to improve themselves. Why do you think we can soar?" Wings suddenly expanded out of his back.

Stella felt the urge to let her own wings expand and to meet the angelic advisor on his terms, but she caught herself just in time. Instead, she began to make a retort when she was momentarily stunned into silence as Lasker sprang to her defense. "What I think Stella is trying to say is that merfolk, like angels, have perhaps developed their minds to the extent that they too can survive in two realms. Maybe all three realms could be one peaceful realm if the three species, which are—as you said—effectively the same biologically, could come together."

The discussion had turned just enough that it made Stella self-conscious. When she looked around the room, everyone except for Akila and Lasker were gaping at her, but it was Daith's expression, a strange, half-cocked smile that really got to her.

He can tell I'm uncomfortable. Her face warmed. *What if he knows?*

Luckily, Baribur, who had been breathing quite heavily a moment ago, turned his back on the candidates, collected himself, and retracted his wings. When he faced them again, his red cheeks had returned to their regular color.

"This is why we need the SSA. Commingling our genealogy with other species dilutes the potential for higher consciousness. However, we recognize that landlings can randomly possess such potential, which is why you have each been brought to the Citadel." He steered the candidates to a new topic, and when the history lecture ended, Orica joined them. Baribur made the announcement that they would be receiving their vizioscopes, the technology Orica had used to scan them that first night.

After Orica had passed out all the vizioscopes, Stella was still without one.

"Miss Merriss, we are still awaiting approval for you to stay," Orica said. The coordinator's tone was sympathetic, but her manner conveyed that she was unapologetically eager for Stella's dismissal.

Panic thundered through her. *What if I'm actually kicked out?*

Baribur patted her shoulder before calling for order. "Power up your devices and be prepared to connect subconsciously with them."

"What?" Fen called out.

"The vizioscope connects with your subconscious mind, reading your thoughts. It's an incredible tool to help you journey from your apprenticeship to the career the Celestial Council assigns you. What that career is depends on what you are deemed best suited for."

"Sit this part out," Baribur said softly to Stella, "but feel free to observe. When you're officially approved, you'll do this as well." He winked at her, and Stella breathed the slightest sigh of relief at this use of *when* instead of *if.*

A loud rattle, which could only have been Sebastian, sounded from the stairwell, and when he appeared in the common room doorway moments later, Orica rushed over to him. They argued in low voices, and when Stella heard her name, she glanced over and saw a vizioscope in the knight's hand.

"They say she gets one," Sebastian said, offering it to Orica.

"And I say she doesn't!" she hissed, pushing it away.

Sebastian tried to push it back, but she crossed her arms and wouldn't accept it.

"Not until I receive a definitive answer from Counselor Fresenius. The Celestial Council alone makes this decision."

"And the Timekeepers say she gets it *today*," Sebastian insisted, holding the vizioscope out to Orica one last time.

Stella was shocked to see him lift his visor, revealing a shiny face with crinkly eyelids and indigo eyes. "Don't let your past determine how you treat one of our apprentice candidates," he cautioned. "Feelings you had for her father are clouding your judgment. Remember the law of polarity—everything has an opposite—hot or cold, up or down, good or bad. For this reason, you must constantly look for the good in others, because all you're seeing is bad."

Orica clenched her jaw, as if biting back her reply. As they stood in what appeared to be a standoff, Sebastian eventually sighed in disappointment and looked down at the tech.

"Then I will give it to her myself." Turning, he called to Stella as Orica huffed out of the room, her heavy footsteps thumping down the corridor.

Stella approached Sebastian tentatively. "Yes?"

"Here is your vizioscope," he said, presenting it to her with a flourish. "The Timekeepers say you stay on at the Citadel. You're important to the realm's future." Then, closing his visor, he clanked back downstairs.

Returning to her seat, Stella felt overcome with gratitude that she could stay—finally, she felt as though she belonged somewhere.

The candidates tapped their vizioscopes, synching their subconscious minds with their devices. As they did, Baribur explained how it worked specifically. "Each vizioscope is programmed to adapt to its recipient's specifications in an exact manner, drawing on such factors as the individual's intelligence, time and place of birth, body measurements, energetic signature frequency, and profundity in the Laws of the Universe.

"The material they're made of is a special non-matter energetic glass that your brain *thinks* is matter, but it's really just energy." Glancing at each of the candidates, he said, "It can be stretched." He pulled on one of the sides of his vizioscope, and it extended to cover his entire body. "Or it can be crumpled like paper." He squeezed it into a ball. "It can also be molded into any shape you want it to be." He pulled it over his head like a hat.

Wide-eyed, the candidates mimicked each of his gestures, laughing.

"You must have it with you at all times. Once you reach cadet status, more resources will be available to you. Until then, your access to information is limited." He went on to explain the LOU function, which would allow them to access their LOU primers without having to carry around the physical tome, and how to use their daily order of business, or DOOB, which showed their schedule.

When Stella pressed her heart-shaped fun labeled DOOB, up popped a list.

DOOB

3:45 AM **Wake up**

3:55 AM **Well-keeping with the mean one**

4:30—5:45 AM **Eat rocks**

6:00—8:00 AM **Free time and meal time: pearlgrain gruel**

8:15—11:00 AM **Vizioscopes with Baribur**

11:15—11:45 AM **Group calisthenics with Bartholomew**

Noon—1:45 PM **Pearlgrain gruel (yum!)**

2:00—3:00 PM **Combat with Thaddeus aka Mr. Few-words**

3:00—5:00 PM **Group choir with Reslan Harmona**

5:00—7:00 PM **Yep, you guessed it. Pearlgrain gruel . . . again!**

7:15—7:45 PM **Group calisthenics with Bartholomew**

8:00—9:00 PM **Study Laws of the Universe primer aka LOU**

9:00 PM **Lights out**

It was clear her schedule had been written using her own thoughts. She cracked a toothy grin at the sarcastic remark that gruel tasted yummy, and then she blushed at the reference to "the mean one." She never would have said that out loud, which probably meant she needed to be more careful with her thoughts. No time like the present for her to start practicing that whole "using her head instead of losing it" idea.

23

CONFRONTATIONS

Weeks later, Stella couldn't get the conversation from that heated history lesson out of her mind. Why was so much effort being invested in keeping landlings, merfolk, and angels apart when, in essence, they were all the same, made of the same flesh and bone? Each was unique, with different consciousness, different strengths, and different weaknesses, but those who believed in their superiority over others were violating several of the *true* Universal Laws.

The SSA was an *angelic* law separating the species, not a natural law, like those of the universe, which made Stella sure there was nothing wrong with a mermaid and an angel being together—or, for that matter, a landling and a merfolk, or even a landling and an angel.

Her thoughts raced as she walked into the rehearsal hall for choir. Was any of this something she could change, or was it all just useless thoughts she'd have to hide from her friends and the other candidates?

Lost in thought, she bumped into Akila, who was checking the printed list showing who had been awarded which singing part for the Sentinel Day performance. "You got the solo!" said Akila, hugging her, and, in her excitement, she knocked Stella's sheet music out of her hand. "Oops."

"No, no," Stella said. "My fault. I'll get it." Stella moved the piano bench out of the way and dropped to all fours, imagining how Daith, who really wanted the solo, would act upon hearing the news.

The two of them were half under one of the pianos, collecting the music, when Stella caught sight of the corner of a sheet sticking out from under the piano's pedals. As she slipped her hand under to retrieve it, stretching her fingers to slide the paper her way, a foot pressed down. The pedal firmly trapped her wrist, the piano even rolling a few inches from the weight of . . .

"Daith!" she spit out. "Get off!"

Putting more weight on the pedal, he scoffed. "You think you're so much better than everybody else—class leader, Guardian of the Well of Life, teacher's pet—and now the solo! But I know the truth about you—you're nothing but a halfwing." His eyes narrowed, his glare full of hostility.

Seeing what was going on, the other candidates gathered around, trying to help Stella. Lasker rushed in demanding, "Get away from the piano or—"

"Or what? You gonna tickle me?" Daith said. "You're scared of your own shadow."

The other candidates were pushing on Daith, trying to get him to budge, while Akila was under the piano with Stella, trying to figure out how to help free her hand.

"Daith! Why do you care if she's *half* angel? That's more angel than the rest of us. We're all landlings," Akila said, scrambling to her feet.

Daith glared at Akila. "So you don't care that her father is a fallen angel? That she, in being here at all, is *illegal*?" He spit out the words like they were all filthy.

"Just lift the piano, Lasker," Stella said quietly. With every second that passed, the pain in her wrist intensified.

"Shut up, you filthy halfwing," Daith said, his knuckles turning white as he held more firmly to the keyboard cover. He'd clearly lost control, and, consumed by resentment, was well beyond the point of reason.

Lasker struggled to lift the piano but to no avail.

I wish I were in "filthy" mermaid form now. I'd whip him with my tail, Stella thought. Then it occurred to her—she could do something similar. Repositioning herself slightly, she lay on her left side, her left arm still trapped, and kicked out at Daith's legs with both of hers. The whip-like motion meant her feet actually slapped the backs of Daith's knees, knocking him to the ground just as Lasker threw every ounce of his strength into lifting the piano off Stella's wrist.

Lasker's side of the piano shot up into the air. The piano tumbled onto its side and slid a few feet. Everyone covered their ears at the cacophony it created—keys coming loose, strings snapping, wood breaking. When the noise subsided, Stella looked around at the damage. "Is anybody hurt?"

"No, all good here," Reginal answered.

"Pretty sure the piano's dead," Stella said flatly, clutching her arm. "Like my wrist."

"Wow, Lasker," Callum said, gawking at the broken instrument. "Bartholomew and I are starting a throwing team. You should definitely join." Offering him a hand, he gave Lasker a complicated-looking shake.

"How'd you do that?" Stella asked.

"I dunno." He looked almost disturbed as he surveyed the heap of parts that had once been a piano. Suddenly he said, pointing at Stella's arm, "Your wrist!"

He was right—the lower part of her arm and wrist had swelled up fast. The adrenaline rush she'd had during the argument had dulled the pain, but now that she saw what it looked like, she got queasy.

The door flew open, and Sebastian burst in. "What's going on in here?" His voice reverberated off the walls of the rehearsal hall. He scanned the room and quickly issued orders. "Akila and Reginal, go get a cherub cleanup crew to come at once. The rest of you, sit tight until Reslan Harmona gets here. Stella, let's get you to the infirmary."

In the corridor, they came across Reslan Harmona. "A little mishap," Sebastian said. "The piano was destroyed, but a cleanup crew is on their way."

Reslan Harmona looked bewildered at first, and then seemed to take it in stride, not asking anything but nodding for him to continue.

"From the look on his face when I entered the room, I believe Daith is to blame. I'm taking Miss Merriss here to the infirmary."

They continued down the hall and when no one was within earshot, Sebastian lowered his voice. "Tell me what happened—the truth."

Stella remained silent, unwilling to identify her attacker. She felt like it was something she could handle on her own—and somehow, she felt it was her fault.

"Oh, I see, you'd feel guilty if you told, is that it?" Sebastian said.

Stella kept tight-lipped.

"I'm going to say something, and if I'm wrong, how's about you jump in?"

Stella gave him a reluctant nod.

"You not correcting me is a good sign." He gave her a small smile as they continued on their way. "Daith did something."

She kept her expression neutral as they walked.

"Lasker discovered his strength."

More silence.

"You're keeping quiet because you don't feel worthy of my help."

Dumbfounded, Stella was startled into looking at him. She'd always been taught to be self-reliant.

He patted her shoulder. "I assure you that you *are* worthy of help. You're highly intelligent, with unique powers, but this doesn't mean you have to do everything by yourself. The weight of the realm isn't yours to carry. How'd you imagine the angelic forces became so powerful? From working together, which sometimes means seeking help. I'm one of those helpers. Whatever you tell me is strictly between us."

As they turned a corner and headed down another long corridor, Sebastian said, "Tell me how you hurt your wrist now."

Perhaps it was his kindness—or maybe his assurance to her that whatever she said would stay between them, because the words just started spilling out: her frustration with Daith, her mistreatment by Orica, her fears about being kicked out of the Citadel.

He slowed their pace and stayed quiet until she'd finished.

"First, you're not going anywhere," Sebastian said, gently urging her toward their destination again. "The Timekeepers have seen to that; never mind the Celestial Council. Second, Daith needs someone like you to stand up to him and hold him accountable, which is why we've let things play out between you. You've been doing a fine job of keeping his bullying in check." He gave her a quick wink. "Nevertheless I'll see to it that he's disciplined properly—because what he did to you back in the music room is a big deal." He pointed at her arm. "For him, the issue is recognizing the error in the way he thinks about life overall. He's a bully and it's not just okay but important that you know you should not tolerate abusive behavior. You're a powerful individual, and Daith senses this. What else would drive his jealousy of you?"

Stella began to clench her hands into fists, but her injured wrist twinged painfully, causing her to stop.

"As for Orica, I'll speak to her about her treatment of you. She's carrying bad feelings from her past and projecting them onto you. She's blaming you for something you had nothing to do with." He trailed off.

"Are you talking about her and my dad?"

Sebastian was quiet a moment before he admitted, "I expected you might've overheard our little tiff about your vizioscope."

"It was kind of hard not to."

"During her apprenticeship, Orica met your father. She had feelings for him, but he didn't feel the same because he was so focused on his career. He only ever considered her a friend. When he left for his work in the field, she convinced herself of a fantasy that they would one day share a life together: marriage, children, the whole shebang. When Magnus informed her your father had abandoned his post to be with your mother, Orica was devastated—not only because she'd lost your father but also because she'd been dumped for a mermaid, which she thinks of as a lower species."

Stella peeked at him out of the corner of her eye. "So you know about me?"

"The mermaid part? Yes, and so does she and probably a handful of others. Not everyone knows what, exactly, your father did. Those who *do* know learned the truth before the Celestial Council was able to erase his record from the mainframe. The Council was trying to save face from the embarrassment of explaining that one of their best commanders had betrayed them by breaking the SSA."

They arrived at a set of double doors with *Infirmary* written across them. A healer rushed Stella inside and, after an exam that confirmed it was a bad sprain, not a fracture, applied a pain-relieving salve and bandaged her wrist.

At the start of the candidates' time with Baribur the following day, he greeted them with the announcement "I have a surprise for you." He quickly led them out into the hall.

Lasker stayed close to Stella as they descended the stairs. "How's your wrist?" he asked.

"Not too bad. The healer I saw said it should be back to normal soon. It already feels stronger," she said, lifting it to show him the bandage. "What I want to know is how you flipped that piano."

He shook his head. "I really don't know. It was like some strange power welled up in me."

Stella grinned broadly. "Well, that should make the bully think twice before messing with you!"

He smiled back at her as Baribur brought them to a stop. They were standing in front of a door that Sebastian was guarding. It opened without bidding and revealed Orica, looking serious as usual.

She looked each one of them in the eye briefly before announcing: "The Timekeepers are ready to meet the new candidates."

24

CAPTURED

When Rand spotted the dahu, it was nibbling moss on an obsidian boulder, oblivious to the expedition's presence. Fawn fur covered its body, and tufts of white hair adorned its hooves like fluffy bracelets.

The team broke into two groups. One moved into position downhill, while the other encircled the animal, keeping a safe distance so as not to spook it until all was ready.

When the dahu bent for a sip of water from a creek, Rand gave the signal. Jakin and the others leaped up, screaming and flailing their arms. Caught off guard, the poor beast turned and attempted to flee. Losing its balance, it thudded to the ground.

Rand was in the second group, waiting some distance below with an extended net. The dahu rolled downhill, knocking loose hunks of obsidian, moss, and muck. The group ran across the hill to better position the net.

"Pull it taut," Rand commanded. The dahu tumbled toward them, landing in the net, its cries echoing across the mountainside.

Jakin and the first team bounded downhill to observe the capture. Rand had a syringe at the ready and stuck the tranquilizing injection in the bleating animal's hindquarters. Instantly, the dahu went limp, it's sinewy body tangled in the net.

Half the team untangled the sedated dahu from the net while the other half assembled a cage, the parts of which they'd carried in their backpacks. They gently placed the creature inside. They mounted the cage on long poles and returned, whistling, singing, and celebrating their prize, to where they'd set up camp the night before.

As night fell with a dahu in captivity for the first time ever, the team eagerly recounted the day's events while sitting around a blazing campfire. For Rand, the victory was bittersweet. He still had Fashion Farm to worry about.

Eventually, the rest of the team went to bed, leaving Rand and Jakin fireside when the animal stirred. It showed no interest in the moss or water placed in its cage. Instead, it bleated in fear. Rand's heart hurt with every despondent whimper. "We can't send him to the Fashion Farm. He belongs in the wild, not a cage. Let's release him."

"Absolutely not." Sparks exploded as Jakin chucked a log on the dying fire. "We are obliged to deliver the animal in exchange for receiving the expedition funds. In fact, tomorrow, the team will take the dahu to Ilya while you and I hunt for Meenah and Hort. I'm worried they're lost or in danger."

"You only care about the money." Anger painted Rand's cheeks scarlet. "You forced Meenah on me even though I wanted nothing to do with her." He slowly rose to his feet. "Hearing the dahu's cries tonight, I realize how wrong it'd be to take him from his home."

Jakin made a wide, helpless gesture with his hands. "We took her money in exchange for turning the animal over to her when you're done studying it. I don't see how we could do that without having to pay her back. If I had to pay her back, I might have to give you up; I couldn't afford to raise you if she took all my money."

Rand fumed, but he held his tongue. Jakin was all he had, but he was also all Jakin had. How could he even mention giving up his guardianship? It felt like a threat, though Rand wasn't sure it was meant that way. Jakin seemed constantly worried about everything: where money was coming from, who would support Rand's theories. His guardian was, truly, a bit of a worrywart.

Raindrops sizzled on the dying fire as Rand stared at Jakin. Rather than argue, he stayed quiet, thinking, until Jakin broke the stalemate and went to his tent, giving his charge a half-hearted goodnight.

When the coals had been extinguished and the dahu's cries had transitioned to snores, Rand slunk toward one of his team's tents. "Psst," he whispered to Garrig, a cryptozoologist buddy from university. "You awake?" With no reply, he unzipped the tent and tugged on his friend's toe.

"What's up?" asked Garrig, pushing himself up on his elbows.

"I need your help. Tomorrow, Jakin's sending the team back to Ilya with the dahu, but—"

"You want me to keep the animal away from the Fashion Farm, right?"

Rand smiled. He was relieved his team knew him so well, knew what kind of a person he was. "Yes. Exactly. Can you do this for me?"

"Sure," Garrig said, "you can absolutely count on me, Rand. I don't want him to go to that horrible witch's Fashion Farm any more than you."

Rand thanked Garrig before retiring to his own bed. He didn't really want to capture any creatures—he just wanted to know they existed.

<hr />

Tracking Meenah and Hort was simple. Given that Meenah demanded easy passage, Hort had slashed a trail wide enough for a train to pass through. Consequently, Rand and Jakin arrived in the lakeside village just before noon, where they were surprised to see that all of the buildings, each solidly constructed of rough volcanic stone block with emerald gruff grass sod roofs, stood empty.

Going from house to house, they shouted for Meenah and Hort, their voices carrying through the deserted streets. Carts, half-filled with rotting fish, sat abandoned, and the wind snapped the rough-hewn fabric separating the market stalls. After knocking on several doors, they understood the town's inhabitants had disappeared.

"Smoke!" Rand said suddenly, pointing toward a plume rising from one of the larger houses. Thrilled to have detected a sign of life, they ran to the house and barged in, not even stopping to catch their breath.

The first thing to catch Rand's eye was the lion skin coat hanging on a rack in the foyer next to a long black cape. A putrid stench permeated the entryway. Fear hit him in the gut.

As Rand and Jakin inched their way down the hallway, they exchanged glances, worried about what they had gotten themselves into. Voices drifted from a doorway at the end. The closer they crept, the easier it was to discern Meenah's voice. Peeking inside, Rand spotted two chairs, their backs to the door and facing a fireplace.

"General Pika won the Hollowilds, but he's old," Meenah was saying. "As the stronger choice, the young Lialian mercenary Phirius is the leader I recommend for general. His record speaks for itself, and I've had personal dealings with him—he sold me a lovely Ilyan emu skin once, which I turned into a fantastic purse. He offers a complete package—he's ruthless but completely loyal as long as you have the right enticements for him."

"And what of Totoq?" Meenah's companion crunched each word.

"He does have good qualities, but—"

A deafening trill erupted, and a black swarm burst from the room, zeroing in on the trespassers.

"Numbats—run!" Rand yelled.

He and Jakin fled, swatting wildly at their attackers. Rand reached the door. He ignored the stinging pricks of the numbat's fangs, shook off the dizziness he was feeling, and jerked the handle open . . . only to slam into a guard.

A whistle called off the bats as both Rand and Jakin crashed, frozen, to the floor. Just as Rand knew it would, the numbat venom had rendered him unable to move any part of his body. From his place on the floor, Rand gazed up at the swinging chandelier, which was heavy with snarling bats.

Meenah, moving into the view of the incapacitated intruders, flashed her teeth. "Well, well, look what the water panther dragged in."

A man limped into Rand's field of vision, next to Meenah. His pale oily skin glistened, stretching taut like a thin crystalline sheath over skeletal features. If not for the paralysis, Rand would have screamed in horror at the wickedness in the man's eyes. "When my new laws are in effect, trespassing vermin like these two will be enslaved," he growled. His pointy nose sniffed twice, "They reek. Remove them."

Rand's head hammered as he sat up. He noticed Jakin lying still, but clearly breathing, next to him. Scanning the room the guards had dragged them to by the light of a small, high window, he spotted a wooden plank with a body on top of it, tubes sticking out of the individual's mouth and nostrils.

As he continued to examine his surroundings from where he sat, Rand realized he was in a root cellar. Baskets of star taters and veiny tubers lined the shelves.

"Uh," Jakin groaned. "Wha happa?"

Rand nearly smiled at that—his guardian's lips were clearly still partially numb from the effects of the venom. Instead, he said, "We were paralyzed by numbat venom. In the wild, they incapacitate their prey to eat later. Good thing they only nipped at us."

"You call this *nipped*?" Jakin lifted his arms to display the rash of bite marks.

"My goodness, it's you two!" a familiar voice screeched.

Rand whipped his head around, and there, in the corner, was a dirty and despondent Hort. "Why are you down here?" Rand blurted, startled to see Meenah's sidekick.

Hort looked close to tears, though Rand knew him to be dramatic, so this could have been an act. "Meenah dismissed me," he wailed. "Me! How could she do this?" He looked truly distraught.

Rand wasn't as surprised as Hort seemed to be. Meenah didn't seem to have much loyalty toward anyone except herself.

"Where are we?" he asked.

"From what I can tell, it's just a holding cell before they ship us off to some work camp where we'll probably starve to death or worse—never see Meenah again." Hort's eyes were wild. "Do you think she'll let me stay? I can't go to a camp. I wouldn't survive."

Rand and Jakin exchanged a look.

"Do you know who that"—Rand gestured with his chin to the figure with the tubes—"is?"

"Those ghastly red-eyed guards said it's General . . . Somebody who disappointed Sylvain." Hort glanced at them. "Have you seen Sylvain? He's got wings and tattoos that move! What sort of creature has beasts crawling under his skin?"

Hort was rambling, and Rand did his best to calm him until the feeling came back to Jakin's lips, and then they both spoke kindly to Hort. Meenah's former flunky seemed to fluctuate between being genuinely relieved to be stuck in the cell with someone he knew and being flabbergasted that Meenah had thrown him in there.

By the time twilight descended, they'd talked Hort down. When the door at the top of the stairs again creaked open and Red Eyes marched in, they all stayed relatively quiet as they were seized, bound with ropes, and forced up the stairs. Soon, rain pelted their cheeks as they flew over mossy roofs in the clutches of Red Eyes. Mud splattered the three prisoners when they were dropped before a large mirror-like orb that hovered above a soggy field. Climbing to his feet, Rand gawked in wonder at the sight, but he and the others were quickly shoved onto a walkway that extended from the floating vessel. Once reaching the belly of what Rand realized was some sort of hovercraft, the door slammed shut.

"We're done for!" Hort shivered with fright.

The gray metal walls around them rumbled, then jolted them to the floor.

Over the noise, Rand said, "I think we're flying."

The three stared bleakly at one another. They were now bound for parts unknown with no chance of escape.

The moment the vessel jolted to a halt, Rand couldn't have said if they'd been on the hovercraft a few days or a few weeks, their captors had kept them so disoriented. Their heads had been shaved, and they wore ill-fitting dark jumpsuits that, as they were finally dragged from the ship's hold by Red Eyes, Rand saw were a grimy gray. Pale, desolate, and a good deal skinnier, the terrified prisoners were deposited onto a creaky dock. For a moment, Rand forgot his desperate predicament and marveled at the stalactites overhead and the hovercraft they'd just left, which floated magically above the water's surface. Two revelations came to him as he took in his surroundings—they were in a huge cave that appeared to be accessible only by undersea, in which case, the hovercraft doubled as a submersible watercraft. Guards nudged the three of them down a steep ramp where more of the Red Eye guards waited.

"Take them to the worksite," a guard ordered.

The prisoners found themselves being herded through a tunnel that seemed to have been carved from the stone rather than naturally occurring. The place smelled of rotted seaweed and dank stone. Water fell on Rand's bare head, and he shivered as it dribbled down his neck and into his jumpsuit.

A guard directed them into another tunnel aglow with dim light, and as they passed a cavern, Rand slowed to stare at a large tank holding two mermaids. The merfolk pounded the thick glass, their eyes pleading for help, their lips mouthing inaudible cries for mercy, making Rand's mind go to dark places.

Mermaids really do exist, he thought, but he had little time to be awed or delighted as he felt a shove from behind. "Hurry along!" the guard at his back said hatefully.

The long tunnel eventually spilled into an open space with high, cathedral-like ceilings flickering with the golden glow of torches. The guards gave Rand, Jakin, and Hort pickaxes and shovels, and they got to work breaking rock, joining a large group of men and boys already there.

Following several hours of backbreaking work, Rand was assigned a blanket. He barely had enough energy to wrap the blanket around him before flopping down on the ground in exhaustion.

The next day, work started early. The three of them tired quickly, not being used to such toilsome physical labor, and Jakin, Hort and Rand developed nasty blisters on their hands. The most impressive prisoners never slowed. One was a tall, imposing presence with shaggy hair and a full beard whom the others referred to as Boss. During one of the meals, Rand sat next to him, and Boss eyed him.

"Can I help you?" Boss asked in a deep voice.

Rand's inquisitive mind wouldn't slow down, and there was a lot he was trying to learn about their situation, so he dove in. "Do you know where we are exactly and if there's a way out of here?"

Boss stared hard at the table in front of him before responding. "I've got a hunch about our location from snippets I've heard from the guards. But I haven't figured a way out yet—to my knowledge, nobody has. They're keeping a pretty close eye on us and wearing us down. On the day I arrived, I saw an angel's wing snap in two—broke his spirit. After that he couldn't work on account of the pain and didn't last another week, poor angel."

"Angels?" Rand asked. Questions flashed like lightning through his mind. A full minute passed before the right question came to him. "They're real—angels, I mean, and they're down here working too?"

"Sure. Beings from all the realms can work, can't they? Our captors have us doing their dirty work, and they don't care if we die doing it."

Something very frightening was going on in Rand's head, and Boss must've sensed it when he cast a sideways look at him. "Don't you worry, son—I'm doing my best to formulate an escape plan. They may take our freedom, our possessions, our livelihoods, our futures by working us so hard, but the one thing they can't take is our ability to think."

Boss turned and looked at Rand full in the face. "The universe is an ocean of motion. Change is the only constant. We've gotta believe that someday, we'll be free again with something better replacing this terrible experience. Until then, stay close to me, and together we'll survive this by focusing on other things—more hopeful things." And with the warmth of a father that Rand had never known, Boss said gravely, "What gives you hope?"

Although frightened, Rand took great comfort in Boss' words, especially the part about hope. It only took him a moment to respond. "Saving my animals." Rand thought about the dahu and took comfort knowing it was safe with Garrig. "How about you?"

"My family—they're out there, and someday we'll be together again."

25

THREAD OF LIFE

"Not a peep." Baribur pressed his finger to his lips. "The Time-keepers deserve the respect of our silence."

Orica waved them all in and then softly closed and latched the door. The candidates settled into a curved row of chairs in front of the three industrious sisters. As Orica walked over to a colossal glass sphere at the far end of the chamber, Stella observed the three energy workers and tried to piece together who they were and what they were doing.

The first Timekeeper plunged her hand into a canister hum-ming with electricity as she coaxed lightning bolts into a copper receptacle on a spinning wheel. To keep the machine whirring, she tapped a foot pedal in a rhythmic *tick, tick, tick*. The wheel twirled the electricity into a single strand of pulsating energy and wound it around a spool. So this was the Thread of Life—Baribur had mentioned it in their history lectures, but they hadn't learned much about it yet. When her spool was full, the first Timekeeper quickly replaced it with an empty one. She passed the full spool to the Timekeeper in the middle.

The second Timekeeper stuck the full spool on a rod. She pinched the loose end of the thread, unwound a length of it, and examined it through a magnifying glass she held so close to her nose that it fogged up. Chewing her lip, she set down the magnifying glass, plucked what looked like a metal pen from behind her ear, and struck the thread carefully, a spark shooting from it where she'd touched. No two measurements were the same. Then she guided the marked thread over to the sister on her left and returned to the spool to measure off another length.

The third Timekeeper accepted the marked thread, spread it across her lap, and reassessed the previous one's appraisal through a monocle that fit over her right eye. She positioned the thread between the open blades of a pair of snippers and cut it at the point of each mark. The loose end's light fizzled, and with the flick of a finger, the dead thread floated into an almost-overflowing canister at her side.

Without stopping their work, their voices rose up, melodic as a symphony:

We are the Timekeepers, forever young and old
Our purpose is to watch you—nothing is foretold
By your own choices, your life thread is spun
We recommend choosing rightly to live a life that's fun
For if you choose poorly, your life may come undone

Clad in thick gloves, coveralls, heavy boots, mirrored goggles, and a protective helmet, Orica stepped forward and collected the full container, replacing it with an empty one. Looking up at her, the third Timekeeper beamed appreciatively. Returning to the colossal clear glass sphere, Orica climbed up a ladder next to it, dumped the container of lifeless threads through a hole on the top, leaped back, and tucked the empty canister under the globe before snatching up her vizioscope.

There was an explosion of light as the sphere sprang to life; filaments of electricity bounced inside the glass like mini lightning strikes. A crowd of holographic people jumped from Orica's screen, similar to how the apprentice's holographic images had appeared on the devise the night they had arrived outside the Citadel's gates. Stella saw a rock climber tumbling down a mountain, a camper running from a bear, even what appeared to be an old lady laying in bed, taking her last dying breath. Each time Orica thumped a holographic head, it disappeared with a puff of smoke and the number of lightning bolts inside the sphere mounted. When she cranked a control panel knob to its highest setting, the foul odor of burned hair rose up as the sphere whirred faster. Stella's cheeks felt warm from the electrical blaze. Eventually, figures stopped popping up on Orica's vizioscope, and the filaments in the machine joined to create one pulsating mass of energy at the bottom of the sphere. The machine sputtered, coughed, and at last seized up. "This batch of energy is ready," Orica said.

The Timekeepers' gray eyes twinkled with energy but clearly also held a sense of knowing, a wisdom that could only come from having been around a long time. Tight bronze-colored buns flecked with nickel crowned their heads, and each had a refined nose, thin lips, and rosy cheeks.

From her lessons, Stella knew the Timekeepers were unique, but being in their presence, she could feel an indistinguishable energy that buzzed around them as if electricity pulsed through their veins. Their translucent skin and luminescent auras fairly radiated. To behold them was to look upon creatures from another dimension—creatures who commanded respect. Their long dresses shimmered around their delicate frames. Their movements, though slight, were deliberate and graceful. As they worked, they sang, each harmonizing with the other.

We are the Timekeepers, always just and true
It doesn't matter who you are—green, white, black, or blue
Your choice, your voice, we are here to observe
We weave, we cut, we measure, we serve
By your choices get the life you deserve

After a time, the first Timekeeper stopped pumping the foot pedal and lifted her head. "My name is Agnita. I am the spinner of the Thread of Life." Her face radiated joy. "What an attentive group of candidates. Quite a difference from last year. True, our training transformed those who were able to endure the rigors of candidacy, but initially they stampeded in here like a herd of wild Lializans."

Baribur dipped his head respectfully. "Hello, Agnita. I hope your work isn't too challenging today."

"Nothing too difficult yet—a rock slide, a bear attack, and old age."

"Don't be so morbid, dear sister. These children don't need to hear about such things. They're far too young." The second Timekeeper stuck her spark marker behind her ear and took in the newcomers' faces. "My name is Agnes, and I am delighted you could come today."

"Ahem—they have to learn about the circle of life sometime," Agnita said impatiently.

"Well, I'd like a chance to get to know them a bit first." Agnes's eyes sparkled as she jerked the electric yarn, making the spool whir.

Agnita glanced toward the children. "When are you planning on telling them your job—or shall I do it for you?"

Agnes laughed. "Dear sister, I will if you'd pipe down and give me a chance. I measure the Thread of Life."

The third Timekeeper looked up as she dropped the snippers into her lap. "And I am Agatha. I cut the Thread of Life."

Agnita's eyes crinkled at the corners. Looking at her two sisters, she inquired, "What do you think, sisters—how much more work should we do today?"

Agnes raised her hand. "I say we keep going."

"That new batch will still be there stewing in the morning." Agatha stretched her arms overhead and yawned. "I say we call it a day."

Agnes grimaced. "You always want to quit!"

"I do not."

"You do so."

Agnita shook her head. "Now, ladies, arguing will give our guests the wrong impression."

Agatha snorted. "Don't mind our bickering. We're just three sisters, poking fun. Otherwise, we'd be terribly bored. Since we've been together forever, it's how we amuse ourselves."

"She's not exaggerating either. We've been together for as long as any of us can remember, since the beginning of time, I suppose."

"I'm sorry, sister," Agatha said. "I should never have argued with you. You're right—we've done quite enough today. There'll always be tomorrow for us to continue our work."

"Shall we explain our job?" asked Agnita. The others bobbed their heads in agreement. Straightening her spine, she began, "Ultimately, we are energy workers. The first law of the universe is the law of vibration. Energy is. Everything in the universe moves— nothing is static. The only constant is change. Each of you has energy coursing through you like electricity."

She pointed to the colossal sphere, and its ball of energy thumped. "We are the stewards of that energy, monitoring it as it passes through you. We evaluate how you use it through your decisions, errors, and judgments and also through the pictures you hold in your mind. Those pictures are, in fact, what determine the length of your life and the amount of happiness you experience. This is your destiny. As the Timekeepers, we're simply observers, watching, probing, examining, studying, and pondering what the conscious beings of the world are up to. We shepherd the energy in when you first breathe life, and we redirect it back to the infinite supply when you die. Nothing is created or destroyed. As the law says, everything is energy—and since energy *is*, it flows infinitely."

The three sisters stood up, stretched their arms above their heads, and then bent over and touched the floor, their joints creaking and popping.

Agatha stretched her arms from one side to the other. "We accomplished a lot today, didn't we?"

"We sure did," Agnita agreed. "I believe we deserve a nice supper."

"Perhaps a ruby mallowmelon soup to start."

"Followed by emerald spinach and sweet ampleroot salad."

"And a hearty hazel-kerneled silver fin with shimmer cress for our main course."

"Cadet cake for dessert, yes?"

The sisters grinned enthusiastically at each other.

"Well, candidates," Agnita said, turning to them again, "have we explained it all enough? Do you understand now what we do? Could you answer questions about our role in the Universe?"

Everyone hesitantly nodded, but the other two sisters looked at Stella specifically, Agatha echoing her sister as she asked, "Well, could you?"

Stella's eyes widened. *Did they expect an actual answer?* "Y-yes, I think I could wing it."

The sisters burst into laughter. Agnes was grinning as she said, "Exactly like your father, I swear, Miss Merriss."

Stella noticed that the sisters suddenly appeared older than when they had first arrived. Their hair was entirely gray now, and it seemed thinner.

"Orica?" The three sisters twirled around to face her.

"Yes, ladies?" Orica said, lifting her goggles.

"Set extra places at the table." There was a lilt to their voices. "I believe we're entertaining guests this evening."

26

DINING WITH THE SISTERS

Orica scurried to open the door for the Timekeepers. "You remember our dinner order, don't you?" asked Agnes.

"Yes, of course. Ruby mallowmelon soup, emerald spinach and sweet ampleroot salad, hazel-kerneled silver fin with shimmer cress, and cadet cake."

They smiled. "Very well. We'll see you in the dining room later," Agatha said as they turned and exited.

Orica jerked open the zipper on her coveralls, threw down her protective hat, and glowered at Stella. "Miss Merriss, you were told to not speak to the Timekeepers, were you not?"

She nodded, afraid to say anything now.

"They're the three most important beings in the Universe. Perhaps puns are not the way to show respect." With a toss of her nut-brown curls, she stomped off.

Lasker jumped to his feet and rushed over to Stella. "I thought it was brilliant." He smiled at her encouragingly, but it didn't help. She'd upset Orica again and Baribur had said nothing to support her, even though the Timekeepers had seemed to want a response and had invited them to dinner after she'd spoken up.

"'Wing it'? Nothing funny about that," Daith said, rolling his eyes.

"That's enough, candidates," said Baribur. "To your dorms to dress for dinner."

Stella tore out of the room, her cheeks on fire.

"Slow down." Sebastian stuck out his arm as Stella came upon him. "That was a gutsy move in there. Few candidates receive an invitation to dine with the sisters until after they've earned their wings." He winked. "But I guess we know you already have yours."

His comment was like a punch to the gut. "What did you say?"

"Worry not, your secret is safe with me."

She waited until her fellow candidates had all passed by before leaning in. "How do you know about my wings? Nobody else knows except . . ." She stopped herself, not sure if she should name her coconspirator.

"Josephine?"

Stella's chin dropped in disbelief.

Sebastian's metal suit rattled as he chuckled. "Ah, I may look like just another pile of shiny metal, but I didn't become the protector of the Timekeepers without exceptional skills— and spies." Pointing to a vizioscope that sat on a nearby shelf, he explained, "I watched everything in the spinning room while you were in there. I have access to many public rooms, since I am in charge of keeping a watch on things. You must know that the three sisters are your biggest advocates. No matter how Orica or Baribur or anyone else may act, you have nothing to worry about. You belong here."

A tentative smile tugged at Stella's mouth.

Sebastian patted her shoulder. "Better not mention your wings to anybody else, as I'm sure Josephine suggested—others won't like that you didn't earn yours the old-fashioned way. Now, go. This dinner is one you don't want to be late for."

In the dorm, Stella hurried to get ready. Knowing that Sebastian knew her secrets—both her wings and her merfolk nature—and embraced her despite them gave her hope. *Is guarding secrets part of higher consciousness?* she wondered. *Do the Timekeepers know my secrets?*

The candidates rushed around, trading out their usual uniforms for the more formal outfits Reslan Josephine had picked out for them. Stella gasped when she saw her reflection in the mirror. The teal taffeta tea length gown Josephine had chosen for her was perfect. Stella reached for the accompanying fire opal and silver halo to complete the look and was quite pleased with the results. Josephine had picked colors that brought out the sheen of her blond locks, and her aquamarine eyes especially twinkled under the glow from the fire opals. Turning to Akila, Stella found her friend daintily stepping into gold slippers that perfectly complimented her white A-line dress with cascading ruffled skirt.

"May I?"

Stella helped Akila sweep her braids into an elegant bun on top of her head, then placed the garnet-encrusted gold halo around it. "You look beautiful."

"Thank you." Akila beamed.

"Did you notice the sisters seemed to grow older in the time we were with them?" Stella whispered.

Akila turned to her, her eyes dancing. "Yes! I noticed their hair got grayer."

"Do you believe the Timekeepers decide when our lives end?" Stella asked.

"No, they don't decide anything—we do," Akila said. "According to the law of vibration, we each create our own lives based on our choices and what we give our attention to. They only monitor our time and our energy."

Stella considered that as Baribur hollered from the common room, "Candidates! Time for dinner. Get a move on!"

They all lined up in front of the angelic advisor, much like they had on their first day. "The Timekeepers treasure cleanliness," he explained. "When invited to dine with them, you must wear spotless garments, sparkle in body and mind, and exude positive thoughts."

He gave them all once-overs as he walked down the line, being sure they were not sloppy or dirty. "I expect you to be perfect angels during dinner," Baribur said. His gaze lingered on Stella. "It's highly unusual for candidates to receive an invitation to dine with the Timekeepers. This is a high honor. Customarily, candidates don't have such personal interaction with the Timekeepers until they have passed their ascendancy exams to become cadets after a full three months of study."

Baribur then led the way to a much more formal dining room than any of the candidates had seen before. Perched on a golden chandelier, a cherub orchestra of sensophones, Sentenelian harps, feather lutes, violetas, huskhorns, and magnetrumpets played as the candidates entered. Tall pillars carved with angel heads and winged swords ran up the walls. Candles flickered atop a rose-colored marble mantel, while a cheery fire crackled in the fireplace. Corner tables with carved Aridian lion paws held vases of starcresters, dragon posies, and moon lilacs. In the center of the room, red velvet chairs were tucked under a long elmlock wood table that was adorned with a lace tablecloth. Beautiful and finely made plates, crystal stemware, and shiny silver cutlery decorated each setting, together with name cards.

When the candidates took their seats, Stella slumped into hers, disappointed to be seated so far away from the Timekeepers.

Orica appeared as they filed in. "Please rise for the Timekeepers," she announced, then stepped aside respectfully. Chairs scraped the floor as they rose while the three Timekeepers toddled in using canes. Stella had been right—without a doubt, they were growing older.

No sooner had the Timekeepers taken their seats than rosy-cheeked cherubs arrived bearing baskets of pearlgrain bread, thick slices of butter, and dishes of zochi berry jam. Their tiny wings flapped as fast as blaze beetles, and one of them flitted past, offering everyone flutes of sparkling zochi berry cider from a silver tray.

Agnita raised her glass high. "I propose a toast to the outstanding candidates we have this year, even though we're still missing the ninth."

The candidates cheered politely, but they all looked around at each other, confused. A *ninth* candidate was supposed to be here? They'd never heard that before. *Didn't Magnus say there were always eight? Was an extra spot opened for a special ninth candidate this year?*

Agnita craned her neck, her eyes searching up and down both sides of the table. "Where's Stella?" she asked, turning to Orica. "I specifically requested she sit next to me." Patting Fen's hand, she smiled. "No offense, dear, but we have a few special things to discuss with her. Would you mind switching places?"

Throwing her hands up at this, Orica huffed and then helped the two switch seats.

"That's better," Agnita declared, squeezing Stella's hand once she had settled into her new chair.

As everyone helped themselves to the bread, butter, and jam, Agnita selected a piece of bread from the basket and offered it to Stella.

"Thank you," she said as they made eye contact and smiled at one another. Stella was eager for a meal other than pearlgrain gruel.

Cherubs flew in with steaming bowls of ruby mallowmelon soup, placing them in front of each diner. In between the clanking of spoons and the slurping of soup, the three sisters asked each candidate a question, beginning with Reginal. "What was your most prized possession in your life before, and what would you say to someone caught stealing it?"

"My books. And I would tell them they shouldn't steal. I'd also tell them that they could earn their own coin to buy themselves a personal library. I might also recommend they visit their local library."

"Excellent." Agnes gave him a thumbs-up. "And what cosmic law would that fall under?"

"The law of vibration. The universe contains such abundance that there's enough for everyone. To take what's rightfully another's is to see scarcity instead of plenty."

The sisters nodded their approval.

As the cherubs cleared away empty soup bowls and replaced them with salad plates, Agnes said, "Akila, how would you explain self-mastery?"

Akila jumped in her seat, knocking her fork to the ground. A cherub zoomed down to pick it up. "It means giving yourself a command and having the discipline to follow through on that command."

"And is it easy?"

"No, it requires sacrifice, invoking the law of rhythm."

Agnes's face glowed with approval. Akila might have been a bit of a klutz, but she was clearly the smartest candidate in their class. Stella smiled at her friend.

"Daith, how fast does a tsunami travel?" Agnita asked.

"Not as fast as a marlin can swim," Daith answered. When the table erupted in laughter, he reveled in the attention.

"Quite right." Agnita pursed her lips. "Marlins are the fastest creatures in the ocean. However, while we appreciate your wit, we'd also like you to answer the question."

Instead of looking chastised, he smiled smugly. "The tsunami's speed would depend on the force causing it."

"And this would fall under which law?"

"The law of cause and effect."

"Very good."

The questioning continued through the hazel-kerneled silver fin with shimmer cress course. Each candidate answered a question related to the universal laws they'd been studying. All their answers pleased the Timekeepers.

When the main course plates floated away in the hands of the cherubs and the cadet cake arrived, the Timekeepers posed a final question. "Stella, please explain what led to your decision to risk your life by jumping off the ship where you were held captive and swimming through shark-infested waters to arrive on the shores of Sentinel Island."

Nobody else had had such a personal story shared, and it caused Stella to stop chewing mid-bite. How was she supposed to answer? Aware that everyone was staring at her, her heart sped up and her back prickled with sweat.

"Well, I wasn't the only prisoner—" Akila's hand went to her mouth in horror, while the rest of her class just stared in shock. "—on the cargo ship. There were about twenty of us, including my friend Sophie. We were almost all free and I was lowering the lifeboat my friend and the rest of the prisoners were in when a guard appeared and almost tackled me. I couldn't let us be recaptured, so I released the lifeboat and just jumped overboard. I didn't think—I just acted on instinct. In that instant, I knew that nothing—not jumping, swimming, or even dying—would be as bad as being a prisoner again."

Stella looked to the Timekeepers. "I don't know what happened to Sophie and the others. We were all in danger from the approaching sharks and I told them to leave me."

The warmth of Agnita's palm bloomed warm over Stella's hand. "We sent Captain Finnegan to retrieve them. After he learned you were safe, he gladly led a rescue mission with the *Capearlus*."

"Really . . . they're all safe?" Agnes and Agatha both nodded in confirmation with their sister. Stella leapt from her seat—cheeks wet with joyful tears—and hugged each of the sisters in-turn while bubbling "thank you, thank you" over and over again.

From her seat, Orica wagged a disapproving finger at Stella, indicating she should remove herself from the elderly Timekeepers and return to her seat. Quickly reseating herself, Stella couldn't wipe the happy smile from her face. *So much for acting the perfect angel*, Stella thought to herself.

"Did that really happen?" Instantly aware that he had spoken out of turn, Lasker reddened. Clearly one of his weaknesses was that he spoke before thinking.

"Indeed, it did." Agatha clinked her spoon on her cake dish. "The truth is that Stella showed great courage in coming here. If the sharks had seized her, she would now be Sylvain's. He's been growing his forces in the three realms. And one of the candidates here tonight is his relative."

The candidates' frightened eyes darted around at their peers, wondering who among them might be Sylvain's relative. Most eyes zeroed in on Daith. He was clearly different from everybody else and mean as a saw-fanged viper—something that was blatant after what he had done to Stella's wrist.

"We determined that, because of your potential for tapping into your higher consciousness, each of you here tonight were at risk of being abducted by Sylvain's army, which is one reason why we sent you notices of apprenticeship," Agnes clarified.

Without warning, Agnita's palms slapped the table and her body convulsed, startling everyone in the room. Her body stiffening, her gaze became fixed on the wall behind Baribur. Her voice hardened and deepened as she said, "Each of you possess unique energy that we need. A team of nine is divine, one of which arrives right on time. Eight together become fearsome, but three of you are the fulcrum. Make no mistake, war is coming unless averted. Take your roles seriously." Her body shuddered, and then she slumped backward in her chair, limp.

"Sister, sister." Agnes took her sister's hand, lightly tapping it.

Orica rushed over with a vial of blue-green liquid, which Stella immediately recognized as elixir. Tilting Agnita's head back, Orica emptied its contents into her mouth. A moment later, Agnita's eyelids fluttered and her head wobbled as her consciousness returned. The corners of her mouth crept upward, and as if nothing unusual had occurred, she asked, "Now, where were we?"

Agatha spoke up. "Agnita has episodes we've learned to heed."

Still a bit unsteady, Agnita waved her sisters away, signaling that all was well. Addressing the entire group again, she announced, "My sisters and I have been watching your progress and have unanimously decided to make you cadets. Congratulations!"

The candidates—cadets—looked around in confusion. They had only been in training for two months, how could they have ascended already? Even Baribur and Orica looked shocked.

"But-but the exam!" Orica spluttered. "How do we know if the candidates are qualified?" She looked directly at Stella as she said this.

"What does the Celestial Council think about this decision?" asked Baribur.

"They've got their hands full running the sky realm," Agatha answered.

Agnita continued, "It's imperative you join in the fight against Sylvain as soon as possible. Sentinel Michael agrees you are all ready to be cadets, contingent upon our queries here tonight. And you all passed with flying colors!"

Agnes rubbed her liver-spotted hands together. "Sylvain is building up factions of his army in each realm, his aim being to replace our harmonious universal laws with ones that promote chaos and corruption. If any of you betray your loyalty to the sky realm and the positive powers our side possesses, Sylvain will exploit you. He will suck out your consciousness and harness it for his evil purposes. Don't be tempted by his false promises."

"You can have anything in life," Agnita said, "anything that aligns with your heart's purpose, that is. The only thing required is to identify what your heart is asking of you, which will empower you to believe, take the required action, and in due course receive."

The sisters explained that the most challenging part of having what you want is painting a vivid picture in your mind of what it is you deeply desire. Many people become focused on material gain instead of what they truly want and what serves a greater good.

"One final thing." Agnita's expression hardened as she took Daith into her sights. "It's our deepest wish that you set aside the differences you have with your fellow cadets and work together. Some of you may resent the strengths others display and the opportunities they may be given, but at Sentinel Island, we collaborate. Do not be jealous of what others might possess. Instead, focus on what you have with gratitude. What strengths can you contribute to the team? With the dangers we face from the opposition, the last thing we need is fighting within our ranks."

Stella considered what her heart longed for, and almost immediately, a clear picture formed in her mind's eye. But dare she will it?

If the sisters say I can have whatever I truly desire, then instead of believing I can't have it, I'm going to borrow their belief that I can.

27

THE FULCRUM

As the new cadets trudged the halls back to their dorms, they peered into the courtyard. Silhouetted in the moonlight, the barren branches of the Tree of Life cast macabre shadows on the ground.

"Oh no!" Akila stopped and stepped up to the glass. "The Tree of Life is dead!"

Baribur put a reassuring hand on her back and gently guided her along. "It isn't dead. It's simply in its winter phase."

Stella had seen the Tree of Life look sparse during her morning well duties, but she hadn't dared ask Orica about it.

"The Tree of Life experiences all the seasons, each day. Winter, spring, summer, and fall each occur within a twenty-four hour period. Nighttime just happens to be the tree's winter," Baribur explained.

"So it has its spring every morning?" Callum asked.

"Springtime, yes. It buds and sprouts leaves." Stella assumed that must happen after she was done at the well.

When they finally made it to the common area, Baribur faced the newly-elevated cadets. "I have two announcements to make before you rest. First, congratulations on becoming cadets. Never has an entire group ascended from candidate to cadet so quickly. Or done so without taking the ascendancy exams."

Stella raised her hand and waited for Baribur to acknowledge before she asked, "Who's the ninth candidate?"

Baribur shrugged. "The Timekeepers tell us we'll know when he or she shows up. No more questions. It's time for bed. Because you are now cadets, tomorrow we are going to visit a new area of the sky realm that none of you have ever seen, so you'll need plenty of rest."

Amid excited mutterings, they all went to their dorms. Akila, Fen, and Vara soon dozed off, though Stella remained wide awake. Flipping over in her bed, she grinned. Her pulse raced as she recalled the colossal clear glass sphere exploding with electricity. *They said I was like my father*, she thought, exhaling a giant breath. In an instant, her mood turned—*I miss him so much.*

But her mother had taught her to turn negative thoughts into positives. Missing someone was an honest reaction, but she could make it positive. Rubbing her face in her pillow, she vowed to make a conscious effort to change her thinking. She focused on the good memories of her parents. There were so many of them—climbing trees with her father, gathering wild mushrooms in the rain, laughing with her mother at the ridiculous games her father would dream up. The more she focused on the good memories, the more they poured in. Her father had always said that where your attention goes, gratitude flows, and profound gratitude welled in her chest at these happy memories. She was at Sentinel Island, where her parents had wished her to come. What did she have to complain about?

As usual, Stella was up and out early to take care of the Well of Life. After completing that task, she checked her DOOB. A meeting with Sebastian popped up following her well duties. *Hmm, that wasn't there yesterday*, she reflected. Tucking her vizioscope away, she raced down the back stairs.

Stella tore around the corner yelling Sebastian's name. Akila and Lasker jumped out of the way to avoid being bowled over. Breathless, she leaned forward, resting her hands on her knees. "What are you two doing here?"

Akila pressed her hands to her hips. "What are *you* doing here?"

"My DOOB changed," Stella said, straightening up.

"Ours did too."

Lasker plonked himself down on the bottom step and rested his head against the banister. "I wish he'd changed it to a later time, so I could've stayed in bed longer."

A clattering rose up from under the stairwell. Stella and Akila spun around, and Lasker leaped to his feet. A moment later, Sebastian appeared carrying an odd assortment of things.

"Right on time, I see," the knight said. A broom, a mop, a bucket, a pair of pruning shears, a few pieces of firewood, and an old saddle landed in a heap on the floor. "Tidying up," he explained, raising his visor to mop sweat from his forehead with a handkerchief. "I wish the other mentors wouldn't clutter my closet. There are important things in there, private things."

"Like what?" Lasker asked.

"Well, that's is why I've asked you here—to show you. But you must swear not to tell a soul, and I do mean *anyone*." He took a deep breath and put his hands on his hips. "That includes the Timekeepers, should they ask. Can you promise me that?"

Eyebrows raised, they looked at one another and then back to Sebastian. The notion of keeping a secret from the three greatest forces in the universe made Stella uneasy, but Sebastian was adamant.

"If you can't, we can't do this."

But now they wanted to know too much, and all three said, "I swear."

"Close the door in case anyone happens by," Sebastian commanded. It was a bit of a squeeze, but the four managed to tuck themselves into the cramped space, which smelled of dust, stale wood chips, and zochi vinegar. Stella tugged the knob until the latch clicked. As she turned around, she noticed a small arsenal of swords, staffs, and even a battle-axe tucked in one corner. Her attention turned to Sebastian as he fiddled with a high-tech lock on a door at the back of the closet, and when it swung open, he ducked into a dark hallway, and waved them in.

After walking about ten steps down the hall, they emerged into a room that appeared empty except for a table in the center. From the ceiling, a spotlight illuminated two clay tablets. "As well as being the protector of the Timekeepers, these are under my protection, which is why I am often at the foot of the stairs. These tablets are inscribed with the Laws of the Universe."

Mouths agape, the cadets approached the tablets in awe. It was obvious that care had gone into creating them. When Lasker reached out to touch them, Sebastian swatted his hand away.

"These are to be shown the same reverence as the Timekeepers. Would you touch them?"

Lasker shook his head vigorously, rubbing his sore hand.

"But you keep them in a *broom closet*," Akila said, aghast. "Isn't that disrespectful, not to mention risky?"

"We chose it because it's hidden and close to the Timekeepers' chamber, so I can protect both."

Stella sounded anxious. "Why are you showing them to us?"

"You heard Agnita's vision last night. I believe you three are the 'fulcrum' she spoke of. If I'm right, then you deserve to know where the tablets are housed. They're just as important as the Timekeepers. Now, away with you, and not a word to anyone."

The next appointment on their DOOBs was a special cadet breakfast. On their way, the three discussed the past twenty-four hours: meeting the Timekeepers; marveling at their spinning, measuring, and cutting the Thread of Life; the dinner; their moving up to cadet rank; and seeing the tablets of the Laws of the Universe.

The trio huddled outside the cafeteria door waiting for their classmates. "That was weird, how Agnita suddenly changed when she had that vision last night," Lasker said.

"Sure was," Akila agreed.

"So Sebastian thinks we're the fulcrum?" Lasker scratched his head. "What is a fulcrum anyway?"

An enormous holographic dictionary erupted from Akila's vizioscope, and she read out the definition. "The support, or point of rest, on which a lever turns. A pivot. Something that plays an essential role in an activity, event, or situation."

After just a few minutes, all of the cadets werwe assembled in the hallway.

"Sebastian thinks we are going to have an important role in an upcoming event?" Stella asked as they opened the doors to the cafeteria. To their surprise, thunderous applause arose from the other diners. A banner draped from one side of the cafeteria to the other read, *Congratulations*. A swarm of well-wishers surrounded the newest cadets, patting them on their backs and shaking their hands.

Stella caught a glimpse of Reslan Josephine standing near an empty table. She raced over to her and wrapped her arms around Josephine's waist. "Great to see you," she said, holding her tightly.

"You too," the clothier responded with an affectionate pat on the head. Then, raising her voice to be heard by all, Josephine announced, "Listen up, my fastest ascending cadets of all time. Come get your new uniforms."

The cadets rushed up and seized their packages. Holding up a blue jacket, Stella remarked how it was similar to those the cavalry sported in the Pageant Day Parade.

Once the other diners returned to their seats, Reslan Belja sauntered over, carrying empty plates. "No cruel gruel today," she said cheerily and motioned to the buffet. "Have at it."

Callum jumped up and raced toward the pastry table, shouting, "Yeah!"

When Daith sauntered up to the table where Callum and Fen sat, Fen frowned. "That seat's spoken for." Spying an open seat at the next table, Daith moved toward it. "Not available," Vara said, tossing her uniform bundle onto the seat.

Plopping down at a table by himself, Daith slouched over his zochi berry pancakes, pushing them around his plate. Leaning over his half-eaten muffin, Lasker pointed at the bully. "Do you think he's related to Sylvain?"

"Given how mean he is, it wouldn't surprise me." Stella jabbed her knife into a pat of butter and slathered it on her pancakes.

"Word is they've put anger management classes on his DOOB," said Akila, leaning in conspiratorially.

"Who told you that?" asked Stella, knowing full well each cadet's DOOB was private, with only the mentors having access to them.

"Glitch—"

Before Stella could ask Akila what that meant, Baribur interrupted them by clapping his hands and announcing, "We're going on a field trip to visit Puff."

The cadets quickly finished their breakfasts and gathered around him. "What's a Puff?" Daith asked as he tried pressing in between the other cadets, who seemed determined to squeeze him out.

"You'll see. But first change into your new uniforms." Baribur turned and walked out of the cafeteria with the cadets hurrying after him.

Akila pointed to the bank of windows that overlooked the courtyard. "The Tree of Life is magnificent this morning," she said. The cadets oohed over the vibrant-green leaves and blaze-red flowers that formed the tree's canopy. Through an open window, sweet spring air wafted in, the tree's fragrance floating on it—a combination of stonerose, silver star, and honeyroot.

Noticing three young girls drawing buckets of elixir from the Well of Life and dumping them on the base of the tree, Stella, pointing, asked, "Who are they?"

Baribur smiled. "The Timekeepers."

"No way," Lasker said, his tone emphatic. "That's impossible."

"Well, it's them," Baribur confirmed, peering out the window. "Much like the Tree of Life, they live a lifetime every day. As Guardian of the Well, Stella retrieves a bucketful of the Elixir of Life every morning and passes it to Orica. At that point, the sisters are just three tiny seed pods. But when Orica douses them with the elixir, they grow and evolve. As each hour of the day passes, they age but at a much faster rate than we do. When they water the Tree of Life with elixir each morning, its life also begins anew."

The cadets waved at the young Timekeepers, who eagerly fluttered their fingers in response. "Come along now," Baribur urged, herding the group away from the window. "We don't want to be late for our appointment with Puff."

Minutes later, the cadets, outfitted in their new blue and white uniforms, paraded through corridor after corridor, all of which contained many closed doors. Baribur stopped in front of one of them and gestured toward a basket of headsets that sat on the floor. Everyone slapped on a pair.

Baribur lifted his hand to the microphone attached to his headset and spoke into it. "Testing, testing," his voice crackled in the headsets. "If you can hear me, raise your hand."

The cadets all raised their hands.

"Good. Now, stay close. We don't want any accidents."

A dense mist billowed in the chamber behind the door, and the intense grating noise vibrated the floor as well as everyone's teeth. Stella nearly tripped and barely avoided stepping on the cadet in front of her.

The group ascended a long set of stairs. By the time they reached the top, they had left the mist behind, and they could see the chaos around them—angels flitted about everywhere, some jetting in through a portal in the roof, others flying out. Farther on, large hovercraft of various designs and sizes were either being loaded with supplies or unloaded. The doors to one of the hovercraft closed up and, once sealed, its engines started with a rumble and it shot out one of the larger portals.

High overhead, a silver-haired, muscular angel wearing a leather jacket and a long scarf waved at the cadets. Employing his sleek wings, he made a rapid descent and then expertly pulled up for a perfect landing beside Baribur.

"Howdy, I'm Puff," he said, his gruff voice echoing through the headsets. "Welcome to Sentinel Island's transfer station. I'm the resident nephologist, which means cloud expert."

Tilting his head, he cracked a crooked smile. "From here, angels transfer exported goods to destinations throughout the sky realm. As you can see, hovercrafts depart or land on the launch pads on the right." He pointed to a group of angels waiting to unload boxes and crates from a vessel that was coming in to land. "Large shipments of whatever we import are unpacked and then distributed throughout the Sentinel Island's angel residents."

Puff pointed beyond the landing strip to where the airships rested. "Maybe you're curious as to why you've never seen these craft overhead? Or angels for that matter? Well, once in flight, they use veiling—part of the Marble Veil protocol—which renders them invisible to the naked eye. Our bracelets make it possible to veil an individual angel in flight," he said, lifting his wrist to show the class. Stella noted that it looked just like the one she'd received from her father.

Puff led their group further down the walkway. "Over here on the left, is where angels depart the citadel under their own wing power. Once you've earned your wings you'll each complete several flights accompanied by an instructor. After passing your flight exam, you'll be certified for solo flight. That means you'll likely be seeing this place often."

In a back room, two large brick chimneys rose up through the ceiling. Glass doors opened to a small chamber at the foot of each chimney, from which emerged an earsplitting, metal-grinding noise. Stella understood now why they had worn the headsets. Puff explained that previous delivery systems used clouds, which were produced from the chimneys. Every load was weighed and the cloud's strength formulated to make sure it could safely deliver the cargo.

"With our advanced technology, we've retired the old system, which means that these days angels don't use clouds to transport goods except under extreme circumstances or for old times' sake. Only a few other nepholigists and I—cloud enthusiasts—keep the tradition alive, but the entire transfer station rests on top of an antique cloud-making machine."

Covering his mouthpiece, Puff leaned over to speak to a worker who was wrenching a bolt on one of the chimneys. Uncovering the microphone again, he announced, "I've whipped up a special batch of strong clouds so each of you can enjoy a ride. I'm not permitted to tell you where you're going, but Baribur wanted you to experience what it's like to fly, and not just by hovercraft."

Stella was flooded with adrenaline. She remembered what it was like to fly on Glowinder.

"Do we have any volunteers?" Puff asked.

Daith's and Lasker's hands shot up, and Puff guided Lasker to one of the weighing chambers. Slamming the glass door shut, he instructed, "Relax and stay on your cloud. Give me a *W* for *wings* when you're ready." Puff raised three fingers, like a *W*.

Lasker gave Puff the sign, and with the pull of a lever, the chamber filled with mist, and before long, Lasker had disappeared into it. The cloud rose up into the chimney and was gone.

One by one, the cadets stepped in, disappeared into a cloud, and floated into the sky. When it was Stella's turn, the chamber filled until she couldn't see her hands in front of her face. As she began to rise, the narrowness of the flue momentarily made her claustrophobic, but once out in the open air, the feeling passed. The fog around her face dissipated and then cleared all the way down to her feet.

The tickling warmth she felt before inched along her spine, and she could feel her wings wanting to unfurl, to help her take flight under her own power.

Breathe, she thought. She had calmed herself before, when her wings wanted to manifest. She could do this.

Her chest expanded as she took in a deep breath, letting her lungs fill up like balloons, and then she slowly let it out. She closed her eyes momentarily, concentrating on her breath, and when the feeling in her wings had stopped, she opened her eyes and found herself perched atop a teeny-weeny cloud. Despite passing through real clouds and being tossed about by powerful upper atmospheric gusts, the cloud's strength held.

Freedom of this kind had eluded Stella since her thrilling Lializan ride on Glowinder. Cloud riding was different from having a thousand-pound beast beneath you, lurching and dipping. The word that came to mind was *peaceful*, and she relaxed.

Observing the entirety of Sentinel Island from up there was exhilarating. The colorful splendor of the land and water realms soon yielded to the vast emptiness of space as the cloud rocketed deep into the sky realm. As moons, planets, stars, and galaxies shimmered overhead, a cozy blanket of tranquility spread over Stella. Although the outside temperature had plummeted, she felt perfectly comfortable inside her hazy cloud cocoon. She floated farther and farther from the island, rising higher and higher, and everything else grew smaller and smaller, including most of her worries.

28

REGENTS IN THE SKY

"Glad your journey took place without incident," Baribur said. The angelic advisor had traveled to their destination by other means and had arrived ahead of the cadets. They marched behind him along the busy landing pad and out a side door. Once in the long corridor, he pulled off his headset, and the cadets did as well.

"On takeoff, an albatross joined me and soared with me all the way to the mountains," Lasker said. "He shrieked and clicked and whistled like he was talking to me. It was so cool."

Akila nearly jumped up and down. "That's a sign of good luck. Albatross almost never approach angels," she said. "I read about it in an article about navigating the skies." They all smiled at each other in wonder—it appeared there was one thing they could all agree on, and that was that flying was truly amazing.

The group entered an anteroom where eight regent angels, wrinkled and dignified, were waiting. Four were males, all of whom had long beards, and four were females with silky, silver hair. They all wore crimson robes trimmed in gold that swooped to the floor and each balanced a vizioscope in his or her palm.

The cadets huddled together as a tall figure stood over them. His ice-gray eyes matched his chest-length beard, and he smelled of pearlgrain gruel. "Welcome to Royomia, the regal city in the clouds. My name is Regent Zaltabur, head of the Regents' Council." He swept an open hand in the direction of his colleagues. "In the usual course of things, we wouldn't be meeting with you yet, but since you are the quickest class to graduate from candidates to cadets, we happily meet with you now. Our intention is to meet with you individually and discuss your apprenticeship training paths."

Light from skylights reflected off Regent Zaltabur's bald head as he scratched his whiskers. A long chain hung around his neck, a scythe brooch at the end of it. Stella saw that every regent had a necklace with Royomia's insignia—the winged scythe—on it.

Stella practically choked when her own holographic head popped out of Regent Zaltabur's screen. The other regents' screens soon produced a holographic head of each of the cadets. Regent Zaltabur summoned Stella, and she hurried to keep up with his long stride as they headed down a corridor.

An automatic door whooshed open, and the regent waved her in ahead of him. *Whoosh*, the door closed. Though the regent had an intimidating presence, there was also a warmth about him. He indicated Stella should sit. She crossed the room and seated herself, placing her still-shaking hands in her lap and intertwining her fingers. Zaltabur took the chair across the table from her.

A cherub flew in and set down a tray of sandwiches, cookies, and zochi berry juice. "Please help yourself," the regent invited, pushing the tray in Stella's direction.

Too nervous to eat, she picked up a glass of juice. While she sipped, the regent peered at his vizioscope, tapping away on it with the fingers of one hand and petting his beard with the other. "Stella Merriss," he said at last. "Yes, well, you are a special angel. Did you know that?"

Stella blinked.

"Yes, indeed." He tugged at his beard. "Being the daughter of a fallen angel and a mermaid is pretty extraordinary. Your story is unique. With the proper training, you'll serve in all three realms. Your father was among the few capable of moving freely among the three, with the help of some angel-mer technology, which is why he was sent on an assignment to the water realm.

"Your father acted the part of merman so brilliantly that the merfolk had no idea he wasn't one of them," he continued. "From what we can piece together, your parents' relationship began at a gala hosted by two prominent merfamilies. Understand, we don't have actual footage of that night as the water realm is not recorded by our technology."

Stella shifted in her chair. They recorded things?

As if he could read her mind, he said, "Missions carried out by angels are recorded for analysis, but our technology does not work underwater." He tapped the screen of his vizioscope and glanced at her face. "When your father's mission ended, he and your mother vowed to stay together. Once they had run away, the Celestial Council required Magnus Garmid, who was his mission partner, to track him down." He outlined the story Magnus had already told Stella and then expanded on it.

"From that point on, your parents were criminals. Your mother renounced her merfolk ways, and your father turned his back on the angels. They lived as a landling couple, but as time passed and you came along, they only felt safe by moving frequently. They were worried about what would happen if someone reported you to the Celestial Council as having been born in violation of the SSA."

After he pressed the screen on his vizioscope, a hologram popped up showing the door of the cottage on Viola Island where Stella had lived with her parents. When a large fist knocked on the door in the hologram, she heard Arago ask, "Who is it?"

"Special package delivery." She heard a throat clearing and then, "*S-P-D*."

Her father peeked through the crack. "Magnus?"

"None other," said the deliveryman.

Arago eased the door open, and the hologram's perspective shifted into the room as Magnus walked inside.

"Special delivery for Stella. It's her notice of apprenticeship on Sentinel Island."

Her mother, who had been sitting on a couch in the room, jumped up in fear.

"Don't worry, Andri," he said calmingly, "I'm not here to take your husband from you. As I said, this is about your daughter."

"But you're here to take her, aren't you?" Andri looked toward Stella's bedroom with fire in her eyes.

Addressing Arago, Magnus said, "I've been sent as her recruiter. It'd be for the best if you'd let me take her as she's to arrive by Pageant Day—and we all know if you bring her yourself, you'll have to turn yourself in." The scene shifted slightly from one parent to the other, the hologram recording was from Magnus's perspective. "You're both aware that Sylvain's forces grow more powerful every day, which means your daughter is in danger. Let me take her tonight. If I can find you, Sylvain can find you."

"Have you considered that they might take my desertion out on her?" Arago countered.

"With what's happening in the realms, it's the only place we can know for sure she'll be protected," Magnus said.

Andri rubbed her eyes. Looking at her husband, she said, "He's right. We should let him take her. It's time."

Arago, shaking his head, turned to Magnus. "We'll bring her to you at the lighthouse ourselves."

"Tonight?"

"Not tonight, but soon. We have a little time before Pageant Day. Let us enjoy our daughter for a little while longer."

Andri rushed to the desk and pulled out the bottom drawer. She scribbled a letter, stuffed it into an envelope, and held it out to Magnus. "Please give this to her if something should happen to us and Stella makes it to the lighthouse without us," she said, "or if we disappear and you have to go looking for her. Or if my family comes for her. Or . . ." Her voice trailed off and a silence fell over the room. Lifting her face toward Arago she added, "It's only right she know the truth."

Magnus took the note, and after several moments, he said, "I'd better take off."

The hologram went dark.

Stella's cheeks were wet, and she realized she'd been crying as she watched her parents.

Regent Zaltabur leaned forward. "You're welcome to ask whatever you want."

The first thing that came out of her mouth was the one question she dreaded knowing the answer to but knew she needed to ask. "Why does Sylvain want me?"

"The fact is, your heritage makes you unique," Regent Zaltabur explained, his voice softening with compassion. "The Celestial Council recognizes your attributes, and the Timekeepers do as well and offered you an apprenticeship to also keep you safe. Sylvain lost track of you and your parents, so he followed Magnus, who led him to you." He folded his hands together. "For Sylvain's army, it's about the long game. Over time, he has slowly and methodically built a following of loyal soldiers—his Red Eyes—in the sky realm. He promises them wealth, fame, notoriety—whatever their hearts desire—and then steals their souls."

"But what about me is so special?" Stella asked.

"Your potential to move between all three realms," Zaltabur said, unequivocally. "By offering you protection on Sentinel Island, we knew we could tutor you in the positive ways of those who have a high enough level of consciousness to manifest as angels. Sylvain recognizes the rare ability your biology gives you—to easily move between the realms. This includes your ties to the landling realm and skills in understanding them. That's why he wants you in his army. And now that you've evaded capture a few times, it has become personal for him. Sylvain will not stop."

29

LIGHT AND DARK

Stella cocked her head. "So the sharks attacked me not to hurt or kill me, but to recruit me?"

"Yes. Those who have joined the army so far have done so of their own accord—because they felt slighted by the Celestial Council, the Panel of Judgment, or the Board of Regents. Sylvain apprenticed here on Sentinel Island when he was younger. Upon graduation, he worked as a clerk for the Celestial Council, but after several years there, he grew angry when other angels earned promotions while he did not. Eventually, he sought a position elsewhere and landed one with Dr. Hargrave, who discovered where the consciousness is housed in our physical bodies— many consider it to be the link between the mind and infinite intelligence."

It sounded complicated to Stella. *Infinite intelligence* felt like more than she could understand, but then again, a lot of what she'd learned in the past couple of months had been overwhelming at first.

Zaltabur went on. "With Sylvain's close relationship to Dr. Hargrave, he gained firsthand knowledge of how to control others by removing their consciousness, and with it, their ability to think for themselves. He has done this to his army of Red Eyes. The process of removing their personal consciousness permanently damages their eyes, which is why they're called Red Eyes. It's good to remember that many of the Red Eyes were trained at the Citadel."

Stella shuddered. Sylvain's minions could approach any of the cadets and recruit them to the opposition's army.

"I've got another question," she said. "Why is it a crime to fall in love with someone of a different species?"

"Angelic law forbids relationships with members of other realms, by order of the Species Separation Act. The SSA was designed to keep the angelic bloodline pure." The regent leaned in before whispering, "As if genetics is the only thing that determines higher consciousness. An elevated consciousness is attained through study, training, and a growing awareness." He paused, took a deep breath, and leaned back in his chair. "For most of us, the wrongdoing wasn't that your father fell in love. It was that he broke his angelic oath. True, angels are fallible, just like anyone else. But your father was of high rank, which makes his fall from grace even more offensive in the eyes of the Celestial Council."

"But if the SSA is wrong," Stella protested, "and the angelic level of consciousness is supposed to be about being in harmony with the Laws of the Universe, why can't it be changed?"

"It can, but doing so requires time and persistence. Perhaps you could work to rewrite the angelic laws one day."

She smiled at that thought. If she managed to do so, it would mean that her parents would no longer be guilty of a crime, that her birth wouldn't be against the law, that her very existence wouldn't be a matter of universal concern. It occurred to Stella that the two forces in the universe both wanted her hereditary qualities, and yet her actual existence was technically illegal.

"Is my father considered a fallen angel?"

"Only a level one," Zaltabur clarified, clearing his throat.

"There are levels?"

"Of course. A level one fallen angel has broken the oath but has no ill intent toward angels or the sky realm."

"Are you certain of that? If he turned his back on his mission . . ."

The corners of Regent Zaltabur's mouth lifted. "It's true we can't know for certain, but none of his actions have shown ill intent. We no longer receive transmissions from him, so we suspect he had his consciousness chip tracker removed, which is how we record missions, but his last transmission was . . . Well, take a look."

As the hologram rose from the screen of the vizioscope, the view swung gently from side to side, and Stella could see two trees, a blue sky, and a baby's head resting on what appeared to be Arago's chest. It took her a moment to realize she was seeing her father's point of view as he lay in a hammock.

She leaned in, beaming—that baby was her. She didn't recognize where they were, but that wasn't surprising, since they'd moved so much.

In the hologram, her mother stepped out of a house and approached the hammock. Her aquamarine eyes were twinkling, and she kissed baby Stella on the forehead.

"You going somewhere or just saying hello?" her father's lilting voice asked.

"Going to the market. We need pearlgrain for dinner, and I want to pick up some fruit for breakfast. You'll keep an eye on our precious sea star?"

Andri walked away, her figure slowly fading into the distant landscape.

A few moments later, a person emerged from a nearby thicket and limped up to the hammock. He seemed out of place in the daylight. Ruts dotted his pasty face, and little red veins wormed around his nose. He had long, greasy, black hair and dingy black clothes, and his eyes darted between Arago and the baby.

Stella shifted uncomfortably in her seat as it dawned on her: "That's Sylvain."

Zaltabur pursed his lips. "Yes."

"Well, well, well, if it isn't the old do-gooder Arago." Sylvain snagged the end of the hammock and playfully swung it, cooing to the baby. "I never thought I'd see a sight like this."

The scene shifted abruptly as Arago leaped from the hammock. "Leave," he commanded.

"But you haven't heard my offer, big brother."

"Don't call me that." A hand popped into view as he pointed to the thicket from which Sylvain had emerged. "I said leave."

"Can't we talk for a moment, angel to angel?" Sylvain smirked.

"I am no longer in the service of angels."

Sylvain quickly backed away, hands up, and Stella surmised Arago had physically threatened him in a way that wasn't apparent from what she saw. "I know, I know, and it's a shame, although it could be an opportunity from which we could profit—all of us." Sylvain looked pointedly at the infant Stella.

"You leave my daughter out of this—" Black wings spread out from Sylvain's back, and Stella realized her father had probably let his own wings unfurl to intimidate the evil intruder. When baby Stella fussed, Arago said, "I'm going to ask you only one more time to leave my property before . . ."

Sylvain furrowed his brow. "Before what?"

"Before I damage your other leg," Arago said.

Sylvain closed his wings and leaned forward. "There's a place for you and any other fallen angel in my expanding army."

"Don't call me that."

"Ah, but you are. Don't ever forget you broke your angelic oath. And if I can't convince you, there's always your halfwing daughter. Her ability to move through all three realms could be useful. I'll be keeping my eye on her." Turning, Sylvain limped away. As the dark silhouette disappeared back into the vegetation, Arago turned his attention to rocking a fussing baby Stella and humming a lullaby.

When the hologram faded, Stella pushed herself away from the table and rose to her feet. Had she heard Sylvain call her father "big brother"? That would make Sylvain her uncle. The room spun. She wanted to throw something.

"Are you all right?"

"It's not Daith," she mumbled. She was pacing, and she stopped to turn and look at Regent Zaltabur. "Sylvain is my uncle?"

30

POOL OF GOOD INTENTIONS

When Stella emerged from her meeting, she saw most of the other cadets talking excitedly, probably comparing what had happened in their meetings with what had happened to the others. Stella kept her distance and stumbled to a private corner, pretending to admire the alabaster dome of the meeting hall, lost in her thoughts.

As the rest of the one-on-one meetings ended, the regents paired up and again held out their vizioscopes, the same holograms of the cadets appearing above them again.

One of the regents stepped forward. "I am Regent Glorious," she announced. "I'd like you all to join the regents who are displaying your hologram."

Lasker and Stella joined their regents—Regent Glorious and Regent Zaltabur—who led the way out a set of doors and into a garden, away from the meeting hall.

The foursome traipsed along a forest trail, up steep cliffs with terrifying drops on either side, and through cloud gardens with giant stands of majestic elmlocks and beechburl trees. The forest abruptly opened into a clearing, and before them stretched the ruins of what had evidently once been a magnificent city.

Pointing to the skyline, Zaltabur said, "This is the ancient capital of Royomia."

As far as Stella could see, massive blocks of white marble and pink granite littered the streets, debris blocking every road. Broken columns had toppled across one another haphazardly, the remains of once-great buildings and temples rendered useless. Bombed-out shells stood with collapsed roofs strewn on their floors. Trees had taken root between the cracks of crumpled homes.

The tallest of the buildings towered above the others atop a knoll in the center of the ruins. Four of its ornately carved columns rose majestically from the devastation. "That was once the Assembly of Nazzabur, our meeting hall." Zaltabur pointed. "In ancient times, every decision that concerned the three realms was made here."

"The city was destroyed by a fallen angel named Mandago and his soldiers," Glorious said. "The attack came at a time when the three realms knew peace and harmony. We were so unprepared. Thousands of angels died when Mandago took control of the three realms."

"How long was he in control?" Lasker asked.

"Far longer than any of us care to remember," Glorious said, a certain gravity lingered on her words.

"Many years later," Zaltabur said, "when a great rebellion broke out in the water realm, we sent reinforcements to fight alongside the armies of mersoldiers. Mandago's army wasn't prepared for the collective strength of the two forces, and we regained control."

When they reached the assembly's grand entrance, Stella tilted her head back to peer up at the four still-erect columns. Three walls were still intact while the fourth had collapsed. Most of the roof had caved in. Still, it was obvious that the building had in its time been an architectural masterpiece.

Stella turned to the regents. "What happened to Mandago's forces? Were they all . . . killed?"

"No," Glorious said. "The Celestial Council gave them the opportunity to turn themselves in and be rehabilitated, but only a few did so. The rest went into hiding; some have been drawn out recently by Sylvain."

Strolling around to the rear of the building, they came upon a circular pool enclosed by a knee-high wall of black stone. Water flowed in from a tall obelisk at one end of the pool and then exited on the opposite side by way of a natural creek. Zaltabur pointed with his chin. "This is the Pool of Nazzabur, where one's intentions can be forecast."

"When you look into the water," Glorious said, "it magnifies your consciousness, which gives you the ability to see the invisible. It's part of the law of attraction. You discover what could happen due to what you are currently paying attention to and the actions you are taking."

Glorious walked over to the obelisk, cupped some water in her hands, and drank. She then knelt at the pool's edge and gazed into the sacred waters. Minutes later, she raked her fingers over the pool's surface, as if erasing the image. "It's as I suspected. Come over here, cadets. Drink and then look into the pool. Remember, what you see isn't set in stone; it doesn't predict the future. You can change it by altering your behavior, if you wish."

The cadets joined Glorious, and Lasker sipped first. Then it was Stella's turn. She shuddered as she dipped her palms into the frigid water and took a sip. On the pool's surface, she watched an epic battle unfold between herself and Sylvain. The vision ended with Sylvain fleeing the scene as, out of the corner of her eye, she caught a glimpse of her father. Rocking back on her heels, she rose to her feet and stumbled backward.

Glorious placed a hand on her shoulder to steady her. "What did you see?"

"I saw myself fighting Sylvain. I also saw my father—he was alive. What does it mean?"

"Oftentimes, visions you have when looking into the Pool of Nazzabur can't be taken literally but must be explored for their hidden meaning," Zaltabur said. "Do you remember any other details—perhaps any symbols?"

Stella's eyes scanned the sky as she thought about her vision. She jumped. "Wait a sec. My father was wearing a necklace with the same design as a drawing on the wall behind him. It was a circle, with six interlocking circles that touched the middle of the first."

Lasker was looking at her oddly as he said, "I saw that too."

Zaltabur nodded. "The Seed of Life. It holds the genetic blueprints to everything. It's symbolic of the mathematical formula that governs the universe and from which the universal laws originate. Royomia safeguards one such seed."

Zaltabur continued, "We brought you here because we'd like to offer you both placement in an elite training program for the Special Protection Division. Your fellow apprentice, Akila, is also being offered this placement. Should you accept, you will begin with the first-year students once you've earned your wings. You would train and learn for five years at the Citadel before you are ready to graduate and take your permanent position with SPD." He pronounced the acronym like *speed.*

Lasker raised his eyebrows. "Why would we do that?"

"We need fresh operatives who can figure out Sylvain's plans. We know it's a lot to ask considering your age and that you've just come to the Citadel, but with more training, we think your open minds and potential will actually be of great benefit in this division.

"We believe each of you, once trained, will offer a unique perspective in this war. You each possess open minds, diverse backgrounds, and distinctive strengths that have given you the potential to be of great benefit to this division."

Stella wavered. "What if we don't want to join the SPD program, what happens to us? Will we be kicked out of school?"

Glorious said, "We honor your choices and understand it's a big decision to make—choosing a career path at so young an age."

"I guess it's nice to know you have such confidence in us," Lasker said, a look of concern still evident on his face.

Stella felt weighed down by what Zaltabur had just said. "Despite Sylvain being my uncle, I have the genetic makeup for this position? Doesn't that relationship make me evil? Or at least potentially evil?"

Lasker's eyes widened at Stella's revelation.

"No," Zaltabur hastened to answer. "Sylvain's choices are no reflection on you. He and your father were half brothers who shared the same father. Look how differently they turned out."

Stella's voice cracked as she said, "Except they're both fallen angels."

Zaltabur patted her shoulder and looked at her with compassion in his eyes. "Yes, but your father acted from love, whereas Sylvain's actions are all hate. And you share their genetics but only partially; you are entirely different and more conscious than both of them."

Just then, a warning siren blared out across the ruins.

Glorious and Zaltabur immediately jumped into action. "Hang on tight," Zaltabur said, giving Lasker and Stella a mere second to wonder what he meant before each regent clasped a cadet and took flight. As they rose into the air, Stella saw that a mosaic of the Seed of Life was spread across the bottom of the Pool of Nazzabur. Soon, the pool's crystalline waters shrunk as the ruins of old Royomia spread out far beneath them. The wind whipped Stella's hair into a snarl, but the familiar feeling of freedom returned, and she could feel her wings pushing against her awareness, a soft warmth tickling her spine.

As they charged toward the dome of the meeting hall, a humungous hole in its side came into view, smoke still lingering in the air from whatever had hit it—there had been an attack.

"Oh no—the Seed!" Glorious exclaimed as the foursome landed in the courtyard. Stella and Lasker followed closely as Glorious and Zaltabur hurried inside, where chaos reigned. Zaltabur disappeared into the building. Several of the massive marble columns had toppled, and two angels and a screaming cherub lay trapped beneath one. A dozen angels were attempting to lift the column with little progress. Lasker dashed to the fallen pillar. Apparently, he was learning how to harness his strength because, knees quivering from the effort, he singlehandedly raised the pillar, though he was certainly straining as he did so.

Those who were closest pulled the injured away, dragging them clear of the rubble.

Clutching her bleeding leg, the cherub cried out, "Thank you, thank you."

Lasker dropped the pillar and stared at his hands. Then hurried over to where Baribur and the other cadets were gathered. Zaltabur returned with the devastating news that indeed the Seed of Life had been stolen.

Baribur quickly directed them all to safety, navigating the crater and the debris strewn all around. Stella looked up and watched as angels chased down fleeing Red Eyes.

31

A CRACK IN THE WALL

Long hours of backbreaking work and lack of food had taken their toll on Rand. As much as he could, he worked at Boss's side, clearing away rock debris they created from pick-axing the cave walls. At night, he still slept near Jakin, though they rarely spoke. Mostly they collapsed, asleep almost before they'd lain down.

Rand wasn't sure how long he'd been there, each new day blending with the last. A general showed up, creating a commotion as the prisoners' guards rushed around to make their progress look better than it was. The general, however, wasn't fooled.

General Phirius could be heard shouting throughout the caverns. "Why have the prisoners fallen behind schedule?"

The head guard was staring at the ground, chastised and clearly frightened. "They're weak, General. They're dropping like flies. Over half the workforce is gone, and we haven't had any replacements since before the attack on Royomia."

"There will be no replacements coming. Our objective was never Royomian prisoners, only the Seed of Life," the general said derisively. Rand made a note to ask Boss about the Seed of Life later. General Phirius looked at the guard as if he'd just scraped him off the bottom of his shoe. "Do whatever it takes. In addition to the digging, the prisoners are to build a platform. Lady Meenah has a sense of . . . theatrics, and Lord Sylvain is inclined to indulge her. Supplies will be brought in. Everything must be perfect for Lord Sylvain's arrival."

Hearing the name, Rand shuddered. As soon as the coast was clear, he hurried back to Boss.

Joining Boss at the cave wall, Rand quickly shared what he'd heard.

"So, Sylvain is finally coming." Boss shook his head in worry as he continued to swing his pickax.

"You know him?"

"I did once." Boss glanced around, and when he spied no guards, he confessed quietly, "I'm actually an angel, like the Red Eyes. Well, like the Red Eyes used to be."

"You are?" Rand swallowed his fascination.

"Yes. Years ago, I was an angelic commander. Over the months I've been here digging, I've come to suspect what Sylvain has us digging for. It's something sacred to the sky realm and is important to winning this war. Sylvain and his army cannot get their hands on it."

Rand's mind raced, "So, what do we do?"

"I have an idea. It's a long shot, but it could work. Will you help me?"

Just then, a guard passed by, so Rand simply nodded and Boss whispered his plan.

Later, Rand approached the head guard. "What do you want, prisoner?" The guard scowled at Rand.

"I heard we're behind and that we have a new task, but I think I know a way to speed things up," Rand said. The guard's face remained expressionless. "It's clear that the work is slowing down and we've not seen any new prisoners since I got here." The head guard squinted, which Rand took as encouragement to continue. "This morning, some of us couldn't even get up to work, no matter what your guards did to prod us."

Now he looked on the verge of interested. "That's true. And what do you propose we do about that, prisoner? Would you like to torture your fellow prisoners for us?"

Rand did his best not to recoil at this suggestion. "No, sir, but if you were to feed the prisoners more food, maybe allow them more rest, they'd be stronger and could dig faster."

"Don't be ludicrous," he snapped, his lip curling in disdain. "Their well-being is the least of my concerns."

"It's not about their well-being, though, sir. By regaining our strength, we can get back on track with our job, er, your mission." He cleared his throat and carefully said, "If we could speed things up, you would earn the recognition you deserve for completing this mission."

The guard glared at Rand for a long moment before he dismissed him. "I'll take care of myself, and you work. Got it?"

Rand bowed his head slightly as he backed away and then whirled around and quickly returned to his position working next to Boss, who asked, "How did it go?"

"I planted the seed, just like you said."

Though it wasn't announced, even just a few days later it was clear they were being allowed to rest a bit more and were given a little more gruel and canteens of water. All the prisoners were feeling stronger and were getting more done. Since they were more productive and even more alert, Boss decided it was time to put his plan into action and get the other prisoners on board.

Rand rounded up small groups of prisoners—to avoid looking suspicious—and told them to check in with Boss, who in turn, explained that he needed to know as soon as someone hit a hollow pocket in their digging.

After two days of Rand constantly circulating in the cave, checking and double-checking to see if anyone had hit a hollow spot yet and distracting the guards when Boss needed to confer with others, Hort excitedly nodded to him on his rounds.

"Well," Hort said far too loudly, pointing at the wall as he spoke, "*hollow* there, Rand. How are you today? Seen the boss lately?"

Rand stood for a moment, perplexed, until it dawned on him what Hort was talking about. After hurrying to get Boss, the two causally worked their way down to where Hort had been assigned to dig that day. Trying not to draw any attention from the guards, Hort showed them what he'd found. Hidden behind the cave rock where Hort had chipped away, they could just make out what looked to be a mortared stone wall. Between two of the stones, a blue-green liquid oozed, which Boss quickly started to collect into his canteen. It would take some time to pull it off, but, the plan was coming together.

32

AWAKENING TO THE TRUTH

Stella was back in the dinghy, surrounded again, this time by circling sharks and Red Eyes. When shark teeth clamped down on her arm, she recoiled, only to bash into the clawing hands of Red Eyes behind her. Their glowing eyes felt like they were burning holes in her skin.

The circling sharks sped up impossibly fast, until they ignited a buzzing whirlpool of energy. Small at first, it quickly became a raging torrent of whirring plasma until the boat was sucked down into it. Pinned to the hull by the force of the boat being sucked into the vortex, Stella couldn't so much as lift her head. When the boat finally tipped, she was catapulted headfirst into a black hole, descending at breakneck speed, with sharks and Red Eyes on her heels.

Sucking in a breath as she lurched upright, petrified, it hit her—she'd been dreaming. In the pitch-black, it took her a moment to regain her bearings, but she wiped her sweaty forehead and sucked in oxygen, willing her heart to slow. This wasn't the first time she had been haunted by nightmares and likely wouldn't be the last.

The Red Eye attack and the theft of the Seed of Life from Royomia had been weeks ago, but it still felt fresh in her mind. She had tried to follow the advice Baribur had given her in the common area the night of the attack. He assured her and the rest of the cadets that being frightened was a normal reaction to events they didn't understand and are out of their control, but that it was important to learn to manage their fear. "It's a phantom in your mind," he'd said, "something your imagination creates if left unchecked."

"But those who truly had no fear were not any better off, as they were not analyzing themselves deeply enough. Some of our greatest fears are hidden so deep in our subconscious that they're difficult to find. If you recognize bad things sometimes happen yet you keep thinking positively, you will be able to react in a way that's more proactive and hence productive," Baribur had explained.

Now, Stella considered all this. She knew Sylvain was a very real threat—she'd seen her mother (and likely her father) swept into shark-infested waters, probably to their deaths. She'd helped nurse her aunt when she'd been attacked by sharks, also sent by Sylvain. But she hadn't expected Sylvain and his truly terrifying Red Eyes would be able to attack anywhere in the sky realm. Since they'd been there for Citadel training, she hadn't really considered that they'd be less safe in Royomia than on Sentinel Island. Seeing the destruction, the angels lying under the pillar Lasker moved—now she knew it could happen. But instead of turning that knowledge into fear that he would soon attack again, she would turn it into a positive and consider how she could be prepared and help in the future.

Satisfied that she was following the Laws of the Universe and would possibly even be able to stop, or at least lessen, her nightmares, Stella swung her legs off the bed, quietly dressed for her duties as the Guardian of the Well, and walked to the courtyard.

After Orica let her in, she went about her duties, tying the knot, attaching the sensor to the rope, and launching the bucket down the well. Since she'd been assigned her own vizioscope, she'd been downloading the sensor's readings to it, to double-check her work and try to learn more about the well in general.

She placed her vizioscope on the well wall and began extracting the bucket. The rope got caught briefly, and as she leaned in to muscle it as much as she could, she bumped her vizioscope, which tumbled into the well but luckily caught on a ridge in the wall a couple of feet down. It was precariously balanced, though, and panic seized her.

She hoisted herself onto the well's rim, and slowly and carefully reached down to retrieve her vizioscope, her fingers barely managing to brush a corner of the device. She leaned just a bit farther, quickly grabbed it, and hauled it, the bucket, and herself up and back onto the grass. It was a silly mistake but one she would have given herself a hard time for in the past. Now, though, she took back control of her thoughts and shifted her attention to how grateful she was that she had been able to reach the vizioscope and that she hadn't knocked over the bucket—gratitude was a powerful function of universal law.

She quickly snapped the lid on the bucket and checked the elixir's levels. The sensor showed they were down just a bit— the normal fluctuations Orica had mentioned—but when Stella tapped her vizioscope's screen to compare it to the historical readings button, she gasped. Compared to recent levels, yes, it was down by only a bit, but it was the lowest it had been at any time in the past five years.

Scampering to the door, she handed the bucket as well as offering her vizioscope to Orica. "I noticed the elixir's level has steadily dropped over the past few days," she said. "You can't tell much when comparing it to recent readings, but I was looking at the historical data, and it's down—it's down the most it's been in years."

"I'm sure it's nothing," Orica snapped, seizing the bucket from her and yanking her vizioscope from her hand. "You probably just don't know how to interpret the readings." She tapped a few buttons, her eyes scanning the screen quickly as she swiped a few times on the screen and frowned. "It's alarming that you can't do anything right or even follow simple directions." Handing back Stella's vizioscope, she dismissed her by saying "I'll double-check your poor work, because I'm sure the only problem here is you."

By the time Stella made it back to the dorm and showered, most of the other cadets were up and in the common room, messing around on their vizioscopes and waiting for breakfast. As casually as she could, she pulled Akila aside.

"It looks like the elixir levels are dropping." Akila looked alarmed but Stella pressed on before her friend could interrupt. "Orica didn't seem to care or really believe me. Being a vizioscope whiz, do you think there's a way to look in the Celestial Council's archives to see if the elixir levels have ever dropped this much before? All I have on my vizioscope are the readings the current sensor downloaded, so I have data going back"—she tapped a few times and turned the screen so Akila could see it—"five years."

Akila glanced at the data and then back at her friend. "I'll put Glitch on it."

"Who's Glitch?" Stella asked just as a figure with bushy gray sideburns wearing an academic-looking gown and cap sprang to life from Akila's vizioscope screen.

"That's Glitch," Akila said. "I created him as an untraceable program to help me access the full angelic database—even restricted files." Akila relayed the information for Glitch to retrieve, and after a few minutes Glitch reported, "I can't find anything about a significant change in the recorded levels of elixir for the past hundred years, let alone the past five."

"Thank you, Glitch," Akila said, tapping him on the head so that he dissipated like a puff of smoke.

Stella shook her head slightly. "That's not good. Something's off. And despite Orica's assumption, it's not me or the sensor."

"What do we do?" Akila asked. "Should we tell Baribur? Or maybe Sebastian?"

"No, not yet," Stella said, making the decision as she said it. "I think we need to be sure we know what we're reporting before we start saying something's wrong and that Orica wouldn't listen."

Akila nodded, and Stella pulled up her DOOB. A promising entry had appeared for later in the day: *5:00 PM Stables with Grand Master Cavish.* Surely Cavish would listen to her regarding the elixir level, or at least have an idea about who she should talk to.

During the course of the day, Bartholomew forced the cadets to start over on their one-hundred push-up challenge five times, leaving them all feeling gutted on the floor of the gymnasium, where their daily calisthenics was being held since the weather had turned cold. Reslan Harmona made the group repeat their performance song so many times Stella's throat felt as though she'd swallowed glass shards by the end of rehearsal. But she was also practicing being grateful and turning negatives into positives, so, looking forward to seeing Glowinder and Cavish in the evening meant that none of this bothered her.

"Okay, everyone, get out your vizioscopes and press the theory of flight function," Baribur said during their lesson.

When Stella pressed it, Puff's face materialized in holographic form. "Hello, cadets," he said. "Are you ready to fly?" Everyone cheered. As Puff spoke, the vizioscopes showed a Sentinelian falcon taking flight in slow motion, against a majestic background of snow-capped mountains, followed by a purple wing-tipped duck crash landing into a pond.

"Angels can manifest wings on their own, but through the years, we've used our technology to streamline the process. Your wings will employ a design that's the result of more than two thousand years of technological advances, taking into account our evolving consciousness. Of course, today's wings use artificial intelligence. You'll learn how to program them with your mind, so they are coordinated with your nervous system and respond to your brainwaves, which are connected to your higher consciousness."

The next holographic clip was, Stella guessed, what the others would experience at Josephine's Fine Garment Shop when they got their wings—she marveled that she'd been able to keep it quiet that she had hers already. Two angels, one young and one old, peered at a variety of boxes. The older of the two selected a box, removed a sapphire gemstone, placed it on the back of the younger, and wings unfurled between the young angel's shoulder blades. Both flapped their wings, whereupon they slowly lifted off from the ground, their faces aglow.

That's not what happened to me, Stella thought, smiling at the memory of her dramatic plummet from the ladder and the way her wings had actually jumped to attach themselves to save her from breaking her neck. For the next half hour, while Puff reviewed wing designs and flying techniques, she was able to apply it directly to what type of wings she had attracted—and realized gaining her wings was the law of attraction in action.

Akila raised her hand after they'd gone over a handful. "So when you say 'design,' you're not referring to who designed them but to the birds they're patterned after?"

"It's both. Our hologram designers program tiny viziochips with bird wing designs. The viziochips are implanted into the hearts of gemstones. With guidance, training, and continued study of the Laws of the Universe, individuals soon achieve the high level of consciousness required to manifest wings. Our designers painstakingly consider how a pair of wings might look and function. This information is then absorbed into consciousness, which is how we are able to create more advanced wing types."

Puff signed off after their lesson. The cadets turned off their vizioscopes and made their way to the cafeteria for lunch.

"I'm starving," Lasker said. He plopped his tray on the table with a clunk, sat down, and then devoured a huge hunk of silver fin in a single bite. "To be honest, I'm a little disappointed. I thought Puff would take us flying for real, not just blab on about it. Wasn't that trip to Royomia the best? And we all might end up training for SPD!"

As her time in Reslan Josephine's flashed into her memory, Stella froze halfway into her first bite of dewberry loaf.

Lasker touched her arm. "Stella, are you okay?"

No, I'm keeping so many secrets from everyone it's ridiculous. But she didn't say that. Instead, she said, "Yeah. I'm fine. Just not hungry anymore. You want this?" She pushed her tray with its untouched food to Lasker, then she got up, and hurried from the cafeteria. She was tired of hiding who she was and what had happened. How could she expect to be friends with anyone if she wasn't honest with them?

Lasker and Akila chased after her and caught her in the hallway. "What's wrong?" Akila asked, touching her gently on the shoulder to stop her.

Stella turned to them. The concern in her friend's eyes tipped her over the edge. *No more lies.* "I want to tell you two something. Will you promise me you'll believe me?"

Lasker and Akila shared surprised looks but promised, and Stella spilled the whole story—losing her parents, the shark bite, the lighthouse, being kidnapped (which they'd heard about at the Timekeepers dinner), and getting her wings early. When she at last fell silent, the two looked shocked, but before she could stop herself, she told them the rest.

"And my family . . ." She took one more deep breath. "Sylvain is my uncle"—Lasker nodded, as he already knew that, but Akila looked pale at the news—"and my mother was a mermaid."

Akila smiled. "That's amazing! You are living proof that the SSA and those stupid ideas about angels being better than landlings and merfolk aren't true!"

Surprised, Stella asked, "So you don't hate me?"

"Never!" Lasker and Akila chorused, hugging her tight. Heart swelling, Stella nearly collapsed with relief, humbled to have friends who knew all her secrets and accepted her anyway.

33

LOCKDOWN

Before Stella and her friends could make their way back to lunch, sirens blared through the halls of the Citadel. Stella, Akila, and Lasker covered their ears and joined the angels and students jostling their way into the cafeteria—one of the designated shelters during an attack. Two minutes after the first alarm sounded, the doors were closed and locked; reopening them was prohibited by order of the Celestial Council until the all-clear horn sounded. Those who didn't arrive within the time frame were left outside to defend themselves. Warrior angels took up defensive positions in the corridor.

The sirens fell silent, leaving the cadets shaking. Akila was frantically reading and searching on her vizioscope and found out that the Timekeepers were sequestered in a secure location. She passed along this information to Lasker and Stella.

"Good. I'm glad to know they're safe," Stella said, sinking into a chair. She felt as if she might come undone. The last alarm had signaled the vicious attack on Royomia.

Several tense minutes passed before the all-clear sounded and the doors swung open again. Sebastian and Zaltabur entered, both of them smiling.

"Congratulations," the regent said, "we successfully completed our first drill. Everyone successfully reached the nearest safe area within the allotted time." There was a murmur of approving sounds as well as relief—from almost everyone—as they realized there was no current attack.

Daith kicked a chair over. "It was only a drill? What a waste of time."

Lasker righted the chair. "Stop," he said, his tone scathing. "Drills prepare us and keep us safe."

But they all looked at Daith a bit oddly as they went back to their regular routine. What did he want? A *real* attack?

"So much for anger management classes," Stella muttered to Akila.

In the gymnasium, Thaddeus's class got underway as the cadets collected their swords from the rack and stood on their usual spots—all except for Stella, who instead grabbed one of the chairs along the wall and placed it on her insignia. When she sat down, the others groaned and looked toward Thaddeus, who was also sitting on a chair. Grumbling, they returned their swords and slid chairs over to their insignias.

Thaddeus stood up and balanced the chair by one leg in the palm of his hand. When the cadets attempted the exercise, chair after chair crashed to the floor. All the while Thaddeus's chair remained perfectly balanced in his open hand. Surprisingly,

Akila managed the feat before the rest of the cadets, but as each of them was able to perform the drill, Thaddeus lifted his chair to his forehead and again balanced it on a single leg. As before, Akila proved to be the only pupil capable of readily mimicking him. Although chairs tumbled from one end of the gym to the other, neither the noise from the chairs nor from the complaining, frustrated cadets managed to distract her.

With slow, deliberate steps, Thaddeus walked to a rope ladder that hung from the ceiling and, with the chair still balanced on his head, climbed it. As if in a trance, Akila followed suit, succeeding without the slightest bobble. Giving up, the rest of the class plonked down in their chairs to watch.

Suspended near the ceiling, a tightrope ran the width of the gym. Thaddeus walked out into the middle, placed two of the chair legs on the tightrope, and sat.

"Whoa," Lasker softly exclaimed.

Daith scoffed. "There's no way that klutz will be able to do that."

Akila eased herself onto the tightrope and, step after step, carefully moved toward the center. When she was within a few feet of Thaddeus, she set two of her chair legs down and took a seat. Her classmates erupted out of the chairs, hooting and cheering.

Startled by the applause, Akila flinched, and her chair wobbled precariously. She reached for something to hold on to and found nothing but air; her eyes grew wide, and she plunged toward the floor in a panic.

The other cadets ran toward her, but Stella knew immediately that none of them would reach Akila in time. Just as she felt a much hotter sensation flash up between her shoulders blades than she'd felt before—her wings urgently telling her they could help—Thaddeus swooped beneath the tightrope, catching both Akila and her chair and placing them back on her insignia.

In his customary fashion, the instructor took up his position at the center of the circle and waited for everyone to find their seats. "Balance and focus will help achieve any objective," he declared. "Dismissed."

Stella ran along the path to the stables in the frigid winter air. She sang her solo for the upcoming Sentinel Day performance, thrilled to get the chance to visit Glowinder and Cavish. It appeared the Lializan felt the same way because as Stella approached, she heard Cavish shout, "Whoa, calm down," and a responding neigh. The horse came charging from the stables, Cavish close on his heels.

The beautiful horse pulled up short as soon as he was within arm's length of Stella, who promptly reached out and petted his muzzle. Glowinder's hot breath puffed out in steamy swirls in front of her.

"I should've known," the Lializan Grand Master said, placing his gloved hands on his hips. "If you're gonna claim him, you'd better learn to care for him. Let's start with penning him. Grab his lead, and I'll show you how to corral him for the night."

Stella and Glowinder followed Cavish to the barn where Stella removed her hat and gloves. She did what he directed her to and they worked without incident, enjoying the peace and warmth of the stables, until Cavish cleared his throat.

"I invited you here today to discuss the Special Protection Division. I'm in charge of that division, and I would love for you to agree to train for this eventual final placement. I think you'd be an excellent addition to SPD. Akila and Lasker have already accepted, so how about you? Do you have any questions?"

Stella hadn't given it a lot of thought after the attack. Really, the attack itself had taken up most of her thoughts, but if Cavish was in charge of that division, and her friends had decided to go for it, she was in. Cavish had always been so kind toward her that she could want nothing more than to work alongside him in the field. "Sign me up," Stella said without hesitation. Leading the Lializan into his pen, she pulled off his bridle and handed it to Cavish, who in turn presented her with a brush.

"He won't let anybody else approach him like he does you. It looks like he's yours. He has chosen you. Or rather you have attracted each other into your lives. The law of attraction is alive and well."

As Stella took the brush and dragged it along the horse's neck, she turned toward Cavish. "Can I ask you something?"

"Mmhmm," he said, spreading fresh hay throughout the pen. As she brushed, she kept talking. "The well's elixir levels are dropping. Orica said it wasn't a big deal, but it seems like one to me. What should I do about it?"

"Well, if the levels drop too low, the Timekeepers and the Tree of Life are at risk. Are you certain the sensor's accurate?"

Combing out a cocklebur from Glowinder's tail, Stella said, "I'm absolutely certain." She thought about Akila, or rather Glitch, hacking into the Sentinel Island database but chose not to reveal that part.

"You and Orica are the two with access to the well's sensor," Cavish said. "Are you sure Orica said it wasn't a big deal? It's her sacred duty to care for the Timekeepers, and she wouldn't risk their well-being. Perhaps she just didn't want to alarm you and is taking care of it. You're only a cadet, after all."

He said it kindly, but Stella felt her face heat with shame. Yes, Orica had actually said she would double-check Stella's figures and reading levels, and yes, Stella was new to Sentinel Island. But *she* was the Guardian of the Well. If anyone deserved to know what was going on, it was her. Why would no one treat her like she had a huge responsibility and was doing her best to take care of it?

PART THREE

SAVING A SAFE HAVEN

34

THE GAZEBO

Sentinel Day fast approached on a warm spring breeze. Preparations for the annual event to honor the peace in the realm and the sentinels' great military service—not to mention the Citadel's graduates—were in full swing. The flowerbeds around the Citadel were carefully tended by cherubs and burst with dragon posies, orelia blossoms, and starcresters. Tomorrow, the cadet's probation would end and they would finally graduate to apprentice status.

Choir practices had gone well, except for the occasional off-key note, and the day before the concert, all went smoothly until Reslan Harmona announced she was scheduling an additional two hours of practice.

A groan rose up from the cadets.

"Sentinel Michael, the Sentinel-in-chief at the Citadel is the guest of honor. To make him proud, you must practice, practice, practice. Okay, class dismissed."

As the cadets filed out, Reslan Harmona approached Stella. "You didn't sing very well today." It was said with kindness, but it still stung. "Why?" she asked gently.

Stella shook her head a little, as though trying to shake off the comment. "Sorry my mind was somewhere else."

"What is it? Maybe I can help?"

"It's . . . nothing. Thank you, though." She sidestepped the vocal coach, intent on leaving without saying more.

Reslan Harmona's voice echoed down the corridor after her. "Get some rest—see you tomorrow!"

Barreling around a corner, Stella ran headlong into Orica.

"Miss Merriss, slow down." Orica took a step back and smoothed her pristine white tunic. "Perhaps if you paid attention to everything around you, you'd create fewer problems for the rest of us."

Stella felt the flush of embarrassment heat her cheeks, but before she could respond, the apprentice coordinator continued.

"Tomorrow morning, your services as Guardian of the Well won't be needed."

"Why?" Stella asked, befuddled. "Is this about the elixir levels?"

"You needn't worry about that." Orica arched a brow as she regarded Stella. "Concentrate on your solo for Sentinel Day. From what I've heard, your part still sounds awful." She brushed by Stella, continuing on her way with her nose in the air.

Slouching, Stella plodded up the stairs. The sensor had indicated the level was down again that morning, but she still hadn't gotten a response from any of the adults. It was like everyone was putting her off, either not believing her or perhaps just thinking she was too young and inexperienced to understand what was going on. She did, though, and being treated like she didn't was frustrating. Why would they make her Guardian of the Well if they didn't want her actually guarding it and caring about its levels?

A private message from Cavish flashed on her vizioscope screen:

> **Tonight at midnight, cherubs will meet you, Akila, and Lasker at the stables and escort you to a secret meeting with me. Wear your father's bracelet for extra protection. Nobody else must know.**

She would have shown the message to Akila and Lasker to convince them to agree to sneak out but it vanished quickly. Slipping out unnoticed would be easy enough, but if Baribur or another cadet realized they were missing, she wasn't sure what kind of trouble they would be in. They'd be with an instructor, but if that was the case, why not just make it part of their DOOBs instead of messaging her privately? If she got caught, would she lose her position as the Guardian of the Well? Could she and her friends be kicked out of the Citadel?

Walking into the cafeteria for lunch, Stella made a beeline for Akila and Lasker and got right to the point. "Cavish needs us to meet him at midnight tonight."

Lasker's brow furrowed in confusion. "Midnight?"

"Yes," Stella confirmed. "The cherubs will escort us to a meeting with him. I'd show you this message, but it disappeared once I read it." She looked around to see if anyone was watching before waving the three of them into a huddle. She pulled at the cord around her neck to show them the universal key

Captain Finnegan had given her, which she always wore. "This will unlock the doors."

Akila turned pale. "Are you nuts? What if we're caught?"

"No way," whispered Lasker, shaking his head. "I'm not risking everything to go on some secret adventure."

"Come on. Grand Master Cavish is our instructor. He wouldn't ask unless it was important. Trust me. We won't get caught." Stella took a deep breath before adding, "I promise." She certainly hoped she hadn't just lied.

Through the crack under the door, Stella finally saw the light in the common room go out. She waited a few minutes before slipping from her bed. Akila joined her, and together they tiptoed to the door.

Earlier in the evening, Stella had collected her father's timepiece as well as his bracelet from their hiding place in the back of her closet—Cavish had only mentioned the bracelet, but something told her she should take both. Stella and Akila ducked out of the dorm together.

Lasker had put up such a fuss, insisting he wouldn't participate, that when he met them in the common room Stella wanted to kiss him. Together the trio walked quickly down the dark corridor away from their dorm. Through the windows overlooking the courtyard, they peered out at the leafless Tree of Life when they heard Sebastian clanging up the back stairs. Alarmed, they scurried away from the windows, to the end of the corridor, and down the front stairs.

Once in the lower hallway, they made their way back toward the courtyard, which was the most direct path to where they wanted to go. They skittered to stop as they caught sight of the back of Orica, who pushed a door open with her shoulder while balancing a tray with three teacups—no doubt a late-night beverage for the Timekeepers. As quickly and quietly as she could, Stella used the universal key to unlock the door to the courtyard, and the three eased inside before Orica could turn their way.

Stella locked the door, and then they ducked into the darkness of the courtyard. Holding their breath, they watched as Orica passed the bank of windows; then the three made their way out through the opposite side of the courtyard and out of the Citidel.

The cherubs Maslo, Larkin, and Grunz were waiting for them. They carried micro-lanterns lit by captured blaze beetles, whose hindquarters glowed in the dark. The cadets followed as the insect-winged cherubs led the way. As they passed, the cherubs vigorously shook the stalks of emerald gruff grass that grew along the path. Dozens of iridescent, nut-size bugs tumbled off the grass, curling into tight balls as they hit the ground.

Maslo and Larkin led the group through overgrown spoolscoke bushes and spindly thimblewood. Grunz was at the back of the group, making sure they were not followed. The path wound downhill to the right, and then to the left, and once more to the right, so it felt like they were walking in circles. Disoriented, the cadets had to trust that the cherubs knew where they were going.

Somewhere below them, they could hear waves crashing against the shore. When they came to a weeping fernlock, its branches hanging low and obscuring a bridge to a small island, they stopped.

"This is as far as we go," Larkin said, landing. "We will wait here for you."

"Take our lanterns," Maslo said, offering Lasker his. "It's quite dark over there. Cavish is waiting for you at the gazebo."

Grunz handed Stella his lantern and then plopped down on a rock. The trio of cadets traversed the bridge, which creaked with their every step. They heard the water churning far below, sending up misty sea spray on the rising breeze. "It's creepy out here," Lasker said with a shiver, huddling close to his friends.

"Don't be such a wimp," Akila said playfully, pushing him forward. "There's nothing to be afraid of."

Once across the bridge, they ran to the gazebo. In its center stood a marble statue of the famous Sentinel Cyrek seated on a fire chariot pulled by a Lializan stallion. They circled it and found Cavish on the other side holding Moonglow's reins.

"Glad to see you made it safely," he said. Unbridling the Lializan, he released her to munch emerald gruff grass growing along the clifftop.

"Sebastian tells me he thinks you three are the fulcrum Agnita spoke of in her episode."

"Well, that's his opinion," Lasker said. "I don't know if anyone has confirmation of that."

Cavish tilted his head at that. "Fair enough. He also mentioned you might know the location of the clay tablets with the universal laws inscribed on them." He watched their reactions.

When Lasker again opened his mouth, Stella elbowed him in the ribs. Then, lifting her face up toward Cavish, she said, "Tablets? What tablets?"

He gave them a curt nod. "Glad to see you're being tightlipped. Sebastian was certain you would be." Pacing in front of them, he said, "The three of you have been invited into the Special Protection Division training program." The cadets stood up a bit straighter. "So . . . how about a taste of SPD life with a Lializan flight?"

"You're kidding, right?" Lasker exclaimed, a smile lighting up his face. "I've been wanting to get up in the air again ever since the cloud flight to Royomia!"

Akila nodded vigorously. "Oh yeah, I'm in."

"Your visit here tonight is classified. Joining SPD requires intelligence, flexibility, and secrecy." Cavish whistled and escorted the three to the gazebo's railing, where a beautiful, luminescent horse was steadily winging its way over the water in response to the whistle.

"Glowinder," Stella breathed dreamily. Even though she had been visiting the stables every day to help care for him for the past few months, just seeing the horse still made her spirit soar.

There were two other horses accompanying Glowinder, though they did not have his glow. They all landed behind a small weeping fernlock tree that sat on the small island. When Glowinder whinnied, Stella raced to meet him.

"Akila, you take Posey, the paint horse. Lasker, you'll have Skyger, the buckskin." Cavish led the cadets to their mounts and gave them instructions on how to ride.

"Hey, why's my saddle different?" Stella asked, pointing at Glowinder's back.

"It's a merfolk saddle. Just put both your feet on one side and wrap the safety strap around your waist to keep from sliding off."

Alarmed, Stella looked at him with wide eyes. "Why would I do that?"

"Because he's taking you under the sea."

This time, she gaped incredulously at him. So he'd lost it, hadn't he? He thought she was going *underwater on the flying horse*? She opened her mouth to protest, but Cavish jumped in.

"Where'd you think his glow came from? He's half giant seahorse, and they're phosphorescent."

Glowinder snorted.

As Stella wrestled herself into position in the unusual saddle, Lasker and Akila straddled their equines, buckled their safety harnesses, and gripped their reins. "A mersoldier commander I've kept in touch with wants to speak to you, so I arranged a meeting," Cavish explained. "His name is Lazeretto. Akila, Lasker, we'll take an aerial tour while Stella goes to her meeting, so you can get a taste of what being in SPD can be like."

Stella's face lit up. "I know Lazaretto. He's the sea cavalry commander. He and his army saved me from a shark attack on Captain Finnegan's ship."

"He's also the special envoy of King Ristaran—your grandfather."

"Wait—what?" Lasker's mouth gapped. "Did I hear that right?"

Stella grinned sheepishly. "Sorry, I forgot to mention it."

"That makes you a mermaid princess then," Akila said matter-of-factly.

From Skyger's back, Lasker stared at Stella, clearly impressed, but then said, "Look, if we are the fulcrum that means we're a team. And that means no more secrets, agreed?"

Stella agreed.

Akila patted Posey's neck and smiled. "Good. That means we're now officially the fulcrum club."

When Cavish whistled, Moonglow pranced up, stalks of emerald gruff grass jutting from her mouth. After bridling her again, he mounted, gave Moonglow a slight kick and said, "To flight."

The sea breeze rushed under the Lializan's extended wings, and Cavish hooked his feet in place as they gracefully lifted off. Lasker, Akila, and Stella followed, whooping as they soared into the sky.

The moon cast shadows on the sea cliffs, its light sparkling on the waves lapping at the shore below. The cove's beach formed a crescent where a narrow inlet stretched to the open sea.

After they circled the cove, the Grand Master's voice rang out, "To sea." At once, Glowinder plunged toward the water.

Stella felt the speed as the wind stretched the skin tautly over her face, and with a splash, the horse punched through the surface of the cold water. Then, as her transformation began, Stella's legs tingled, gills sprung up behind her ears, and her lungs filled with water. She was a mermaid again.

Glowinder's coat illuminated the dark waters as his hind legs transformed into a tail, propelling them into the deep. Near the seafloor, he slowed, his ears perked in the direction of distant clicks. When he swam left, the sound grew louder until a royal-purple glow illumined Lazaretto strapped to a mersaddle atop a giant black seahorse, the modest current billowing his hair about his head.

Heyho. His declaration was telepathic.

Heyha, Stella instinctively replied. It was the same way she and her mother greeted each other.

Lazaretto bowed his head. *You know the traditional merfolk greeting, and you speak our language—impressive. A good night for riding, isn't it?*

Stella returned his bow. Glowinder swam closer to Lazaretto. *Why have you called me here? Do you have word of my mother? Or Esmi?*

I have no word of the princesses. I come to issue a warning of odd occurrences in your waters. A group of renegade merfolk, mercenaries really, from Abalonia has been circling the island. They also guard an underwater sea cave. I thought you'd be the right one to tell. I am not allowed to divulge the goings-on down here to any angels. But since you are part of the royal family . . .

Stella shook her head ruefully. *Strange things are happening on land too. No one will listen to me, though.*

Angels are stubborn. Lazaretto curled his lip. *They act superior to merfolk and landlings, citing their deeper understanding of universal law, though they're blind to their own violations of it. They sever ties with the other realms and then withhold their technology, even though if shared, it would wildly improve the lives of everyone.*

Stella considered that carefully. She only really knew angels and landlings, though landlings had never talked about any of this, of course. *Angels are certainly not perfect*, she finally messaged, unwilling to speak badly of them but aware that they did, certainly, think themselves superior.

Your grandfather, King Ristaran, regrets missing your childhood and continues to strongly and publicly oppose the Species Separation Act. He wants to make amends when you're ready. He wants you to come home.

Home. The word reverberated in Stella's head.

Glowinder suddenly jerked his snout in the air and gnashed his teeth. The sudden shift in his mood unsettled Stella.

Lazaretto drew his trident and raised his shield, sending Stella the message, *You must flee.*

Three shadows rushed at them from the inlet.

Go to the surface and fly. Lazaretto prodded Glowinder's rump with his weapon, and Glowinder lurched away. Almost immediately, they became entangled in a giant net. Glowinder went wild, kicking, biting, and thrashing. Stella looked around for a means of escape, but quickly realized she was utterly helpless. They were trapped.

Lazaretto hacked at the net with his trident, yelling, *Knockout darts—watch out!* Stella ducked as a dart zoomed past. The net tightened over them, but Lazeretto hurled his shield at it, slicing a window to freedom that Glowinder quickly swam through. He rocketed toward the surface. Free of the net, Stella remembered she had her father's bracelet and willed it to activate, sending electricity tingling up her arm. A glowing globe formed around both her and Glowinder just as another volley of darts shot toward them. The darts ricocheted off the protective orb. Heart pounding, Stella clung to the horse's neck as they broke the surface.

On the shore, Cavish, Lasker, and Akila waved and shouted. The sandy beach was approaching fast, but both she and Glowinder still had their tails. As they skidded into the shallows, drenching those on the beach in a torrent of seawater, Stella released her safety harness and dove toward Cavish.

Cavish snagged Stella under her arms and dragged her to higher ground. Seeing her tail dig a groove in the sand, slowing Cavish down, her friends lifted it.

"Glowinder still has his tail," Stella screamed. "You have to help him."

Moonglow galloped to her son and bit down on his reins. With a forceful flap of her wings, she pulled him clear of the water.

Lasker crouched beside Stella. "What can we do?"

"I'm not hurt," Stella assured them, pushing herself upright as her tail began to dry and manifest back into legs. "There's a group of merfolk renegades lurking in the waters around the island. They're guarding a sea cave. I don't know for who or what, though."

"What's that?" Lasker asked pointing at her father's timepiece that had fallen from her pocket onto the sand.

Cavish picked it up reverently. "A Magnetic Temporal Cata-pult—your father's?" He asked Stella absently, clearly impressed with what he held. "This is an advanced piece of technology used to manipulate time." He cracked the lid, and its glass face burst to life in ice blue light, making it easy to read the dials and spinning hands.

"How does it work?" Stella asked.

"I don't know exactly, that was your father's area of expertise," he said, looking closer at the device, "but . . . see how the hand on this dial is pointed at the five? I believe that means it's set for five minutes." He caressed the button on top, with its see-through hinged cover. "And I believe pressing this button activates it."

"But to do what?"

"To stop time, of course"

The three kids gaped at Cavish in doubt.

"That's impossible!" Lasker blurted.

"Actually, it is very possible." He cracked a smile. "But there are rules to it. I seem to remember that you have to be touching the MTC or touching the person who is touching it for it to work."

"What happens if you aren't touching it?"

"Time would stop for you, not to mention for everyone and everything. It's a quite an impressive piece of technology. Pure genius, really."

"Let me get this straight," interrupted Akila. "For anyone not touching it or in contact with it secondarily, time stops. But anyone touching it or touching the person touching it, time continues normally, is that right?"

"Exactly . . . except for one additional caveat. Because no one can beat time, anyone who wasn't affected when it's setoff, is then frozen. Time then catches up to them."

It was mindboggling, but Stella was pretty sure she understood the basics—time stopped; then you stopped for time to catch up.

"Oh—and one other tiny detail—if a person causes anyone harm while time is frozen, that harm is reflected back on that person once time unfreezes."

"Tiny detail?" Lasker coughed. "That's pretty important!"

Cavish handed the timepiece back to Stella. "Now it's late,and you kids should get going. I'll see to the equines and report what I've learned to my superiors. Don't worry. As the head of SPD, I have the discretion to not mention the three of you in my report." Recalling the injured Glowinder, they turned to find him now standing.

Placing a hand on Stella's shoulder to get her attention, Cavish quietly said, "It's quite an honor to have a Magnetic Temporal Catapult, Stella. It's a powerful tool. Guard it with your life."

35

TEST RUN

"Quickly, cadets," Grunz urged impatiently as the kids trooped across the bridge.

"Sorry," Stella said, handing him a lantern, "we had to retrieve these."

Lasker passed his to Larkin and the six of them headed back to the Citadel. Trailing the back of the group, Stella slipped the time-piece into her pocket, careful not to disturb the button's cover. She worried that if she held it, she might accidentally activate it.

The warm, late spring night sky was bright with the rising moon lighting the path, so the cherubs released the blaze bee-tles from their lanterns. At the stables, the cherubs said goodbye, and traipsed off to wherever they made their beds, while the cadets prepared to sneak back inside. But when entering through the courtyard gate, Stella froze, throwing both arms out to stop the other two from advancing.

"Something's off," she warned. Up ahead the three could see Orica pacing back and forth in front of the courtyard windows. Clearly, she was agitated.

Ducking behind an orelia bush, Akila asked, "Do you think she knows we snuck out?"

In his shining armor, Sebastian came into view. He rushed up to Orica, and they began talking.

Certainly the three cadets didn't *have* to be the topic of discussion, but if they weren't, Stella didn't want to know what was so important in the middle of the night because it couldn't be good. She turned to her friends. "So, are you ready to give this MTC thing a try?"

Lasker looked pale. "You want to *stop time*? Are you serious?"

"Why not?" Akila challenged. "Cavish explained it wel enough. I'm ready." She winked at Stella.

"Okay," Stella said, "grab hands. Whatever you do, don't let g

Akila grabbed Stella's hand and then offered her other o to Lasker, who took it reluctantly. Stella slipped the cover off timepiece and pushed the middle button.

Akila gestured with her chin to the window, where Se tian and Orica could be seen standing completely still. Orica mid-gesture with her arm raised over her head. It looked to S as if Orica were smelling her own underarm. "It worked!"

"Quick," Stella said, "before our time's up." She showe other two the face of the device—the five-minute coun clock had begun.

The three moved swiftly across the courtyard and un Tree of Life, until they reached the locked door. Stella unl with the universal key, and led the way as they hurriedly vered through the door and around the frozen Orica and S

It proved awkward for the three to serpentine all the way up the stairs and around corners, squishing together, but they managed to arrive in the common area just as 1:32 flashed on the MTC.

Stella pulled the others toward Lasker's dorm. When she opened the door and peered inside, she saw that these quarters were essentially the same as hers, except for the piles of dirty clothes littering the floor.

"Are you always this messy?" Stella asked.

"No." Lasker said, kicking off his shoes and sending them flying across the room. "Well—hardly ever." With his clothes still on and one arm stretched out to keep hold of Akila's hand, he pulled back the covers and crawled into bed. When he released Akila, he instantly froze in place.

Akila and Stella made their way to their dorm; once there, they placed their shoes under their beds, and Akila clambered under her sheets. She and Stella exchanged a nod, and Stella let go of her friend's hand. Then Stella dove into her own bunk, shoved her hand under the pillow to hide the MTC, and let go.

MISSION CRITICAL

with a start, feeling hands on her shoulders, almost
see Orica doing the shaking as she was to be woken
ly.

rica said in a desperate croak. "Get dressed—NOW!"
d to shake off the sleep that still clung to her
I...? I thought I wasn't needed this morning as
f the Well."

a "hurry up" motion with her hand. "You weren't.
led for something else. Now, hurry."

Stella was dressed, out in the hall, and scurrying
o was practically racing down the corridor. It was
g at this time of day for the Tree of Life, with the
pers frolicking under its canopy. But this morn-
sed the courtyard window, Stella noticed that the
nd still bare and wintery.

e way to the room where the cadets had first seen
nd Agatha spinning, measuring, and cutting the

ENTER THE DARK ANGEL

With Sylvain's arrival imminent at last, the cave bustled with activity. Most of the prisoners had been redirected to either finish construction of the platform or to clear away rubble, leaving only a handful of prisoners at the wall to dig.

Phirius paced back and forth, tapping his chin and barking orders, and the prisoners watched when they could, anxious about what was going to happen.

A guard approached Boss and handed him a sledgehammer and a spout. "General Phirius wants an able-bodied prisoner." As he led Boss away, Rand followed behind. He'd learned that he was small enough that if he also stayed quiet enough, he could sneak practically anywhere without the guards noticing him. Typical adults, thinking he wasn't worth paying attention to since he was a kid.

They stopped at the mouth of the dark tunnel and the guard looked at Boss. "The general needs you to tap this wall during Lord Sylvain's visit for the liquid inside. Stand here until you get specific orders otherwise."

A loud hum reverberated through the tunnel and into the cavern, echoing off the walls. Staying in the shadows, Rand stealthily made his way toward the source of the sound. When Phirius yelled for the guards to prepare for Lord Sylvain's arrival, Rand scurried along behind them, passing the cavern where merfolk floated in a large tank. A new addition, a merman with black hair, glared at the scene unfolding before him.

Rand felt the anticipation, hot and fiery, like the torchlight dancing on the walls. Phirius waited on the dock to welcome his leader, his head held high with pride. The guards faced forward, tense, their eyes darting down toward the dock.

A submersible watercraft surfaced and docked. The hatch on top opened, and an entourage emerged. Ten Red Eye guards came first, their glowing eyes casting a disturbing hue in the dim light of the undersea cave.

Wearing a full-length black cloak, Sylvain climbed out of the transport. His boots were polished to a mirror sheen. His oiled hair, pulled back and bound with a black ribbon, gleamed. Meenah Batelle emerged next, wearing her lion skin coat yet again. Rand nearly fell over at the sight of her. In her arms, she cradled two clay tablets.

Stepping up to Phirius, Sylvain wasted no time. "Take me to the platform. I want to make final preparations for the ceremony."

"Yes, my lord." The general turned to lead Sylvain through the corridor, who followed with a limp.

Torch flames lit the cave from the submersible docking station all the way to the newly constructed platform.

The prisoners observed the procession, and Hort caught Rand's eye as he scowled at Meenah parading up the stairs. Rand raced

back to join the others. The gua
the prisoners, though stationed
been working, were no longer bu
still all held their work tools, b
from Boss to attack.

Stella woke
as startled to
up so physica
"Get up," C
Stella trie
thoughts. "Di
the Guardian
Orica mad
But you're nee
In no time
after Orica, wh
normally sprir
young Timeke
ing, as they pas
tree was alone
Orica led th
Agnita, Agnes,

Thread of Life. As they came to a halt outside the door to the sisters' sleeping chamber, Orica announced, "They're in a terrible state. Agnita asked for you. Agatha and Agnes are, sadly, catatonic."

Stella wasn't sure what *catatonic* meant, but when she followed Orica in, she knew it was not good. Agatha and Agnes lay motionless, their eyes opened but fixed on nothing, staring without seeing. She had never seen the vibrant sisters looking this old, sick, and skeletal. What in the world had happened?

Agnita's head turned toward her. "I've been waiting for you," she said in a whisper. Stella rushed to the bed and knelt, taking Agnita's hand in hers. Although the Timekeeper's face was as dry as a dehydrated zochi berry and her hair thin and wispy, there remained a twinkle in her eyes.

When Agnita squeezed her hand and tried to speak again, Stella leaned in until she felt warm breath on her ear.

"Thank you for coming," Agnita said with a rasp. It was clear that even that much took a tremendous amount of energy, and Stella simply smiled in response.

"The well has run dry."

Stella swallowed her shock. The Timekeeper had asked for her to come here. She had to stay focused and discover exactly what she could do to help.

"Because . . . of . . . Sylvain," the Timekeeper whispered.

Though squeezing her hand gently and trying to convey strength, Stella could feel her own heart thumping against her ribcage as if trying to break free.

"His thread . . . strong . . . but yours . . . stronger . . . strongest I've ever seen."

Pride filled Stella, though she wasn't sure why. It wasn't as if she knew why she had such a strong life thread, but the pride was there nonetheless, making her feel stronger. She looked at Agnita so weak, so frail. Surely she wasn't going to die—it couldn't possibly be her time. She was one of the most important figures in the Universe.

". . . Stop him." Agnita's breathing was becoming even more labored, and it startled Stella—so did what Agnita said.

"How can *I* stop him? He's an adult with an army; he's a fallen angel—my life thread may be stronger than his but I am not powerful or strong enough to stop him. I can't ki—" Stella stopped speaking in the middle of the word she didn't want to even think, let alone say. She swallowed hard. The Timekeeper hadn't said *kill*. She'd said *stop*. "I can't stop my . . . uncle."

Agnita took in a deep breath that seemed to rattle about in her lungs. "Yes . . . you . . . can," she insisted. "The laws . . . need . . . protecting." She looked relieved as she stopped speaking and took in another laborious breath. Her body heaved with the effort, and the hand that was still in Stella's clutched more strongly. Visibly weaker by the moment, Agnita coughed.

Stella's mind was turning over everything she'd learned since coming to the Citadel, everything anyone had told her about Sylvain and what he wanted. He already had the Seed of Life, and the Well of Life was dry, which meant the Timekeepers were weak—she refused to admit to herself that they were dying.

Now it dawned on her—the clay tablets that Sebastian had shown them, where the laws were written down. She wasn't sure why they were so important, but she assumed they were still with Sebastian. Surely, he would protect them.

"You want me to protect the clay tablets?" she pressed, confused and desperate to understand.

Stella stole a quick glance at Orica, who shrugged, perplexed as she was.

Mustering her last bit of energy, Agnita rasped, "Find the golden tablets . . . and keep them away from Sylvain." Then she froze, her eyes fixed unseeingly on Stella in the same catatonic state as her sisters.

Stella turned to Orica. "Do you have any extra elixir to give her?"

"Sadly, no. It doesn't keep." Orica's eyes drooped.

"Do you know where the golden tablets are kept?"

"No clue—" she said absently, clearly in deep thought. Orica suddenly reached out to clutch Stella's shoulder. "Go to the well. Bring some elixir even if it's only a few drops. I'll stay with the Timekeepers."

Racing down the hallway, Stella was intent on getting the elixir and discovering the location of the golden tablets. She needed to find Sebastian and go down the well as quickly as possible. Lasker and Akila could help. Together, they were the fulcrum. She tore in to the common room, where she found them up and waiting for breakfast.

"Fulcrum!" she shouted, making everyone in the room jump. Akila and Lasker didn't need more than that. They chased after her as she ran out, heading down the stairs.

"Whoa! Slow down." Sebastian was exactly where they thought he'd be, in front of the staircase, in view of the broom closet door.

Stella leaned over, her hands on her knees, to catch her breath. "The tablets," she panted out, clutching the stitch in her side and pointing toward the broom closet. "I know those clay tablets aren't the real laws. Where are the golden tablets?"

Sebastian's eyes softened. "Only the Timekeepers know where the real ones are—"

"Well, the Timekeepers are dying. The Well of Life has dried up, and the elixir isn't replenishing itself for some reason."

"Something's definitely amiss," he growled. He rummaged in the broom closet for a moment and produced some weapons. He held out a smaller version of the blade he always wore, sheathed in a sword belt, to Stella. "Take this sword—you may need it." Stella gingerly took it. "Go to the well and see if you can't collect any elixir. I'll guard the Timekeepers." His armor clattered as he ran toward their chamber.

Stella looked down at the short, double-sided blade of quarried gem glass, expertly tempered in the forge fires of the mountain bluffs of Arid. It was broad and razor-sharp, with swirls of Aridian gold wrapped around its helm and cross guard, lacing its way up to the fine point. The pommel, dotted with sky-blue sapphires and yellow diamonds, glittered. As she raised it the way she'd been taught in combat class, she realized it was perfectly balanced for her.

Stella's mouth fell open. Words to describe what she was feeling escaped her. She wrapped the sword belt around her waist and clasped it shut. Slipping the sword back into its sheath, she realized how natural it felt hanging there.

Then she motioned to Akila and Lasker, who had strapped swords of their own to their belts. "Let's go. We have a well to climb down."

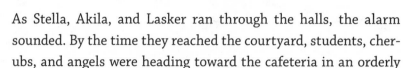

As Stella, Akila, and Lasker ran through the halls, the alarm sounded. By the time they reached the courtyard, students, cherubs, and angels were heading toward the cafeteria in an orderly fashion, just as they had practiced during the drill.

The three of them stepped outside and stood beneath the Tree of Life. The hot sun beat down through the leafless branches, and chunks of bark fell from the trunk as if it were disintegrating before their very eyes.

Stella untied the rope ladder and heaved one end down the well. She peered into the dark shaft. It was a long way to the bottom.

38

BUCKETS OF ELIXIR

"Grab the buckets." Stella pointed, and Akila ran past the Tree of Life, snatched up two buckets normally used by the cherubs to collect zochi berries, and raced back to the well. She tied the buckets to a rope and pitched them into the hole, peering down as they whizzed to the bottom. Then, stepping over the wall, Akila bit her lip.

Stella looked over at her. "One rung at a time. If anyone can do this, it's you."

Stella and Lasker eased themselves over the edge, following Akila, and clambered down the rope ladder.

"Whoa, I hope we don't fall." Lasker hooked his arms around the swaying ladder.

Stella smiled, even though she knew there was no way he was looking at her at that moment. "If you can knock over a piano without help, you can do this," she reassured him. "Hold tight and concentrate on one foot at a time."

He breathed deeply and began his descent.

Perched on the ladder's top rung, Stella paused briefly, suddenly struck by the memory of standing on the deck of her kidnapper's ship facing one of her biggest fears—not knowing how to swim—and jumping overboard anyway. She felt a similar fear now, but she also felt certain that she must act. She stepped into the belief the Timekeepers had in her and the faith that everything would work out for the best, and followed her friends down the ladder.

Once the darkness of the well shaft had swallowed them, it felt like a long time before they finally saw light. Reaching the bottom, they jumped off the ladder, and Stella examined the crack in the well where a bit of light shone through.

Closing one eye, she peered through the crack into what appeared to be a large cave. She could see a large group of prisoners off to the side watched by a few guards. A man dressed all in black and woman in a lion skin coat stood on a platform across the cave. They were accompanied by truly frightening soldiers with glowing red eyes. She knew him, the man in black, though she had never before seen him in person. Sylvain. But now wasn't the time for fear. They had a mission.

Akila bent to grab the buckets. Stella stuck Sebastian's sword into a crack between stones in the well wall from which a trickle of elixir wept. Poking the sword in deeper and wiggling it from side to side, she got the elixir to run along its blade. Akila held a bucket so the elixir could dribble into it. "When it's full, take it to the surface," Stella instructed. "Pour some on the tree and give the rest to Orica for the sisters."

Once both buckets were full with the Elixir of Life, Akila lifted one, grabbed hold of the ladder, and stepped onto the first rung. Instantly, the ladder started swinging, and a splash of elixir sloshed over the rim. She dropped back to the floor of the well and set the bucket down. "I can't do it." Akila's face fell into despair. "I can't climb up with one hand."

Stella grabbed Akila by her shoulders. "The whole Citadel has put their faith in us. We each have unique talents, and if we harness them, we can do this. You just need to bring your full consciousness to what you're doing." She lifted the bucket of elixir off the ground and placed it on Akila's head and then guided her friend's hands up to balance it. "If you can climb a rope ladder while balancing a chair on your forehead, then you can easily do this. The Timekeepers are counting on us."

Akila straightened her shoulders, drew in a calming breath, and took hold of the rope. "You're right. I can do this." With steps that began tentatively but gained confidence as she went, Akila began her ascent and soon disappeared upward into the darkness.

Stella peered into the cave again. A shiver darted through her as her eyes landed on her uncle. Rubbing her temples, she took a calming breath, then pressed her ear to the crack to try make out what he was saying to the gathered army.

"—and these tablets Meenah is holding have been inscribed with the new laws of the universe—MY LAWS. Once the new laws are anointed with elixir, I will command all three realms. The Laws of Chaos will reign. How sweet it will be for the power of the angels to fail on this, their day of highest military honor. As my army of Red Eyes attack from above, so shall we attack their precious Well of Life from below. My ultimate power will rule the realms." He turned and shouted in Stella's direction. "Tap the well, General."

Stella stumbled back, in a panic, while Lasker looked at her in confusion.

Another voice immediately called out, "Boss, get over here and tap the well."

A loud *thunk* sounded, a metal peg breached the wall directly above Stella's head. She stopped herself from crying out and watched as Lasker's eyes became impossibly wide.

"Finally!" the voice yelled. Murmuring could be heard and then a crash. A voice just on the other side of the wall said with cold anger, "Where. Is. My. Elixir?"

"The angels must have drained the well, my lord." General Phirius was sniveling, clearly doing his best to avoid punishment for his failure to find elixir.

Stella shook her head, confused. She knew the angels hadn't drained the well. So if neither Sylvain nor his soldiers had done it, who had?

Before she had the chance to consider that question, her uncle— she was sure that's who she could hear now—shouted, "Knock down the wall and go right to the source. I will have my elixir."

Stella heard a loud whack as a tool hit the well wall. She and Lasker sprang to their feet; they had to get out of the well. Stella reached up and yanked at Sebastian's sword from the crack in the well wall. Halfway out, it caught, and as she adjusted her grip, the sword jiggled, and with a pop, a rock door swung open into the well shaft, exposing a stairway that led up.

Stella and Lasker looked at each other, and Lasker raised his eyebrows, as if asking, *Should we?* Stella nodded, and they entered into a small chamber with a long spiral staircase of rock, snaking up the side of a shaft toward a golden light. As they raced up the stairs, the odor of mud and dank wood got stronger the higher they climbed. At the top of the stairs they stepped onto a landing that led into a round room.

Stella got tingles when she brushed her hand across the smooth lustrous mahogany walls. "I think we're inside the tree of life."

Positioned side-by-side on a small table at the center of the cavity, two tablets shimmered.

"The golden tablets!" Lasker exclaimed. The elegant letters engraved on the tablets were an ancient language neither Stella nor Lasker recognized.

The distant sounds of pickax blows and rocks tumbling continued to come from the long shaft they'd just ascended, jarring Stella back into action. Sylvain and his army of Red Eyes were only a crumbling wall of rock away and their escape up the stairs to the tree's heart had only led them to a dead end—there was no other exit from the room except to go back through the well. They needed to get out of the well now, and they needed to bring these tablets. They could hear Sylvain's minions still attacking the well wall, trying to break through. Stella attempted to lift one of the tablets. When it didn't budge, she said, "We'll need your strength, Lasker."

Lasker gripped the edges of one of the tablets and lifted it easily. Stacking them on top of each other, he hoisted them off the table and tucked them under one arm. "I'm not sure what to do with them other than take them to Sebastian," Stella said. "He'll know where to hide them."

Lasker nodded and they descended the stairs together. The sounds of Sylvain's attack on the well wall were getting louder. Back in the well, Lasker headed to the rope ladder while Stella closed and latched the stairwell's rock door, which sealed with a click.

The metal peg was now gone and the small hole it left behind was beginning to grow. Boss kept chipping away on the other side with his pickax. The noise stopped, and suddenly Stella saw a face appear in the hole. She watched as an emaciated boy fanned the dust away with his hand and caught her eye. When he gasped, Stella placed a finger to her lips. He nodded his understanding.

"Hurry up, boy! Clear the rubble," ordered Phirius. Rand's face disappeared from the hole as he started clearing away the rocks.

Peering up the well, Stella saw that far above it looked like Lasker was approaching the surface with the golden tablets. She stepped close to the wall, and touched her father's bracelet to reassure herself it was there.

When the next blow was delivered to the wall, Stella was ready. Dust billowed in clouds as large chunks of the wall caved in, crashing to the floor. Stella stepped forward into the opening, her wings spread and the sword shimmering in her hand.

From the platform, Sylvain scoffed upon seeing her. Recognition flared in his eyes, but it turned to dismissal just as quickly.

"PHIRIUS!" yelled Sylvain, limping to the edge of the platform. "Hurry up with my elixir." His irritation filled the cave. He turned and limped a few paces away, expecting his order to be obeyed without hesitation.

"Don't just stand there," cried Phirius, pointing at the other prisoners. "All of you, get to work." Guards hurriedly started shoving prisoners toward Boss and the well. But Boss stood unmoving, just staring.

"Stella?" Boss whispered quietly as if speaking to an apparition. Their eyes met. "My sweet angel."

The familiar voice tumbled from the mouth of the gaunt figure before her. "Father?" He was a shadow of what he had been. In her memory, he had been big and strong, but now he was reduced to skin and bones. His jet-black hair seemed too long, and it was matted with gray dirt clods, his beard equally unkempt. But there was no doubt he was her father.

Behind her father, Stella saw Sylvain turn back toward them and throw up his arms in disgust. "Incompetents!" he yelled. "I'll get it myself." He manifested his black wings, ready to head toward the well. Arago stood to his full height, turned around, and manifested his enormous honey brown wings.

"You!" Sylvain hissed contemptuously as though a ghost had flashed in front of him.

Arago spun around. "Quick, toss me my bracelet, Stella."

Stella flashed him a smile and sent the bracelet spinning through the air. After snatching it, he jammed it onto his wrist. He rose up over the assembled group and, in his most powerful voice, yelled, "Attack!"

Whooping and hollering, the prisoners responded to his command and turned on the guards, using their tools as weapons. For the last week, they'd been drinking as much of the elixir as they could collect without notice by the guards, and though many still looked thin and weak, they easily overwhelmed the Red Eyes, who were taken by surprise.

As the personal guards Sylvain had brought with him joined the fight, the melee intensified. Sylvain's companion in the lion skin coat held a set of clay tablets and cowered next to a wall. Sylvain took to the air with a powerful flap of his wings. Taking flight, he zeroed in on Stella's father.

"Father, behind you," Stella screamed.

Twisting in the air, Arago hurled himself at Sylvain. He caught his half brother in the midsection and they grappled above the rest of the fight unfolding throughout the cavern. Sylvain tried to throw a punch, but Arago held him tightly and wrestled him back to the ground.

Stella realized this was her moment to act. The tablets bearing the new Laws of Chaos had to be destroyed. She rose above the battle with a few quick, strong strokes of her wings, looking for the person she'd seen with the tablets. The woman's coat was easy to spot among the throngs of prisoners who were overwhelming the guards and the small contingent of Red Eyes. The woman darted toward the entrance to the cave, holding on to the tablets for all they were worth. Stella's wings seemed to know what she wanted them to do—as if they were directly connected to her consciousness.

Unfortunately, Sylvain seemed to know as well, and he shouted, "Meenah, guard the tablets with your life!"

But it didn't matter. Stella was infinitely faster now that she could engage her full angel form. She bowled over the whimpering Meenah, who was screaming nonsense, and snagged the tablets. Meenah took off down the tunnel, screaming, "Red Eyes! We need reinforcements!"

Rocketing to the highest point of the cave, Stella chucked the tablets to the floor, confident they would shatter as they hit the hard ground. But again, Sylvain was one step ahead. He threw off Stella's father and shot toward the falling tablets. The first one shattered just as Stella had intended, but Sylvain caught the other and handed it off to one of his nearby guards.

Arago was right behind him, breathing heavily from the effort, while Stella swooped toward Sylvain's surprised guard. She lunged and thrust Sebastian's sword toward the guard now holding the tablet. As he jumped out of the way, he dropped the clay tablet, and she scooped it up.

The boy she'd seen through the wall of the well crouched by the hole he'd helped create. Stella instinctively felt she could trust him. She flew toward him, hurled the tablet near him, and yelled, "Break the tablet!"

He grabbed a pickax and slammed it against the tablet with such force that it smashed into myriad pieces.

Fuming, Sylvain cried, "Seize her!" As he boiled with rage, his flesh bubbled and moved, and Stella could hear the muted cries of . . .

Were those monsters moving *under* his skin?

"Come forth, my dragon!" he commanded, opening his cloak to bare his chest. The whites of his eyes turned blood red, veins snaked purple under his skin and, stumbling backward, convulsions ripped painfully through his body. A shriek of agony roared from his throat and echoed off the rock like a thousand tortured souls crying out at once. The stench of charred tissue hit Stella's nostrils as a dragon clawed through Sylvain's blistered flesh into the three dimensional world.

Sylvain steadied himself, satisfaction arising with his narrow smile. "Join the fight! Protect your master!"

Together, Sylvain and his dragon took flight and resumed their pursuit of Arago.

Landing, Stella beckoned to the boy who'd broken the tablet. Stella said, "I don't know who you are, but I need your help. I'm going to stop time with this device." She yanked the MTC out of her pocket and waved it at him. "When I do, you follow my instructions to the letter. What's your name?"

"Rand."

"Okay, Rand, I need to get my father back here. To do this, the three of us have to be touching when I push the button." She glanced around at the fight still raging and then back at the small device, wondering if it was even possible to be sure all three of them could come together in this chaos. "I need you to get him close to me."

"I can do that," Rand said. "Anything else you need me to do?"

She gave him a serious look. "Yes, don't get hurt. Hide until the time is right, and try not to get drawn into a fight."

Rand gave her a short nod and slunk behind a pile of rocks.

When Stella looked back at the fight, she saw Sylvain and his dragon flying side by side in pursuit of her father. When they got close, the dragon unleashed a torrent of flames at her father. Luckily, they couldn't penetrate the protective globe of light that engulfed him, and with daring turns and swoops, Arago continued to evade being either captured or killed. But Stella knew he probably couldn't last much longer. He looked so sickly, so weak. She was terrified about what was going to happen when he tired. And though Sylvain might have limped when he walked, he flew with prowess and grace—and so did the dragon. Stella's father was good, but for how much longer?

When the dragon's fire ceased, Arago let his shield dim for just a moment, but it was long enough for Sylvain to seize the opportunity to head-butt him. Together, they plummeted to the ground. Sylvain landed on top of Arago when they hit the cavern's floor directly in front of the well. They were caught in another wrestling match and in his weakened condition, Arago was quickly overpowered by his younger half brother.

Rushing forward, sword in hand, Stella took a swipe at her uncle, slashing his arm, but not before Sylvain released a furious punch to Arago's jaw. As Arago fell, knocked unconscious, Sylvain lunged at Stella. Frightened, it was as if her wings had a mind of their own as they carried her farther into the cavern, away from Rand and her father.

"Elixir!" Stella yelled to Rand and pointed to the hole in well.

Rand popped up from his hiding place behind the pile of rocks, sprinted into the well, snatched up the bucket of elixir, and raced back to Arago's side. No sooner had the elixir trickled into his mouth than his eyes bolted open. Stella felt her body relax in relief, but there was no time for rest. She saw the dragon land directly in front of the two of them, and Rand looked up into the golden glare of the menacing beast. When the creature let out a roar, Rand threw the bucket into the dragon's open mouth. Sputtering and coughing, the monster stumbled before its entire body began to shrivel, smolder, and burn.

The beast withered away and smoke rose from where it once lay. A scream of pain echoed through the cavern as Sylvain fell to his knees. His teeth clenched, back arched, eyes burned red again. A wisp of dark vapor surged from his chest and floated over to the smoking ash that had been the dragon. For a moment, smoke and vapor swirled in a dance of black magic before shattering into a luminous foul-smelling dust. Sylvain swayed side to side, panting for breath. Stella presumed the dark vapor had been a part of Sylvain's consciousness, but despite the pain he was in, it took but a moment for Sylvain to recover. Slowly, he turned his head, his blood-red eyes narrowing as they zeroed in on Stella. Rising haltingly, he stared, his onyx black eyes drilling into her as he rose into the air once more and flew toward her. She recoiled, the evil in his hate-filled gaze causing her to lose her focus. Time seemed to stop, and she remembered—yes! Time *needs* to stop.

Agnita's premonition flashed into her thoughts: *Take your roles seriously.* The harmony of the universal laws of vibration, attraction, and cause and effect were in imminent danger. The darkness that would descend on the universe if she allowed Sylvain to win this battle was harrowing—he would create chaos and promote hate. She swore that she would not let it happen. "Never," she quietly vowed.

Using all she'd been taught, Stella focused on goodness, on the positive in the universe, on manifesting the beautiful world she wanted. An explosive flash of light radiated from her heart, and the energetic eruption pushed Stella and Sylvain apart as though they were two magnets with the same polarity.

Though Stella had been knocked to the ground, she was still brimming with energy. She jumped up just as Arago mustered every last ounce of his strength and rushed between her and Sylvain. "You will not harm my daughter," he declared through clenched teeth. An electrical charge like Stella had seen only in the Timekeepers' colossal clear glass sphere shot from her father's hands, keeping Sylvain from rising from the ground.

Her father lowered his hands and approached his half brother slowly.

"Father, wait! We need to—" But Stella didn't get to finish her thought. Sylvain lurched for Sebastian's sword that she had abandoned on the ground. He grabbed it and jabbed at Arago. Luckily, her father managed to dodge the first thrust, but Sylvain lunged forward with all the strength he had left, anticipating his brother's next move, and stabbed Arago in the stomach.

Stella screamed as Arago clutched his abdomen with both hands and doubled over. Blood oozed out from between his fingers as he dropped to his knees. Easing forward, he lowered his forehead to the ground and succumbed to his agony. A victorious grin spread across Sylvain's face as he raised the sword above his head.

Stella thought she and Rand must have had the same thought—or the same instinct—because they both yelled and ran for Arago at the same time. But as Stella began to crouch at her father's side, Rand knocked Sylvain to the ground, taking him out at the knees from behind. Sylvain let out a bellow and popped up quickly, as though Rand tackling him had energized him, and swung the sword for Rand's head. Resigned to his fate, Rand stood and simply closed his eyes . . .

Stella tugged on his shirt. "Come on!" she shouted, pulling again, so he'd open his eyes. When he did, he saw Arago had a loose hold on her ankle and she'd stretched to grab Rand, the device in her other hand. Time had stopped.

Rand looked from Stella to the frozen Sylvain. "We should kill him while we have the chance."

Stella shook her head. "No—we can't. Any harm done to a person when time is stopped will reflect back on the person doing the harm."

She yanked harder on him this time. "And I need your help. I have to keep touching this thing and can't let go of my dad or you." They looked down at Arago, who was bleeding badly. "We only have five minutes to get him to the surface," Stella said. "Help me lift him. And don't let go. If you do, you'll be frozen too." The two managed to drag him along the ground and into the well, but Stella quickly realized the idea of carrying her father to the surface was futile. "He's too heavy," she said, looking around and assessing their options. He was bleeding too much. She was going to lose him.

Blood pooled beneath Arago as his wound continued to seep. Pressing her hand to it to try and stop the flow of blood, it occurred to Stella that if she just let go of him, he would freeze as well. She touched Rand with one hand and lifted the other away from her father. He was fine for now, but they were on a countdown, and she needed to figure out something fast.

"We need to give him more of the Elixir of Life, and we need to go up to the Tree of Life . . . Oh." She looked toward Sylvain and then back at her father.

"What is it?" Rand asked.

"The Seed of Life that was stolen from Royomia. I bet Sylvain has it with him. I have to get it."

Holding hands, they clambered over the fallen rocks. When they reached Sylvain, Stella fished through one of his pockets and Rand through the other, glad that touching a person after they'd been frozen didn't unfreeze them. "I've got it," she exclaimed, holding up the little seedpod triumphantly, then slipping it safely in her tunic.

Rand pulled his hand from Sylvain's pocket and swayed on his feet. "Are you ok?" she asked.

"Fine," he replied, shaking his head as if to clear it. Stella tugged on his hand and they dashed back to the inside of the well shaft, where they found it empty. "What? Where did he . . . ?" Rand looked around, shocked.

"Well, we were out there and then there was only one way to go, and that's up," Stella said. "Hold on to me. I'll fly us up." As Rand wrapped his arms around her, they raced against time. Stella flapped her wings as carefully as she could so they wouldn't catch in the narrow well shaft.

Just as the time on the MTC ran out, she got them over the well wall.

Then time stood still.

39

REUNION

Stella's eyes fluttered against the dappled light shining through the budding branches of the Tree of Life, her awareness slowly returning. The air outside the cave was fresh. Stella glanced at Akila and Lasker, who had helped her ease down to sit on the ground, looks of concern on their faces.

"My father . . . Where's my father?"

Baribur placed a hand on her shoulder. "Rest," he said kindly. "You've been through quite an ordeal."

"I want to see my father." Stella struggled to stand, but Baribur gently kept her down. "At least tell me if he's alive."

"He is, but from what I've been told, he's in pretty bad shape."

Orica squatted next to the two of them. "Sentinel Michael took your father to the clinic. He was bleeding pretty badly. Thanks to you and your friends, there was sufficient elixir to douse his wound, so they're confident he'll make a full recovery."

Stella decidedly removed Baribur's hand from her shoulder and scampered to her feet. "I want to see him."

Baribur stepped in front of her, blocking her way. "You're not going anywhere. Let him rest for now as he's—"

"Release her," Agnita's young voice demanded. Her two young sisters flanked her. The three Timekeepers, now appearing to be around Stella's age, had been fully restored to vibrant health. "We will take you to him," she said, extending her hand to Stella. "It's the least we can do to thank you for saving us."

All three Timekeepers said in unison, "You've been very brave."

Stella gratefully grabbed Agnita's outstretched hand and finally took in everything else going on around her. The scene was one of nonstop action as warrior angel after warrior angel expanded their wings and disappeared down the well shaft and angels of other ranks bustled about, organizing, helping, and bringing supplies to the courtyard.

Slumped on the ground, his thin face smudged with grime, Rand winced. Fine rock powder colored his hair gray. He looked even paler and scrawnier than he had in the dim cavern, and he swayed a bit, as if he could barely sit up on his own. Catching his attention, Stella mouthed hello. He managed to acknowledge her with a meager bob of the chin, though he couldn't hide that he was bewildered by everything going on around them.

"You saved the golden tablets," Agnes said, a big smile on her face.

"*And* the Tree of Life," Agnita chimed in.

"Yes, and us," Agatha said. "We were attacked by Red Eyes from above here on the island, but our forces were, thankfully, prepared. A battle is still happening below, but word is we are off to a good start. Once we defeat Sylvain and his army, the well will be sealed off and will replenish again." Stella looked around wide-eyed at the damage the aerial attack had caused. Glass debris littered the courtyard and Stella saw that several panes of the glass dome had been broken.

"Come now," Agnita urged, squeezing her hand. "Let's go to your father." Stella helped Rand to his feet, and they walked to the infirmary. Stumbling from exhaustion, Rand almost fell on the way, but Stella caught him.

When they finally entered the infirmary, Agnita called out, "Can we get some help?"

A healer swooped over and picked Rand up. "I'll fix you right up."

Continuing deeper into the infirmary, the visitors came to a long row of beds, and Agnita pointed to the far end of the room, where a curtain was drawn around one of them. "Sentinel Michael brought your father here, but"—she held Stella back by placing a hand on her forearm—"he has been restrained."

It hadn't occurred to Stella before, but why hadn't Sentinel Michael been frozen by the MTC? Then Stella realized what Agnita had said about her father.

"What? Why is he restrained?" Stella asked.

"Your father was a fugitive, and he has turned himself in. The angelic forces have taken him into custody."

"But . . . that's not fair. He fought Sylvain and defended Sentinel Island." Anger rose inside her. He had helped *save* them all. How could they do this?

"You're right," Agnita said in a calm voice. "It isn't fair. Just the same, the angels have their methods."

Stella shook her head in disbelief.

"The law of perpetual transmutation shows that everything in the universe is always in a state of movement. What goes up must come down. Understand—you must relinquish control of uncontrollable circumstances. Accept this moment for what it is."

Stella hung her head and nodded.

They slipped through the curtain around the bed. Sentinel Michael was down on one knee whispering into Arago's ear. Absorbed in conversation, they didn't notice her immediately, but Sentinel Michael soon rose up, towering above Stella and the three sisters. The halo of ruby red gemstones resting on his head gleamed and his gold-embroidered cape glowed, lending to his aura of strength and power. The Aridian gold sword and its swirling silver sheath that hung from his thick armor belt was a reminder that the sentinel was, at his core, a fighter.

As Stella craned her neck, she noticed that the sentinel's face was a study in opposites. The law of polarity did state that everything had its opposite, and there was something kind about his face, but it also projected an authority that Stella would have been afraid to challenge. Bowing, the sentinel backed away to make room for her at her father's bedside.

"Go on," he encouraged, motioning for her to approach.

A combination of anguish and relief washed over her as she leaned down. Never had she imagined that her father, always powerful and robust, could be reduced to such a puny state. When she kissed his sunken cheek, he tipped his head toward her.

"Father, it's me." When she tenderly brushed back his hair, he closed his eyes, their corners wet.

"I know," he whispered, wrapping his arm around her and pulling her close. As she buried her face in his neck, she slowly breathed in his familiar scent.

"Let's give them a little privacy," Sentinel Michael said, ushering the sisters out.

The world stopped while father and daughter embraced. When she at last released her grip, Stella felt her mind swim with the many questions she longed to ask and the many stories she had to tell. "Where do we start?" she said.

"From the beginning," her father said, "and one thing at a time."

The words burst from her. Matters she had mulled over for many months bubbled to the surface as she babbled. She peppered him with question after question, and shared everything that had happened to her since she'd last seen him during the storm.

"Slow down, my sweet angel," he said, smiling. "We will get to it all. But I am still weak."

Tears pricked her eyes, and she did her best to blink them away. "I'm so sorry, Dad. I had no idea where you'd gone or if you'd left on purpose when Mom went into the water. What happened to her?"

"I don't know. There was so much going on that night. Wind, waves, sharks—then your mother was swept of the boat and you smacked your head and was knocked unconscious. I scrambled to get you secured in the boat just in case we were hit again, and was checking your head injury when I was slammed by a sudden swell." He breathed in trying to keep his composure. "There was nothing I could do as I was swept over the side and into the sea, leaving you alone and defenseless in the middle of a storm." His chest heaved with emotion. "I'm so sorry. I wasn't strong enough to get back to you." He hugged her close. "I knew your mother would survive in the water, she's a mermaid for goodness sake. But—there was a split second after she went in and before you stood up where I had a choice, and I chose you." They openly wept in each other's arms as they both thought of

Stella's mother. How could she ever have doubted his love for her? "After my capture, my only concern was to find you and your mother again. So for these many months, I kept my identity hidden from everyone—guards, prisoners, even little Rand, knowing it would give me the best chance to escape and find you both. If Sylvain had the slightest notion that I might be one of his prisoners, he would've killed me. I am a threat to him since I would never join his cause."

Stella shook with relief as she realized just how close she'd come to losing him. If Sylvain had visited the caves earlier to check progress on the digging . . . she may not have found her father.

"I experienced true cruelty in the cave that no daughter should ever have to know about, let alone save her own father from." He kissed her hand and held it to his heart. "The thought of you and your mother kept me going every single moment of every single day. My hope is that the three of us will be together again someday. I-I have no idea whether she's alive for sure, but—"

"She is," Stella stated with conviction. Without knowing how, she just knew it.

"I can believe that—your mother is tough. And you're alive, and as long as you are alive, my brother or his soldiers will try to use her as bait. My brother is exceedingly clever, the most manipulative being in the universe. Using loved ones to achieve his objectives is something he has done for as long as I can remember."

Stella held her breath. Somehow hearing it from her father's lips made the terrible truth that she was related to Sylvain so much worse. "I'm scared that I might turn out to be like him," she whispered, crumbling into his arms.

"He may be your uncle, but his choices have nothing to do with blood or genes. Be assured that as long as you embrace the positive in the universe, you won't be anything like him."

"Father, in all those years of hiding, did you know that the angels would eventually find us?"

"In my heart, I knew they would. I always understood that you can't outrun the law, your responsibilities, or your problems. It's best to face them head on. But I guess I had hoped they'd leave us alone. Looking back, I realize now that the decision your mother and I made was immature and irresponsible. We were young, in love, and ready to turn our backs on everything we had worked for as individuals for that love—but I would do it again. I love you and your mother too much to not be willing to go through it all once more. But I am sorry for everything I put you through." It was now his turn to crumble.

A wave of gratitude swept over Stella. His words, his heartache, and his apology expressed a kind of openheartedness she'd never before seen from him.

"When Viola Island was attacked, we left our home to take you first to the lighthouse, and then to Sentinel Island." Arago looked away. "I intended to turn myself in so I could meet with the Panel of Judgment and finally take responsibility." Pulling back the covers, he revealed that he was, as Agnita had warned, shackled to the bed frame.

Stella brushed the hair from her face as she did her best to hold in her tears. She tried to bolster herself for the wave of emotion that would surely come with losing him again.

"Stella, darling, don't cry," he pleaded. "When your mother and I decided to come back with you, we knew the consequences. I will have to plead my case before the Panel of Judgment. It certainly helps that I have a daughter who turned out to be the key to saving the universe."

"Is there anything I can do when you go before the Panel of Judgment?"

He barked out a small laugh. "So ready to do what needs to be done, aren't you, my angel? You have grown so much in the time we've been apart." His eyes held pride but also a touch of sadness. "Perhaps." He paused for a long moment. "Or it may be better for you to keep doing what you've been doing. I've known ever since you were little that I wouldn't have to worry about you. I sensed you'd fulfill your destiny. I just never imagined you'd do it so soon."

Stella reached into her pocket, pulled something out, and slipped it into his hand. "Would this help?" Leaning forward to give him a kiss on the cheek, she whispered, "It's the Seed of Life."

Arago stared at the seedpod in his hand, his eyes widening. "How did you—?" Arago quickly put the Seed of Life back into Stella's hand and pulled her into a hug. "It doesn't matter. You must keep it safe. They'll find it if I have it. I know this is a lot to put on you, my angel, but I don't know who can be trusted with this in the sky realm. I know you will do the right thing."

Interrupting their tender moment, a healer whisked the curtains open and barged in. But her father nodded weakly at the healer, acknowledging her politely.

He turned back to Stella. "Please, my angel, let your father rest now. I need to sleep."

40

JOINING THE RANKS

As Stella walked back to the front of the infirmary, she saw the Timekeepers amble down the aisle and stop in front of Rand's bed.

The now-teenage sisters clasped their hands together in front of their chests. Addressing Rand, Agnita said, "We've been waiting for you, and at last you are here, though by a very different path than the others."

Stella's brow furrowed as she approached them, and Agatha explained, "He's the ninth candidate. Sentinel Michael himself scanned him for higher consciousness."

Stella's eyes widened. "Oh!" She turned to the healer who was tending to him. "May I speak with him?"

"For a brief moment," she said, tucking a blanket around Rand. "He's weak, though it's nothing some rest and decent food won't cure." The Timekeepers, as well as the healer, looked benevolently on, and they backed away.

Stella turned to him. "How are you feeling?"

"Better, thanks." He struggled to sit up and free his legs from beneath the blankets that had been tucked so tightly around him. "I need to contact my guardian and my team and let them know where I am."

Sentinel Michael, who had been standing nearby, listening, stepped up. "We can arrange that after you regain your strength. You've experienced tremendous suffering at the hands of Sylvain."

Rand looked at the mighty sentinel and held the angel's gaze intently. "Have you seen two other prisoners named Jakin or Hort?"

Sentinel Michael's lips pressed together in a thin line. "You and Arago are the only ones who came up from underground but there are still people below. I assure you we'll look for them and let you know as soon as we find them."

"Thank you."

The Timekeepers rejoined Stella and Rand as Sentinel Michael directed his words to Stella. "Today, you acted with tremendous bravery. You faced mortal danger selflessly. For this we are not only grateful, but we also know we owe you an explanation for a few things.

"Good and evil have always battled each other," Sentinel Michael continued. "Since the beginning of time, the struggle has been unrelenting. Fortunately, because of souls like you, good has always prevailed."

When he placed his hand on Stella's shoulder, she dropped her gaze to the floor. His presence was almost too much, and she was humbled by his praise.

He reached out and lifted her chin. Once they'd made eye contact, he went on. "We live in perilous times. Our way of life is threatened. What you achieved today was critical. Our struggle isn't over by any means, but today was an important battle won, for which we owe you a great debt."

The pride that swelled in her chest made her feel like she could take flight, even without her wings.

"When the Timekeepers asked for your help, you agreed to act. Enlisting the help of your two friends was a brilliant display of leadership. As Agnita suggested, you followed your instincts, and it paid off." His expression turned grave. "But you also endangered yourself and your friends' lives. Remember: just because you are told you are an important part of something does not mean you need to go off on your own."

"But we saved the tablets! We stopped Sylvain!" Stella protested.

"Of course you did, and we are truly grateful. In and of themselves, however, the tablets don't have any power. They are symbolic of laws that were put in place at the beginning of time. The architect of the universe created them to be as definitive as the physical laws, such as gravity—unchangeable and constant. To apply the laws consciously or unconsciously is one's choice. But you must understand that they are constantly in play whether you work with them or not."

"Are you saying that had Sylvain found and destroyed the golden tablets and then anointed his own clay versions, the laws would have remained in force?"

"Correct."

Stella frowned, her brow wrinkling and lips pursing. "So everything we did today was for nothing?"

"Stella, so many angels have faith in those tablets and the laws inscribed on them that, in spite of the laws themselves remaining intact, Sylvain destroying them would have been a serious blow. By protecting the tablets and destroying Sylvain's before he could anoint them, you prevented Sylvain from spreading doubt and chaos. There is great power in belief. Believing in the tablets' powers is what matters most, not any kind of mystical power they contain. You saved everyone in the three realms from falling into darkness by protecting the tablets."

Agnita chimed in. "Everyone is so intimidated by us that they do not ask questions—but you are willing to. We love your boldness and courage. You must question everything, especially yourself. It's a quality we three admire, as does Sentinel Michael."

An angel approached and thrust a vizioscope into Sentinel Michael's hands. "Forgive the interruption, but footage of the battle below has been processed."

The group huddled around to watch, and a holographic image of the cavern popped up, startling a gasp out of Rand. The hologram showed the viewpoint of a warrior angel hovering above the battle in the cave below. Warrior angels rushed to defend the still-fighting prisoners from the Red Eyes pouring in from the tunnel. Sylvain, weak and unsteady, screamed out in frustration, realizing the battle had been lost. Two Red Eyes hurried to their lord, taking position under each of Sylvain's arms, and carrying him away from the fighting and into the tunnel as quickly as they could.

The hologram's perspective gave chase, as the warrior angel fought her way through Red Eyes and down the long, dark tunnel. Far ahead, silhouettes could be seen entering a larger space, where a submersible watercraft waited. From the dock, Meenah was screaming and waving frantically to the Red Eyes carrying Sylvain.

"Get the merfolk," Sylvain ordered before disappearing into the submersible. As the hologram moved closer, Red Eyes could be seen pulling two struggling mermaids from the tank, as well as a severely injured black-haired merman, whose right arm hung limply at his side.

Stella jumped. "That's my mom. Esmi and Lazaretto too." As she turned to run to the well, Agnita caught her arm.

"Let go," Stella said, panicked. "I need to rescue my mother."

Shaking her head, Agnita tightened her grip. "This is only a recording of what has happened. Sylvain got away, Stella."

It took a lot of effort for her to not fly back down the well and check for herself. Did her father know her mother had also been held down there? No, if he had known, nothing would have stopped him from trying to get to her. And what about Magnus? Was he okay? The last time she'd seen her aunt, she'd been safe at the lighthouse with him.

"There's still hope—keep watching," said Agnes, pointing at the screen.

She gulped and looked back at the holographic battle, though now it was more of a retreat than anything.

Sylvain's soldiers tossed the merfolk down the hatch and then climbed in. Just as the vessel was about to disappear beneath the water, a figure catapulted into view. He slipped aboard an instant before the submersible pulled away from the dock and then disappeared underwater.

"That's Thaddeus!" said Stella. "What's he doing?"

"His intentions are obscured, even to us, but we trust that he is pursuing Sylvain," said Agnita.

Stella had grown to admire Thaddeus as a mentor and couldn't believe that her combat coach could have been one of Sylvain's operatives all along. The idea that he could have approached her or her fellow cadets any time to recruit them into the army sent a shiver through her, until Agnita's whispered in her ear. "Thaddeus is a member of the Special Protection Division. He's likely on a secret mission."

Stella's thoughts turned back to Sylvain. "What were those creatures that came from his skin?"

"Products of a dark magic practiced by one who peddles in the blood and venom of every type of beastly creature," Sentinel Michael explained. "Sylvain has starved his consciousness, magnifying his narcissism. Everything is about him, rendering him incapable of caring for others. His whole focus is on fulfilling his own needs, wants, and objectives, and turning your consciousness on yourself creates a void that can only be filled by hurting others."

"You saw what happened when Rand tossed the elixir into the dragon's mouth," Agatha said. "The Elixir of Life destroys that which has been created out of death and hate, so when the dragon was destroyed, part of Sylvain's strength was destroyed as well."

Stella turned that over in her mind. "What *did* happen to the elixir in the well? If Sylvain wasn't taking it . . ."

Rand cleared his throat. "I think I can clear that up. Boss . . . er, I mean, Arago knew that Sylvain's army was using us prisoners to tap and drain the well, so he had us drain it before they could. He knew it would be a risk to the Timekeepers and the Tree of Life, but he figured the prisoners being strong enough to revolt and, hopefully, defeat Sylvain's guards would be better than Sylvain himself having it. He also hoped the dropping elixir levels might alarm those in the sky realm and possibly lead to the discovery of the prisoners and Sylvain's evil plan."

The sisters nodded, seemingly agreeing that he had made the better choice, even if they had nearly died because of it. "Sylvain was long jealous of anyone with access to the elixir. In fact, all his issues stem from his jealousy," Agnes said. "By comparing ourselves to others, we risk growing resentful of them and end up wanting to lash out at them. Sylvain is an extreme example of this, which is why he's so dangerous."

"Why was Sylvain jealous?" Stella asked.

"Someone is only jealous of another when they haven't done the inner work of exploring their own consciousness and the ways in which they are unique," Sentinel Michael said.

Agnita turned toward Stella. "Your altruistic actions contributed greatly to this victory. You have risen to the challenges put before you at every stage of your journey and have embraced the unique talents you bring to this fight. You are not jealous of others but instead encourage them to use their own talents as part of a team to help."

"We owe you a huge debt of gratitude," Agnes said.

Stella bit her lip. "In that case, I have a few more questions. If angels want others to learn about and live within the Laws of the Universe, then why does the Marble Veil exist? Why the SSA, keeping my parents apart? Don't the landlings and merfolk deserve to learn about and believe in the laws too?"

It took Sentinel Michael a moment to find the right words. "Those are insightful questions that need to be addressed, and we need truth seekers like you to ask them, answer them, and bring about change. I want to affirm how much we want you to join the ranks of the Special Protection Division and help us battle the negative forces in our universe, wherever they may be. We could benefit from having you onboard."

Stella looked puzzled. "I thought I already was."

Everyone chuckled, and Sentinel Michael smiled warmly. "You have free will, young angel. You can make your own choices, including changing your mind. We can't force you."

"Well, I have my father back, but my mother is Sylvain's prisoner. So of course I'll fight alongside you." She looked around at them all and straightened her spine, pulling her shoulders back. "Plus, we have a few laws to change."

The Timekeepers smiled, while Sentinel Michael offered Stella his huge hand and shook her whole arm with it.

"Now, we need Lasker and Akila and the other cadets to join us as well," he said.

"*All* of us?"

Sentinel Michael nodded. "Instead of heading to the safe area, your fellow cadets ran into the fight. Though we certainly could've had a bit more"—he cleared his throat—"rule following from the group, we have been impressed with how quickly you've progressed and how willing you've all been to learn and grow. You all embraced the Laws of the Universe today and fought to maintain that positive order in the universe. We will be quite the force if we continue to recruit apprentices like this group."

41

A Reason to Celebrate

From the wings of the stage, Stella looked out at the monumental interior of the concert hall with its wooden beams adorned with intricate gold leaf patterns, an opulent gold and crystal chandelier bathing the space in its golden glow, and rows of ornate seats filled to capacity. Behind Stella, the other cadets fidgeted with pre-performance jitters as they waited to sing their choral number for the Sentinel Day celebration. Stella looked at her classmates with a sense of wonder. Just a week ago they were peacefully rehearsing this number, ready to perform the very next day. Then Sylvain and his army attacked and the cadets were thrown into their first battle.

Now, after spending the last few days helping to clean up after the destruction from the Red Eyes assault and repairing the Well of Life, they were ready to participate in the postponed celebration along with the rest of the sky realm. At first, it had seemed wrong. Yes, they'd all graduated to apprentice status, but Sylvain was still out there, waiting to strike, to create chaos, to turn angel against angel.

In the end, however, they'd all realized the celebration was a good idea for everyone's sake. As the law of polarity said: as above, so below. So they would celebrate and revel in the good, in the positive thoughts, while they could. If the pendulum was going to swing back the other way at some point, at the very least, they would enjoy their victory now.

A movement on the opposite side of the stage caught Stella's attention. Sentinel Michael saluted Stella, who acknowledged his salute with a nervous wave before turning her attention back to the audience.

Orica was sitting in the front row, looking the happiest Stella had ever seen her. Just like the first time Stella saw her, she was wearing a beautiful white gown, and her black-rimmed glasses and curly, chestnut-brown hair framed her face that now looked softer somehow. A few days ago, she had pulled Stella aside and told her that she had spoken to Arago.

"I have been holding on to a hurt that was not caused by you nor was it anything you should have had to pay for." Orica had looked at her feet, her eyes full of regret, as she'd explained, "Truthfully, it was nothing anyone should have *paid* for. It was simply a situation that upset me and that I held on to for far too long. No one is to blame for my actions but me. I'm sorry for how I've treated you." She had smiled at Stella tentatively, and Stella hadn't known what to do, so she just nodded.

Orica concluded, "You will return to your duties as Guardian of the Well tomorrow, since the well has been repaired, and I hope you will let me start over with you. I'll do better in the future. I promise."

Stella looked at her now and couldn't help but smile. She would never know what had been said between Orica and her father—and part of her wasn't sure she wanted to know—but she was happy in the knowledge that whatever had been said meant that Orica could move on. Or at least she hoped she could.

A few seats down from Orica, Stella's father sat with Rand. The Council had been too busy with planning their next steps in the fight against Sylvain and repairing the damage done to the Citadel to have held Arago's hearing, which meant they were still very unsure what his future held.

Stella glanced up to the box seats where the Celestial Council sat with regents, high-ranking sentinels, and angelic dignitaries. The sight of the Celestial Council infuriated Stella as she thought about the unfairness of their laws and the consequences those laws had on her family.

Stella was happy, though, that her father had been allowed to come to the celebration. He'd been resting and eating well and was now cleaned up. He almost looked like his old self again, and Stella knew that, no matter what, they'd get through whatever his punishment was together.

Rand looked good too. He caught her eye and waved. He was the only candidate from her group who hadn't graduated to apprentice, but she supposed that made sense. He was certainly going to join their ranks eventually, and probably soon. In visiting him the past few days, she'd quickly come to realize just how smart Rand was. He'd pick up the Laws of the Universe at least as fast as the other candidates had and would be a cadet and then apprentice in no time. She smiled back at him and ducked back behind the curtain, hoping no one else had caught a glimpse of her. Applause rose up to greet Sentinel Michael as he walked on stage to the podium.

Akila pulled Stella over to stand between herself and Lasker as Sentinel Michael, the host of the evening's celebration, welcomed the audience. He spoke a few words of gratitude, and, finally, introduced the choir of new apprentices about to take the stage.

"It's time!" she whispered to her two best friends, excitement dancing in her eyes.

Everyone was silent as the curtain floated up and revealed the eight shimmering in their billowing robes. As the young apprentices sang their first notes, Stella knew they were *all* a part of something special. The smile that bloomed on her face as she took in her friends and their voices almost hurt it was so big.

As Stella's solo approached, a vision formed in her mind's eye—a goal she would pursue ceaselessly and with all the joy she held in her heart in that moment. It was a vision of her father, whole and happy and free, her mother smiling and thriving by his side, and Stella herself standing in front of them, each of her parents with a hand on their daughter's shoulder.

She sang the first note of her solo but knew she was not alone—she had so many people rooting for her, and her friends by her side, as the pure sound burst from her soul.

Lost in the joy of the moment, Stella manifested her wings and slowly drifted up to the thunderous applause of the audience. She was finally comfortable enough in her own skin to let herself soar.

Flying on Glowinder had given her a sense of freedom unlike any she'd ever known. But flying on her own now and being with her friends, with the people who had trusted her, stood by her, fought beside her, with her vision for the future so firmly in place—it was the kind of freedom that only came from knowing how fully one can be oneself and still be loved.

ACKNOWLEDGMENTS

None of this would have been possible without the encouragement of my best friend, Peggy McColl, *New York Times* bestselling author—the first person who truly believed in me and my vision with certitude. She stood by me during every struggle and all my successes. That is true friendship.

I'm eternally grateful to my grandparents, Lester and Vivian Opal Finley, who took me in as an eleven year old after my family's home, nestled on the banks of the Rio Grande river in New Mexico, had burnt to the ground. They taught me hard work, discipline, how to deal with adversity gracefully, and so much more that has helped me to become the man I am today. I truly have no idea where I would have ended up if they hadn't provided me a safe haven from life's tumult, something I desperately needed at that age.

To Phil Goldfine, who took a chance on me as a new author with a big idea and provided me with the creative space to write at his bungalow on the Universal Studios lot in Hollywood. He never saw me as anything other than a writer hungry to learn, excited to grow, and willing to do whatever it took to succeed. I borrowed his belief in me, which has never wavered once; he encouraged me to focus on the bigger dream and to believe it was already here.

Although twenty years as a flight attendant was filled with many ups and downs and takeoffs and landings, my time in the airline industry has been worth it, affording me the flexibility to travel, read, and work on my writing. None of this would have been possible without the help of my supervisor, Ginny Coronado, who cheered me on, occasionally helping to adjust my schedule when staring down a deadline.

A very special thanks goes out to my publishing team at Beyond Words in Hillsboro, Oregon. For an Oregon author to have the opportunity to work with a world class Oregon publishing house is a match made in heaven. To Richard and Michele Cohn, who caught my vision and enthusiastically locked arms with me, together we brought this wonderful dream to reality. Emily Einolander, my developmental editor—it was a golden time sitting around the conference table and gossiping about my characters as if they were old classmates. You helped me to expand my thinking about the depth and richness of Stella's world and the lives of its inhabitants. Emmalisa Sparrow Wood, my production editor—thank you for gently but firmly holding your position as an advocate for my characters and my readers. You have challenged me to become a better collaborator and writer. Lindsay Easterbrooks-Brown, my managing editor, thank you for your patience with me. Your attention to detail and straightforward comments brought clarity and reality to the process and, ultimately, to the work.

Acknowledgments

To Jade, Mirinda, Paige, Jace, and Tairus: you have always filled my days with enchantment and laughter and gave me a place to live when I needed it most.

To my mom: you always treated me like a golden child even when I deserved coal at Christmas. To my dad: you knew deep down I would amount to something in life, even when you thought I should get my head out of the clouds. To David and Mary, my parent's partners—you're both angels! Thank you for taking such good care of my parents. I am eternally grateful to you.

To Aunt Jan: you have always been that special person I could turn to during both turbulence and smooth sailing in my life. You supported me in ways that I never knew I needed.

To Debi Anderson: thanks a million for giving me access to your beach house, which is the perfect place of peace and creativity.

To Elaine Herin: you're the best sister a brother could ever ask for. I love you dearly and can't wait to go back to the cabin with you.

To David Ord: thanks for inspiring in me the desire to write about manifestation.

To all those who have played a part in my journey: Bob Proctor, Ken Goldstein, Jennifer Salyer, Jeff Berry, Jeanette Steiner, Barbara Najera, Kevin Smith.

Finally, to anybody who has ever been rejected or ever been made to feel inadequate about your life's passion: I dedicate this book to you . . . the dreamers and artists of the world, you know who you are—You have a vision. Don't let the dream stealers take it away. Hold fast to your vision until it becomes a reality. You are the only one who can give yourself permission to become the person you decide to be.

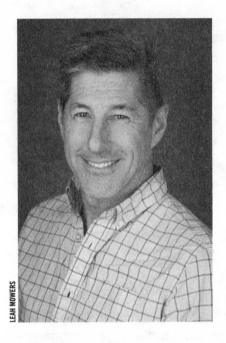

M. Shawn Petersen began to tell stories almost as soon as he could talk, but it took him years of traveling the world to discover Stella's story. When he is not writing, he loves to travel, create new stories, and passionately pursue personal development. *Stella and the Timekeepers*, Petersen's first novel, originally came to him in a dream, but it wasn't until he committed it to paper during National Novel Writing Month that this epic story sprouted wings and took flight.